Living for You

LEYA LAYNE

Trigger Warnings

While this book is meant to be a cozy romance with spice, there are discussions of topics that could be triggering for readers. To be respectful to those who need warnings and those who see them as spoilers, I have placed the trigger warnings on my website. Scan this code to check the site.

Living for You was originally published in part within Snowed-In in Cole County: A Cozy Romance Anthology in 2024 as Charmed by the Pixie.

LIVING FOR YOU

COLE COUNTY MEMORIES
BOOK TWO

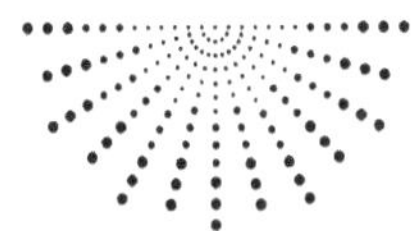

LEYA LAYNE

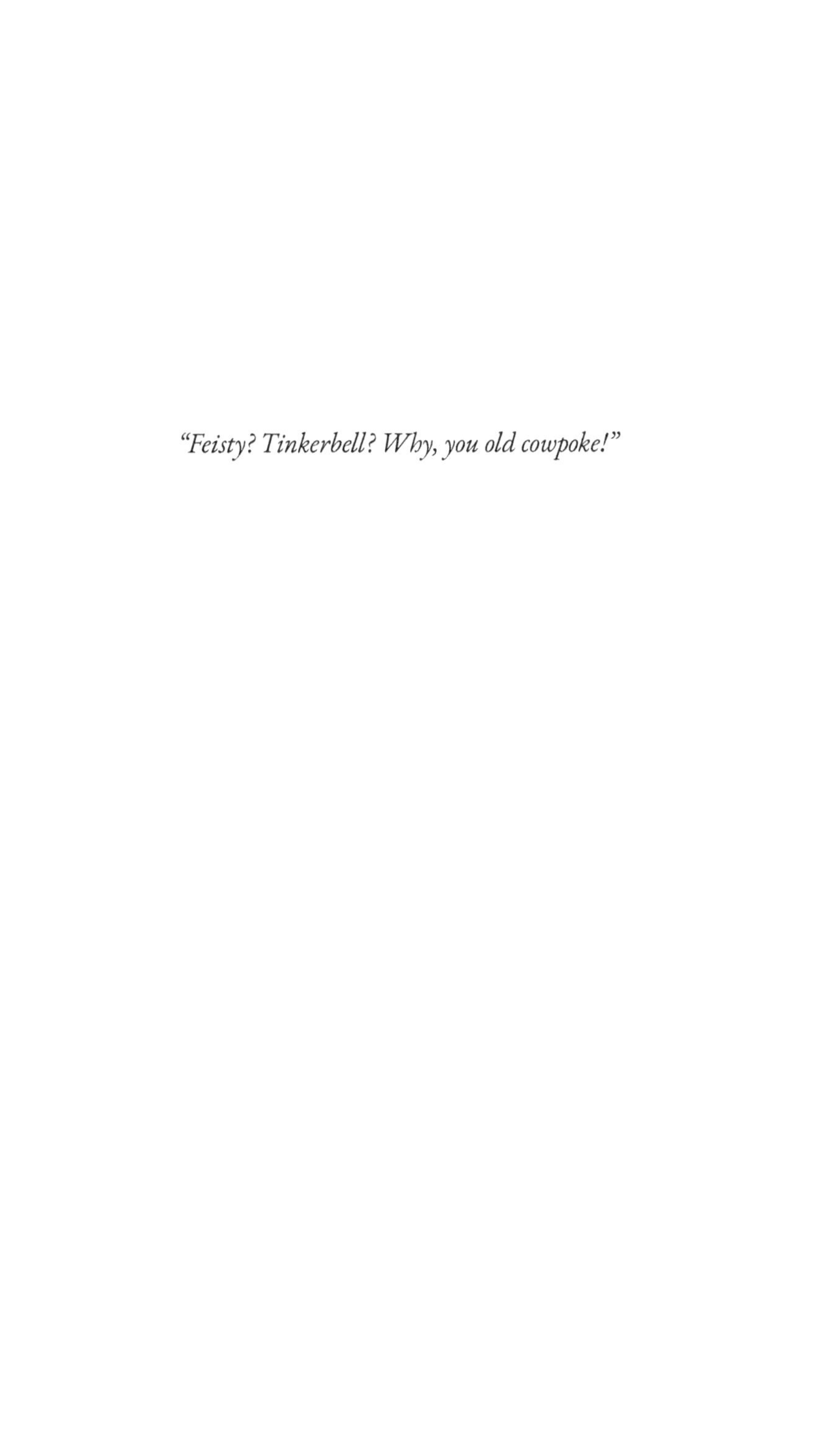
"Feisty? Tinkerbell? Why, you old cowpoke!"

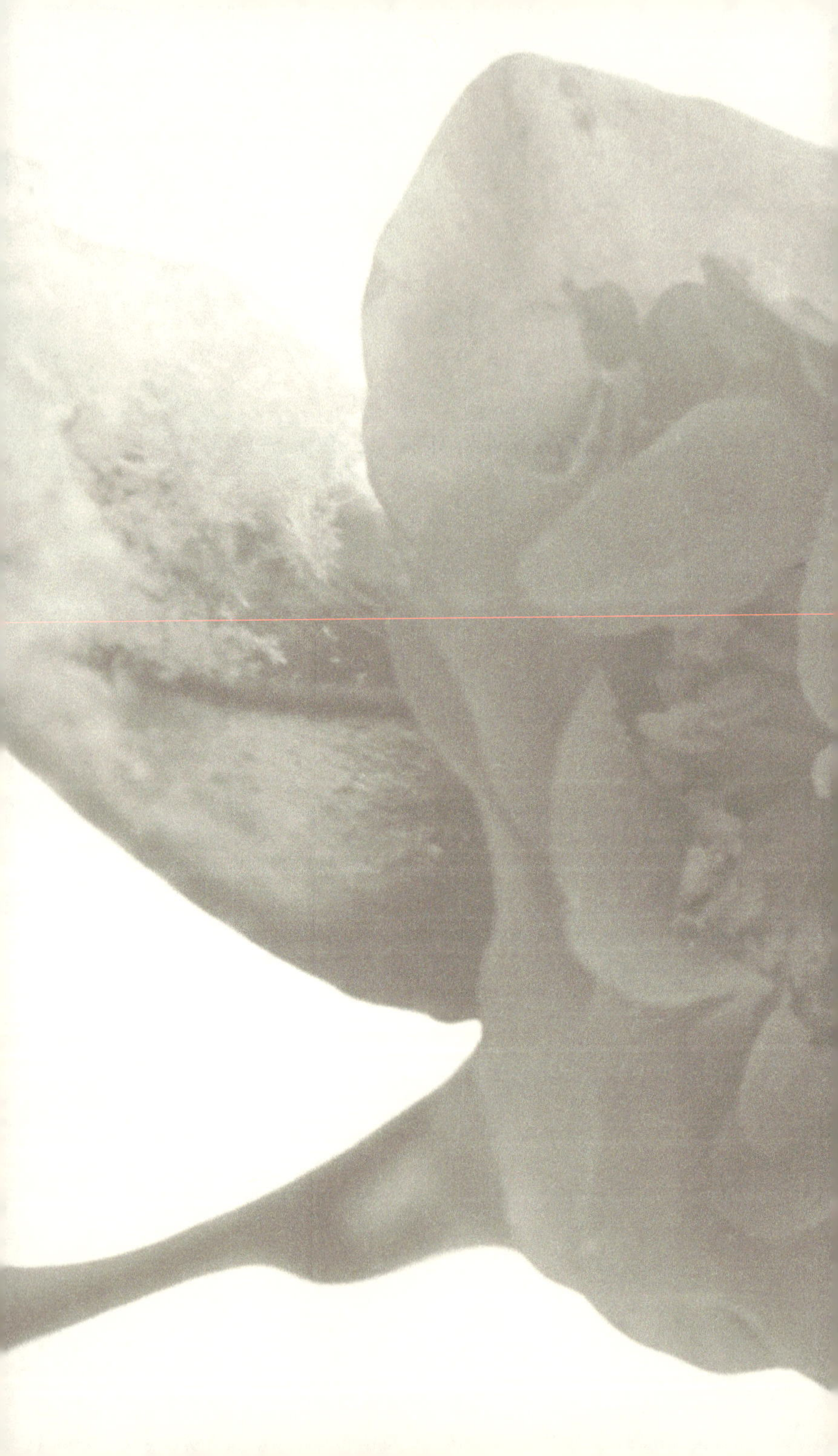

JUST BE YOURSELF

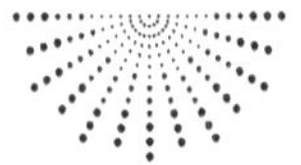

aylor

The alarm blares, and I throw an arm over my eyes to block out the sun streaming through the shades. My other arm flies to the side of the bed to find my phone. God, I hate mornings. Who in the hell thought it was a good idea to make the sun the reason everyone gets up regardless of the hour they go to sleep or where they sleep. I've been sleeping in my car these past couple weeks, only coming to Jordan's house every few evenings to shower before my shift at the hotel. If not for that job, I'd not only be in my car but also starving. There's no way life can continue like this though.

As the foghorn of a fucking phone continues to blow, I fight to unwrap myself from the massive comforter that somehow twisted into a tightly-wound rope around my body. I need to shut that alarm up before I lose it. My thoughts start spiraling when there's a knock on the door.

"Get up, T, or you're gonna be late!" Jordan's sing-song voice rings through the wooden barrier.

"What time is it?" I yell back. "I can't find my fucking phone."

Jordan pushes the door open and stops in her tracks. Her lips pull together, and her eyes go wide. When her whole body starts shaking, I glare at her.

"It's not funny!"

At that, Jordan doubles over with laughter, her breath catching. As soon as she seems to get herself together, she straightens up, looks at me cocooned in the covers, and bursts into giggles again.

"Help me, or don't, but find that damn phone and throw it against the wall!"

All my patience is gone. The repetitive sound, much more than my bestie's laughter is making me crazy. I've always hated hearing an alarm. It reminds me of all those mornings when my stepfather would wake me for school and dress me while my mother slept in. I shudder at the thought and squeeze my eyes tightly closed to get the image out of my head. When Jordan presses the stop button on the phone screen, thus quieting the room, I keep my eyes closed, fighting down the panic.

"Sorry, T. I forgot how much an ongoing alarm affects you."

Jordan's apology is sincere. I know that. I just need a moment to take a few steadying breaths before I can open my eyes and respond. As soon as I renew my fight with the comforter, though, Jordan snorts. My eyes snap to her face, taking in the flare of her nostrils and quiver of her lips. I barely hold the glare a few more seconds. The corners of my lips tick upward and laughter bubbles out of me. Jordan flops on the bed in a fit, and I squirm to get to her, both of us cackling at this point.

"Stop," Jordan says after a few minutes. "Let me get you untangled, so I can go pee before this becomes a waterbed." She grabs what appears to be the corner of the comforter but is simply a folded part of one side and tries to unravel me from the knotted wad like one might a kitten wrapped in a ball of yarn. "How in the hell did you get yourself balled up like this?"

"I don't fucking know. I woke up like this."

"That was NOT what Beyonce meant, T!"

We laugh again. After much tugging, repositioning, and flipping over, I finally emerge from the comforter looking like I'd just been thrown in the dryer and left to wrinkle overnight.

"Girl, you better go get yourself spruced up for your interview. That right there," Jordan says, gesturing her hand from my head to my toes, "is not a good look."

In a moment of peak maturity, I stick my tongue out and stomp into the bathroom across the hall, sticking up my middle finger before closing the door. I look at myself in the mirror, think about the morning's fight with the covers, and chuckle quietly before going about the business of making myself presentable.

Jordan is seated on the already-made bed with a steaming cup in her hand. I go straight to my overnight bag and pull out the clothes I had planned to wear—a pair of black slacks and a long-sleeve, button-down, white shirt. It's my hotel uniform, but at least it's clean and looks professional. From the corner of my eye, I catch a glimpse of Jordan, her brows drawn together.

"What?" I ask.

"You're going to go to your interview looking like a fucking restaurant hostess?"

"What do you mean? This is professional?"

"Yeah, if you're going to a stuffy, upscale corporation in the city, which is totally not your scene. Didn't you say this place is a new bed and breakfast just opening up. When I looked at the website...don't look at me like that Taylor Marie Wright! Of course, I checked out the website. Anyway, when I looked at the place, there were before and after pictures that show the transition from dark, traditional, and boring to bright, colorful, and hip. You," she says while getting up from the bed and walking around me like an art critic, "are bright, colorful, and hip. But not in that ensemble."

I really do hate the monotone look. It's not that I hate either color, but stark white with stark black always makes me feel like a penguin, cold and aloof. My shoulders droop.

"What if I go as myself, and they hate it? I need to find another job, and maybe getting out of the county will let me find somewhere I can afford."

"You know you could just stay here until you get settled. I have this room, and you're welcome to it for as long as you need. I'd love to have you as a roommate."

"I can't do that, Jordan. I can't pay. I'd be more like a glorified houseguest soon to overstay her welcome than a roommate, and I wouldn't do that to you."

Jordan releases a heavy sigh that means she disagrees but won't argue. It's not like this is the first time we've had this conversation. She does, however, have more to say about the interview.

"Okay, look. You can go as a penguin, or you can go as you. If they hire you based on the clothes, ignoring the woman with the pink streaks in her hair and bubbly personality with a dangerously sharp edge, then you'll never feel like you belong. You'll be worried every day that they may decide to go with someone more traditional. But..." she starts with brows raised in challenge.

"But, if I go as me, and they hire me, I'll know they know what they're getting. I won't be walking on eggshells."

Now it's my turn to sigh. I quickly throw the penguin suit back in my bag and dig around for something more comfortable. When I'm fully dressed, hair and makeup as good as it's going to get, Jordan nods in approval.

"There's my best friend, the woman who can take on the world. I've missed her!"

I walk over and sit on the bed next to Jordan, putting my arms around her shoulders.

"Thank you for being my friend and keeping me straight. I don't know what I'd do without you."

"Just remember that when you're 'out of the county,'" she says with air quotes.

"Oh, I will. Now, wish me luck!"

Rather than saying anything, Jordan holds up a small bottle of Diet Coke and smiles. I return the smile, grab the drink with a wink, and leave to make the nearly hour drive.

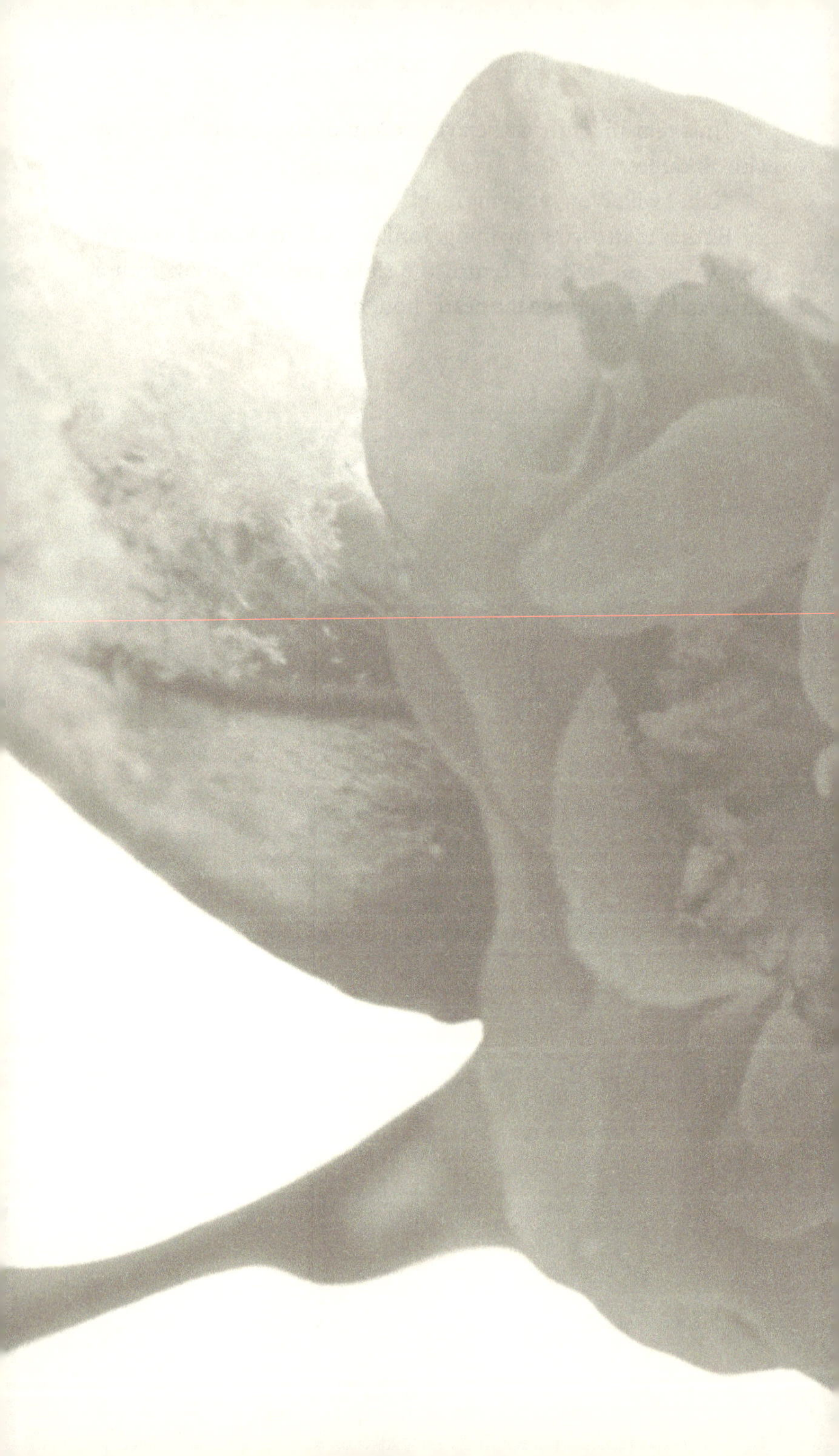

WAKING UP

Garrett

"I can't!"

Sweat pours from my face as I sit bolt upright on the bed with Rosie's voice playing through my head the same way it's been doing for the past month. *How am I supposed to let you go?* It's been five years, and I've barely started leaving the house, dread hanging over my head every time I pull back up the driveway. She's not here. She's gone and never coming back. "Dammit, I miss you!" I cry into the early morning silence, but all that answers is the ghost of her last words in the dream...*Let me go, Sweetheart.*

It's barely 5am, but I can't lay here anymore. It was the same that first night Rosie came to my dreams, the night Jake proposed to Morgan. I hate she couldn't be here to see that, to see him finding his happiness. Twenty years in the making, and she missed it. I cried myself to sleep that night, angry at God, the universe, cancer, and the fucking doctors who failed her. I've cried many nights over the past five years, but she'd never come to me. That night, she told me to stop crying over her. Her words flash through my mind, *Jacob isn't the only one who deserves to find happiness again, Sweetheart.* I shake my head. That ship has sailed. It took her away from me.

I can't shake the dream, so I shuffle into the kitchen in search of coffee. Joanna's standing there with a mug in her hand and a confused twist to her brows. "You good, Pa?" she asks, putting the mug on the counter.

"Coffee," I grunt. I don't have words for her yet. I'm not even sure what to say. Am I good?

She grabs another mug from the cabinet, turning back to look at me like she's afraid to take her eyes off me. What in the hell have I done to my children if I can't get up early and have a cup of coffee without worry screwing up her face? With the first sip, my head finally starts to clear. Joanna's gaze stays locked on me over the top of her mug, and it's honestly beginning to piss me off.

"Stop looking at me like that," I bark. "I'm not a zoo attraction."

Her lip quirks up in the corners, and a brow raises. Joanna's never been overly affected by my surly demeanor, not like her brother. She's always given it right back. Jake, on the other hand, has always been softer. The only time he ever got in someone's face was with some bullies back when they were a kid. A smile plays across my lips when I remember the boys' parents coming to talk to us about Jake's anger issues. Of all the people in this family, he's the least angry, except maybe for Rosie. My smile drops. She was my balance, and I'm all over the fucking place without somewhere for these emotions to go.

"You hungry, Pa? I got a few minutes and can make something," Joanna says, breaking me from my rogue thoughts. One look in her eyes says she's doing it to distract me, and I sigh.

"You always were a stubborn girl, JoJo."

At the use of her childhood nickname, she smiles. "I get it from you, old man." I nod because I can't argue with her when she's absolutely right. "So, breakfast?" she asks again.

"No," I say, shaking my head. I can't remember the last time

I've sat down to have breakfast, and I don't plan to start that shit today. Instead, I say something that I know she's not expecting.

"Your brother mentioned Morgan needing some daytime handyman help to get things finished up. You think she'd settle for a washed-up, old man?"

Joanna's eyes widen before a smile transforms her face. "I think she'd be thrilled at the chance of bossing around the town's curmudgeon."

My initial reaction is to bark out something about no one bossing me around, but the wink that follows her words elicits a chuckle instead. If anyone would be willing to take me on and not get on me about missteps, it's Morgan.

"Don't tell her I'm coming, okay. I need to be able to walk in there and ask myself. Let me do that much."

Joanna eyes me skeptically, like she's not quite sure I'll follow through, but then she agrees. "You'll have to get ready to drive me into the store then. I'll work on getting my car fixed if you're going to be using the Mustang again."

Garrett

Morgan is standing at the door, surprise written on her face when I open the car door. I take a deep breath and let it out. I was afraid Joanna would've called and warned her. Though I don't want my future daughter-in-law looking at me like a lunatic, it's better than feeling like a charity case if my daughter would have begged Morgan to find something for me to do. I climb out of the car and smile in her direction.

"Mr. Daniels? What're you doing here?"

I grab my tool belt from the backseat and sling it over my shoulder before walking toward the house. "A couple of birdies told me that you were closing in on the opening of a new business and needed a daytime handyman to help finish up the odd jobs that aren't done. I found myself with some free time and thought I'd offer my services." I look down at the ground for a second before saying the uncomfortable truth. "I admit I'm a little out of practice, but it should be like riding a bike, right?"

She stands there with an expression somewhere between being stunned and curious before settling on admiration when she says, "You know what, I do have a couple small jobs. How are your locksmith skills?" Without batting a lash, she's accepted my offer and given me a chance to breathe. "Not gonna lie," she continues, "you might just be taking down the whole damn door."

I laugh at the way her eyes sparkle. "Oh, I am good at demolition!"

"Where were you months ago?"

"Wallowing in the pits of despair where my children left me."

"Well, Mr. Daniels, it is good to see you back on Earth."

"Thank you for giving them something else to focus on, so I could focus on me for a while."

Before I can make it into the house, Morgan wraps her arms around my waist in a tight hug, and my chest swells. I may have felt guilty for how we as a town treated this girl when she was a child, but the woman she's become in spite of it all is admirable. My son is blessed to call her his.

"So, where is this lock that's going to be my ruin?"

"How about a grand tour first?"

I take her up on the offer. Gretna Humphries, Morgan's grandmother, was a hard woman to get close to, and she rarely invited anyone into the house. Though she had known my family my entire life, I can't remember one time where we'd been invited over or even sent to help out with shoveling and raking like we'd been for many of the other families in town. The Humphries house just wasn't one you visited, especially not after Morgan's grandfather died. It was as if the air grew stale and stagnant all around this place. Now, however, I can feel a difference in the land, so I look forward to seeing Morgan's vision for the house.

The house is huge, much bigger inside than I had imagined. Three floors, giant rooms with even bigger pieces of furniture, most of it too big for the space it's in. A twinge of guilt creeps up my neck when I think of how Jake had asked me to come help when they first started the renovations. He and the girls had been out here doing everything themselves. The work is impressive, but there's still so much to get done. I'm surprised the only thing Morgan is worried about me doing today is changing out a lock and door handle for a room she plans to keep private.

"This was my grandmother's suite, and while I finally found the right keys to get in here, I don't want to leave the door like this." She physically shudders as if caught in a memory. "Let's just say, I need this done to feel like this is now my home."

I understand what she's saying. One of the hardest parts of losing Rosie has been learning how to live in that house without her. Everything reminds me of her and yet I can't bring myself to change anything. I got stuck somewhere between wanting to burn it all down and needing to enshrine the memories. If I ever want to move on, there are some things I'm going to have to change as well. I look down the hall to where Morgan has disappeared back into the formal dining room. She has the right idea about how to move forward.

An hour later, I'm eating those words. I may have spoken too soon when I silently praised Morgan's plan to purge Gretna Humphries and the locks she'd put up around herself. Nothing has worked to remove this doorplate. Whoever installed it must have used construction grade adhesive beneath the metal. I look through the toolbox I retrieved from the car and pull out a hammer and chisel. If nothing else, maybe I can break pieces off this thing or make a dent in the wood for the pry bar. Instead, I manage to take a chunk of skin out of my own hand.

"Son of a bitch," I yell, unable to stop myself. That shit hurt.

"Oh my God, are you alright?" Morgan asks, running down the hall in my direction.

I'm here on my knees, clutching my hand with the other, and wondering whether or not her grandmother's ghost really is trying to keep us from making this room inhabitable. "We're going to have to change out this door when Jake gets here. I'm pretty sure your grandmother's ghost is trying to kill me."

Morgan doesn't laugh, but I catch the twinkle in her eye. Maybe I'm being a little dramatic, but damn it, I've tried everything I know to remove this damn plate. "Nothing I've tried has worked, and now I've cut my damn hand," I grumble, showing her the blood running down the side of my arm. "Bested by a fucking door."

"Stay there," Morgan says, when I won't let her look at my hand. It's embarrassing to have injured myself the first day. All the work these kids have done, and I can't even get a lock off a door.

When Morgan comes back, she has a red plastic box labeled first-aid kit on the side. It has to be new. I doubt Gretna Humphries had updated medical supplies hanging around here, not with the way her personal area of the house looks. I apologize again once she's got my hand cleaned up and bandaged, but she cuts me off with a new plan. I start cleaning up the mess I've made, and she heads back to where she's been working on the business side of things.

"In the meantime, I'll just focus on hiring an assistant."

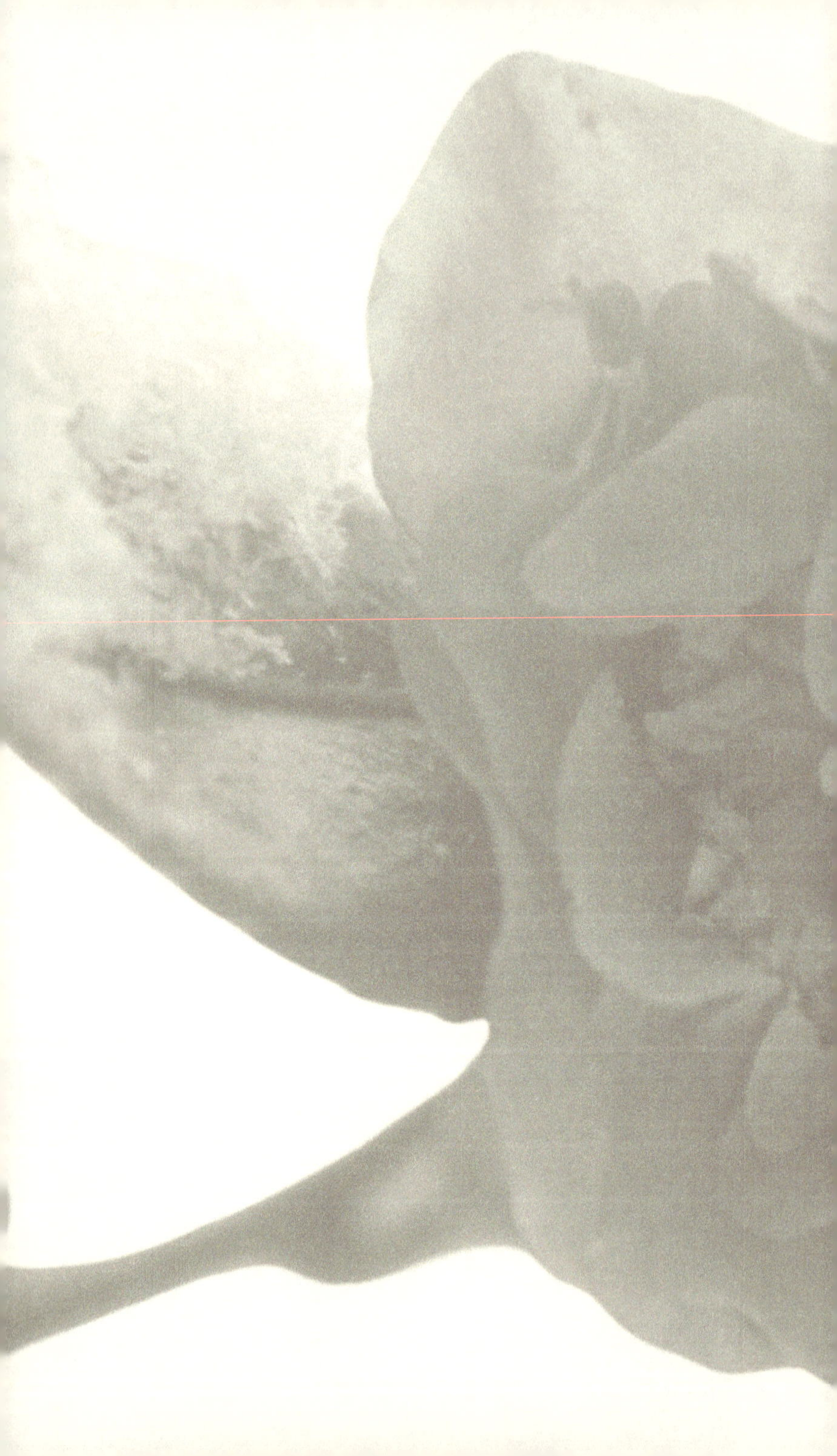

3

INTIMIDATION AND EMPATHY

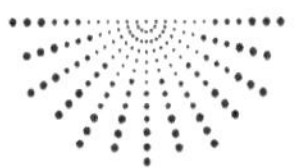

Taylor

If anyone asks, I'll never admit to being intimidated by Gretna House. Hell, I can barely admit to myself that the house is foreboding and has me rethinking the plan to work here. The dark, three-story monstrosity is probably haunted. "I'm kinda haunted myself," I say aloud with an uncomfortable chuckle before stepping out of the car. Grabbing my extra-large bag with the huge 3D magnolia blossom on the side out of the passenger seat, I look at myself in the side mirror. My hair still holds the puffy curls I'd put in it that morning. The curls help integrate the pink stripes in my short hair rather than drawing stark attention to them. Not that my hair matters when I'm wearing powder-blue slacks with a pinstripe button-down and chunky-soled, cow-print shoes. As much as I love these shoes, I can admit they might be a bit overkill. Taking a deep breath, I let out an audible sigh and turn toward the house. It's too late now to second-guess my attire.

Looking up at the front of the house again, I give one small shudder and then step onto the front porch. A sign saying, "Come in, we're open," is clearly posted in the window of the large entry door. Even the size of the door makes me feel small and

15

insignificant. *Just breathe, T,* I tell myself and step over the threshold.

"Hello? I'm here about the job." Sunlight illuminates the entryway, showing a narrow hallway with multiple doors, but as soon as I let the front door close, shadows cave in from all sides. Nope, this isn't scary at all.

"Back here. Come straight down the hall and into the kitchen," a woman's voice calls from beyond the long hall.

I take a deep breath and square my shoulders. I'm here for a job, and I'm good at my job. I could be good for this one. More of the house's structure becomes visible with each step into the dimly lit space, and my unease dissipates. This place definitely isn't like the contemporary hotels I'm used to with their bright lights and pristine front desks, but it's got good bones. There's a large staircase leading up to the second floor from the end of the hall that explains why it feels so narrow and dark. More lighting is needed in this area. If families come to stay with small children, they'll be frightened as soon as they walk in the door. There are two doors off to the right, and one to the left before I reach where the hall opens up more near the bottom of the staircase. Still, there isn't much light. To the left, is a set of double doors, presumably hiding the dining area. Even in many traditional hotels, those doors are kept closed except for breakfast hours. Another hallway leads off the right side, adjacent to the kitchen door. That hall isn't as long as the entry, but that's all I can see for the shadows. They need lighting everywhere.

"Welcome." A brunette with bright eyes stands from the massive island in the kitchen and holds out her hand. "I'm Morgan Humphries, the owner of this monstrosity."

I chuckle as I cringe inwardly. Discomfort must be written on my face for the woman to describe the house, her new business, as such. Morgan Humphries is wearing black leggings stretched over thick thighs and a full midsection, much like my own. She also has on an old, worn t-shirt that is missing the collar, so it shows her bare shoulder and bra strap. She might actually be a little bigger than I am, but she surely doesn't dress that way. She's dressed for comfort, and I'm glad to see it. I breathe a little easier and am able to hold myself steady when Morgan's gaze takes me in from head to foot. Thankfully, the woman's smile is warm.

"Coffee?" she offers.

"No thanks, I'm not a fan," I say, trying to keep the trepidation from my voice.

Morgan shakes her head. "I can't stand the stuff either, but I know we would be throwing away any chance at success if we didn't serve it. So, I plug my nose, grin, and bear it."

My smile widens. Morgan is right. People at the hotel go through pots of coffee each morning, and some come back throughout the day for cups. "Coffee lovers are like a cult and can't believe there are people out here who might be disgusted by the taste or even the smell."

Morgan gives a nod of agreement and gestures at the stool next to her. "Shall we get on with it then? If you'd like some water or something else, just let me know."

Several minutes go by before the interview begins in earnest. Morgan asks all the usual questions, and I answer flawlessly, my training kicking in regardless of my nerves. My high school specialized in preparing us for jobs in hospitality, and I've been working in the field since completing my associate's degree at the community college. A big part of our training had been participating in mock interviews. I know to give away a little of myself without sharing anything too personal. I'm the eldest of five children and no longer living at home. The hardest part is trying to keep the sadness from my expression when I talk about my siblings. A lump forms in my throat at how much I miss them. Thankfully, Morgan transitions us to another topic.

"Now, for the most important question," Morgan begins, and my back stiffens. "Why are you in Colliers Town? You're obviously not from here, and most of our young people are looking to get away."

Shit! I wasn't expecting that question. How honest do I need to be? Would some generic 'I'm looking for a change of scenery' answer satisfy Morgan? Do I want to be generic? I think back to my conversation with Jordan this morning. If I were going to be generic, I might as well have worn the penguin suit. Instead, I clasp my hands and take a deep breath before responding.

"I hate to say that I'm running away from responsibilities at twenty-five, but I had to get away. I had to move far enough from home to find myself and reconnect with the parts of me that were withering. Yet, I don't want to be too far from my siblings. My stepdad just...well...let's just say, I had to leave." There, that's as honest as I can be without turning this interview into a therapy session.

Morgan's eyes shine with empathy, and she nods silently. I incline my head and take a steadying breath. I'm grateful when Morgan stands and gestures for me to do the same.

"Let me show you around," she says, and I follow her out of the kitchen and up the stairs. A change in scenery is just what I need to get my head back in the game.

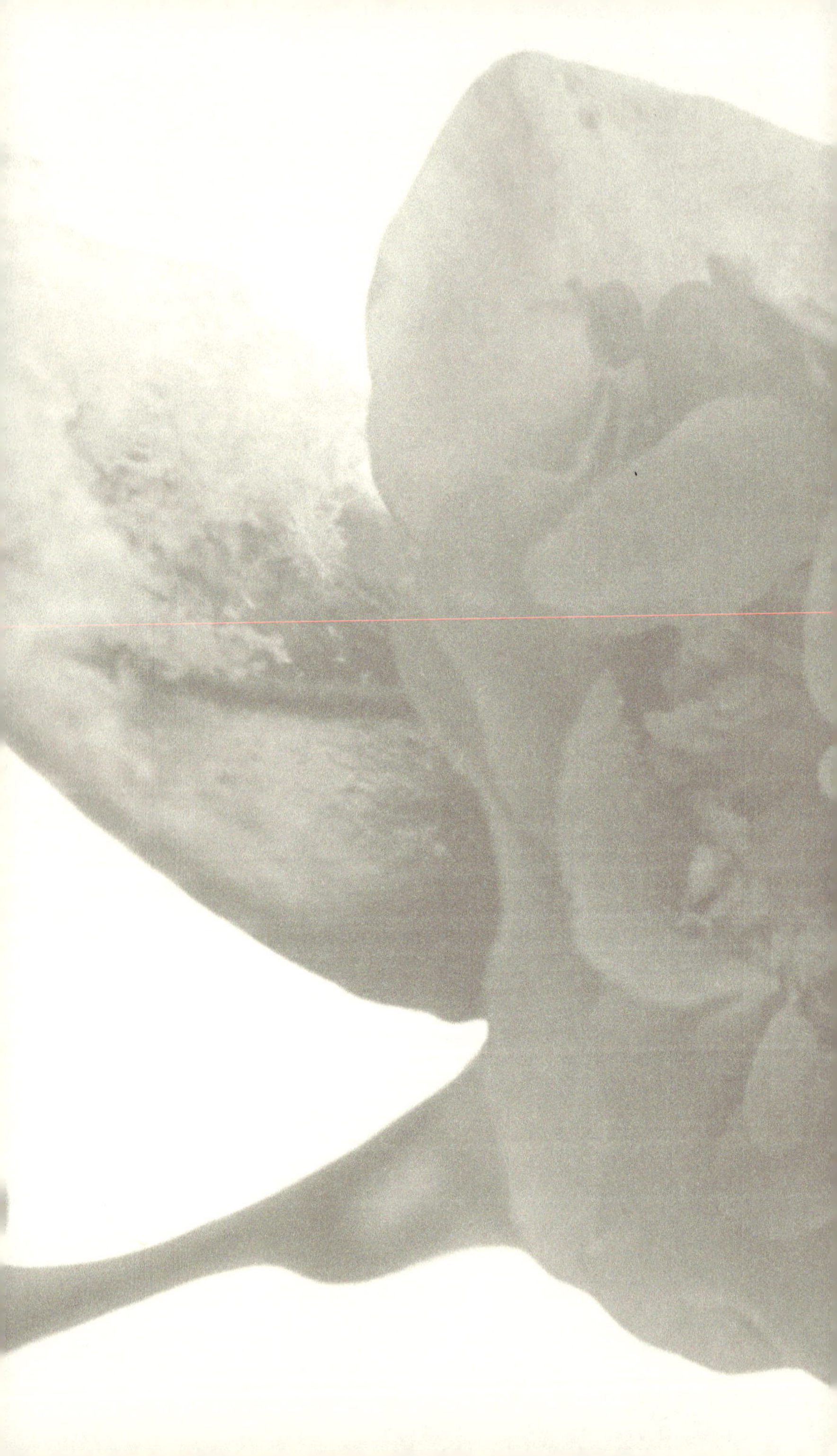

4

PLAN FOR THE WHAT IFS

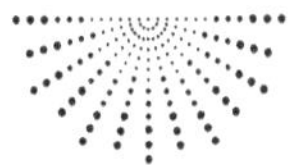

aylor

The house is bigger than I thought. It doesn't just have three floors. It also has an attic in the back and a full basement that serves as a larder and wine cellar. I'm genuinely surprised to find out that they originally had 20 rooms for patrons to rent back when it was a rooming house for those who worked in the coal mines. Morgan has begun to convert those individual rooms into suites, and the plan is for each suite to have a room with either one or two beds and its own bathroom. I can't even imagine how much that costs, but the work she's done already is amazing. There are currently five rooms on the second floor ready for patrons. She moved herself from the second floor to the third and converted the hall bathroom to a powder room rather than an extra shower. There's still so much to do, but with everything that's already been done downstairs, and that will continue to be worked on, this bed and breakfast is going to be one of the hottest rentals in the county.

In the past eight months, she's had the ground floor completely repainted, trying to bring some brightness into the space. When I make suggestions on how to provide even greater light, Morgan appears pleased, which encourages me to share more ideas. We could easily create a library, sitting room, and small workspace for any business travelers in the large parlor. The one room I can't imagine changing, however, is what had obviously once been a formal dining room with its grandiose fireplace at the end of the room. Morgan has created different seating options for various patrons. There's a high bar along the wall with internet hookups and outlets, communal seating for those who don't mind sharing a space, and then a more intimate set of tables separated by a beautiful, hand-painted partition that accommodates couples and small groups of three or four people. It really is a great use of space that keeps some of the traditional aesthetic but adds a modern flair.

Close to an hour after we'd left the kitchen, we return in fits of laughter. I really like this woman. Though she's older, nearing 40, she has a vision that can withstand the test of time. She's forward thinking while wanting to remain true to the essence of the house. The biggest thing, though... Morgan listens to all my ideas and not once brushes me off as being too young to have anything worthwhile to contribute.

"What's down that short hall there?" I ask.

At first, Morgan doesn't look like she's going to answer. An unfamiliar emotion flits over her face, but then she turns back to me and smiles.

"We will cordon off that area once we're ready for guests. That was my grandmother's suite, and her mother before her."

Apparently, there are plans to renovate that space for Morgan to move into and make her living quarters and office. Unfortunately, the amount of work needed cannot happen prior to opening weekend, so it will be put on the back burner, as will the third floor. The house will open at half capacity in less than two months.

"I'm sorry. I know it must be difficult trying to renovate the house and having to clean out your grandmother's space. It's no wonder you've put that off until last. Take all the time you need."

Morgan's smile is tight, but she reaches out and pushes the kitchen door inward, gesturing for me to go first. I don't get but two steps through the doorway when I'm stopped in my tracks by a vision of two strong backs that taper down to tight asses in denim. The first thing that goes through my mind is 'Holy shit!' but all that comes out of my mouth is a squeak. Then, the men turn around, and I nearly faint. They are absolutely gorgeous, even with arms and hands covered in suds that are dripping onto the floor. Though I'm sure both of them are probably too old for me, their light blond hair, brilliant, clear eyes, and tanned skin damn near take my breath away.

"Gentlemen, you're dripping, not to be confused with drooling," Morgan says with a shake of her head from my left, where she's stepped around me to see what I've squeaked about.

Both men look down and laugh before turning around to rinse their hands and arms, fighting over the tap. I look back and forth between the two men and choke back a groan that catches Morgan's attention. When Morgan's eyes turn away from the man whose ass she'd been checking out, I try to keep my face as neutral as possible.

"Let me introduce you," Morgan says as one of the men squats to dry the floor with a rag. "The one who looks good on his knees is Jacob Daniels." Jacob sighs and shakes his head with a chuckle. *Off limits*, I say to myself, instinctively knowing there's something between himself and Morgan. The other man barks out a laugh at Morgan's description. "The taller one with the booming laugh is his father, Garrett Daniels."

Father? I nearly choke, unable to break my stare from the man. Though I can obviously see the salt and pepper stubble along his cheeks, there is nothing in his face, not even a wrinkle, that makes him look old enough to be Jacob's father.

"Don't worry," Morgan continues, "his bark is much worse that his bite." She then gestures to me with a smile. "This is Taylor Wright. She is here about the assistant position, and I'm hoping she takes it."

I stiffen in surprise as Morgan's last words filter through the haze that is whatever I've been feeling about the two beautiful men in the room. A huge smile spreads across my face as I turn to face Morgan. "Really? I mean, thank you! I mean, yes, I'd love to!" I know I'm rambling, but my heart is racing. Though I'd hoped to get the job when I left Jordan's house this morning, touring the property and spending time with Morgan has me wanting it more than I've wanted anything else in a long time. "You are serious, right?"

"Of course," Morgan says, looking surprised at the question. "Honestly, I knew I wanted to hire you before I gave you the tour, but your ideas and eye for details solidified the decision. These guys here have been helping with the heavy lifting and construction until we're up, running, and making money, but you and I will talk logistics shortly."

"Nice to meet you, ma'am. You can call me Jake," the younger of the two says, extending his hand to shake mine, and heat crawls up my neck. I've never been called ma'am before. Considering I am, by my account, somewhere around ten years younger than him, I certainly didn't expect it. "I'm here to do whatever it is Morgan needs," his gaze shifts to the woman, and there's adoration in his eyes. I let his hand go. *Definitely off limits.*

Mr. Daniels' laughter once again fills the room. "Get a room, you two," he bellows with a shake of his head.

"We have one, old man, but you need my help cleaning up the mess we made out back," Jake says with a glint in his eye.

"Don't get embarrassed in front of your woman and her pixie," the older man says before extending his hand toward me. He keeps his eyes on Jake and Morgan as he introduces himself. "The name's Garrett. I can't get Morgan to stop calling me Mr. Daniels, so please don't start. Makes me feel old, and my children do enough of that."

I simply stare at the man, ignoring his proffered hand. Did this old guy just call me a pixie? What the fuck is that about? Who says shit like that about people they are being introduced to? When I fail to respond, he finally turns and looks at me directly. I don't even try to fix my face. My brows scrunch together as I work out whether to ignore all the lessons about respecting my elders and hit him over the head with my oversized bag.

"Ma'am? Did I say something? Do I stink? I just washed my hands." He holds them up in a placating gesture.

Ma'am? Jesus Christ, did this guy live under a rock? Foregoing the physical violence I'd contemplated, I try something less overt. "Pixie?" I ask in as scathing a tone as I can muster, brow raised in challenge. "You told Jake not to embarrass himself in front of Morgan and her pixie. I can only imagine you meant me, and I'd like to know what you meant by it, Mr. Daniels."

His brows furrow at my use of his proper name, and I see Morgan grab Jake's hand to pull him back a step. They're going to let my challenge stand, which makes me smile inwardly. I'm going to really like working for Morgan if she allows me to address bad behavior from anyone, regardless of their position and age. It takes a few moments of silence before Garrett responds.

"Shit," he says with a chuckle, "I didn't realize I'd said that aloud."

I'm not buying it, so I cross my arms over my chest defiantly. "If, at your age, you don't know how not to say the inside thoughts aloud, you should be able to explain them." He is too old to be playing games, and I'm having none of it.

From the kitchen door, Jake says, "Oh shit!" before Garrett formulates another response.

"Okay then, Pixie Girl. If you must know, I took in your colorful self and thought, I bet that's how Tinker Bell would look if she were real and walking around today. And now that I've seen your feistiness, I think I was right."

"Feisty? Tinker Bell? Why, you old cowpoke!"

I take a step forward, ready to swing my bag for real when Morgan and Jake finally step between us. My face is flushed, though I'm not really angry. I just want to knock him down a peg, or at least knock the amusement from his eyes.

"Mr. Daniels," Morgan interjects, "if you and Jacob would please go finish whatever you were working on, I can finish up with Ms. Wright."

He holds my gaze for another minute before turning. When he kisses Morgan on the cheek, a look of contrition on his face, something flutters in my stomach. I haven't seen a gesture that sweet in years, not since my grandparents passed. Morgan says something in his ear, but I can't hear the exchange. It's only when she turns my way to apologize that I stop looking at his retreating backside. I say the first thing that comes to my head to help swallow the lump of embarrassment that forms under her scrutiny.

"They are actually father and son? I would have never guessed his age."

Morgan chuckles, but I can't tell if it's for the question or my earlier fixation. "Ironically," she says, "I guessed your age wrong when you first got here, so there must be something in the air. The twins are barely six months older than me, so I can vouch for Garrett's age."

"Twins? Do I even want to know about another tight-assed hunk in that family?"

The laugh that springs from Morgan at this question rivals Garrett's, and it takes her several seconds to catch her breath enough to respond. I actually look around, thinking I might have to search the kitchen for glassware to get the woman a drink of water. It would be terrible to kill my new boss before I even sign a contract.

"Jacob has a twin sister. Joanna is my best friend."

"Best friend's brother, huh?" I say under my breath, but the return of Morgan's laugh says I hadn't been quiet enough. This time, I join her, letting the whirlwind of emotions that have been swirling since this morning finally break free in the laughter.

"Yep, we're a walking small-town romance: Best friend's brother, second chance, the one that got away...all the tropes."

I chuckle again at Morgan's description of their relationship. I've not been a big romance reader, but maybe I need to start. I only know about the best friend's brother trope because of social media. Morgan breaks me from my thoughts when she asks if I'm second-guessing the job.

"I hope we haven't made you change your mind. Mr. Daniels is part of the package, as he's doing work around here, and he's my boyfriend's father."

I love her use of the term boyfriend. Morgan and Jacob are cute together, even if they're a bit old for the boyfriend-girlfriend thing. No matter what, though, I'll find a way to put up with the old man if I can't just keep away from him altogether. Shouldn't be too hard.

"Oh, he couldn't scare me away, but I might be able to scare him off if you ever want him to be scarce," I respond with a wink, and we both laugh again.

The next twenty minutes are spent reviewing the expectations and needs of the position and the start date. I try to keep the disappointment from my face at the delay in it being a full-time position, though I fully understand the reasons. Morgan has just moved back to Colliers Town; all of her money has gone into renovations, and there's no income yet from the house. There is literally no money with which to pay staff, including this position, which would be more of a manager than simply an assistant. I want this job, but I'm not sure I can wait to start and wait again to get the full pay. As I'm thumbing through the employment contract, I notice an addendum that says "if needed."

"Wait, what's this clause mean?" I ask Morgan who is watching expectantly. In fact, she looks downright nervous. What does she have to be nervous about? She isn't the one who needs a place to live and enough money to pay for it.

"Oh," Morgan says with a start, looking at the page, "I forgot about that. It's there in case the person who takes the position needs somewhere to stay. Basically, you would have a room here in the house for your use and be able to take meals in the kitchen once it's up and running. There might also be times when I might need to be out of town, and my assistant would need to be on hand for guests overnight, so I've included a room in the contract."

My eyes burn as I try to hold back the deluge of tears threatening to spill out of me at the realization that this clause might just be the miracle I need.

"Is everything alright?" Morgan asks, walking around the island toward me.

I jump to my feet. "Can I hug you?" I blurt. Morgan responds by enveloping me in her arms and holding on until the urge to sob fades, and I'm able to pull away. "I was so worried I would have to say no to the job because of the low hours and pay to start, but a room changes everything. I've been sleeping in my car most nights and only went by a friend's house on the county line to shower this morning before coming here."

Morgan sniffles before saying anything, and my regard for the woman grows. Very few people have been empathetic to my situation. Pretty much, Jordan is the only one who supports me in any way. Everyone else who knows thinks I'm crazy and should just go home. They believe I'm just being ungrateful, or worse spiteful, toward my parents. The fact that I've found someone who cares enough about others to write a clause for a free room into an employment contract as a "just in case," is amazing.

"Unfortunately," Morgan says, "I cannot start paying you any sooner than outlined here in the contract, but if you would like to start sooner, I can get you a room ready for this evening."

"Really?" I ask with a sob.

"Yes, now, if you wouldn't mind, I have a few things to do, and I need some things from the hardware store downtown. Could you go for me?"

"Absolutely!" I would do next to anything for Morgan. Going to the store for her is nothing. I jump from the stool I've been sitting on and grab my purse.

Morgan gives me a huge smile and some money for gas. Apparently, JD Hardware belongs to Joanna Daniels because Morgan says her best friend will have everything ready by the time I get there. More importantly, Morgan will have the contract corrected when I return to the house, and I'll have a bed of my own to sleep in tonight as part of my compensation rather than living off a friend or anyone else. Once we work out a schedule for the coming weeks prior to opening, I'll give notice to the hotel and be glad to start working toward my future.

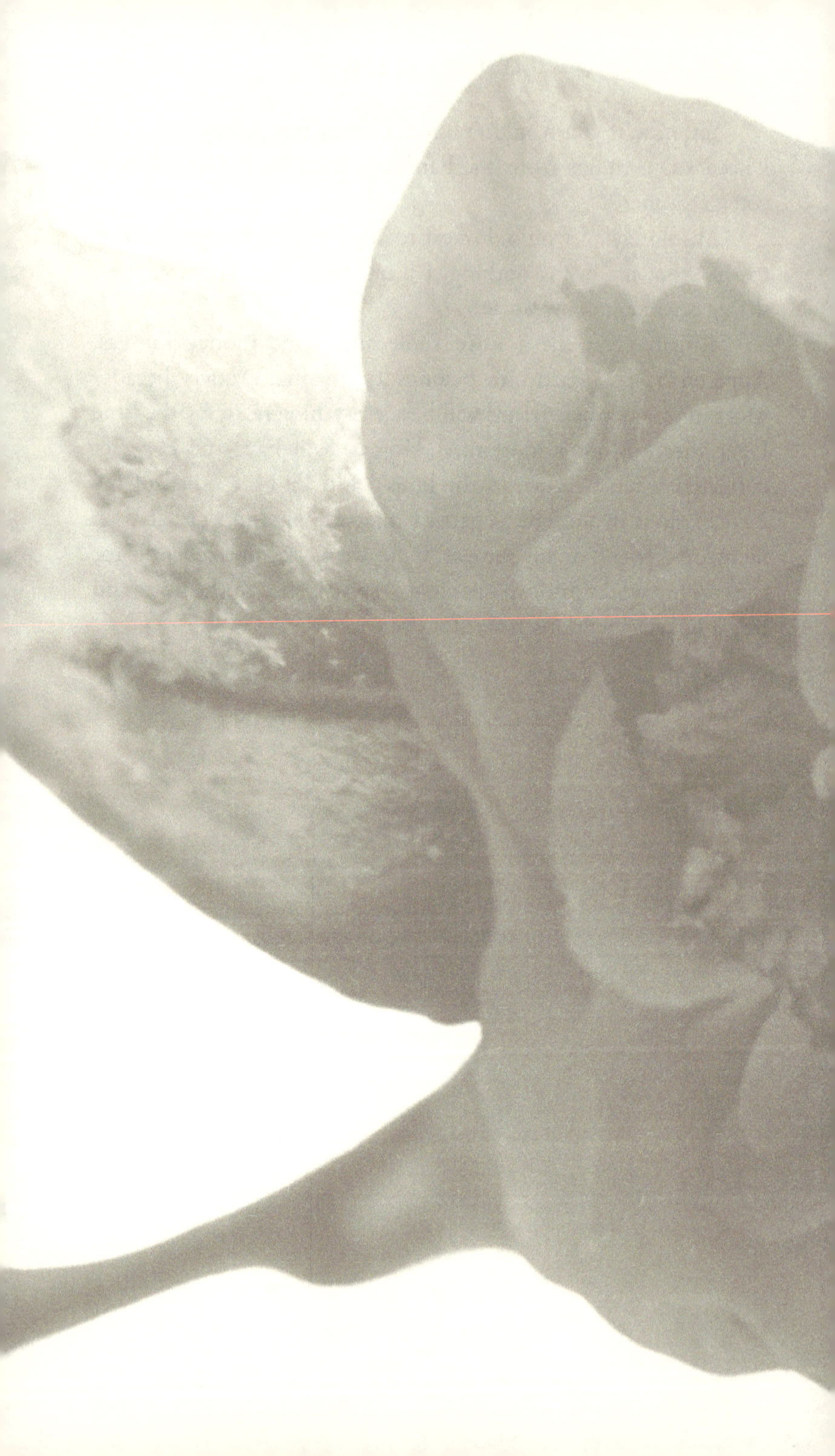

5

THINGS ARE LOOKING UP

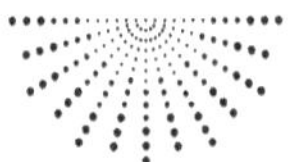

*T*aylor

As soon as I get in the car and set the GPS, I text Jordan.

> Me: You are not going to believe this!

> Jordan: You just gonna leave me in suspense?

> Me: LOL. No, but I'm about to drive into downtown Colliers Town. Apparently, this town has a downtown. Anyway, can you talk?

Within seconds, my phone rings, and Jordan's face pops up on the screen.

"Hey."

"Skip all that. I only have a few minutes before I have to run back inside. What's up? How'd it go?"

I laugh at her antics. I knew Jordan wouldn't have been able to wait for news, even if it meant leaving the store unattended. She works at the boutique whenever she doesn't have classes. One of these days, her boss is going to fire her for things like this.

"You know, you could have just said you were busy."

31

"Stop wasting time with the small talk. Tell me!"

"I got the job! But that's not the best part."

Jordan doesn't say anything right away, and I wonder if the call has dropped. I toggle from the GPS and see her face on my screen.

"You still there?"

"I'm waiting for you to tell me the rest. I told you to make it quick, and you keep dragging things out."

I laugh. "Seriously. You could at least sound happy about the job."

"I want to make sure I'm celebrating the right things. Now, tell me, or I'm hanging up on you!"

I laugh again. "Fine. Not only did I get the job, but I won't get full-time pay for at least a month or so."

"What? Please don't tell me that's the best part!"

"No, silly. The best part is that, though I won't get paid, I'm getting a free room to stay in, and I can move in as soon as tonight! I don't have to sleep in my car anymore, and I'm working for the room, so I don't have to feel bad about it either."

"You're for real? They're giving you a room in the B and B?"

"Yep. There was a clause in the employment contract about the use of a room if needed, and once I told her my situation, she determined it fit the 'if needed' part. I couldn't believe it and had to hug her. She's super cool."

"Wait. I really do have to get back inside, but wait. If you move in tonight, when are we going to celebrate?"

"I'll come by this weekend and hang out. I need to tell you about the other people I met today, including this old dude I nearly beat in the head with my bag."

"Girl, shut up! I'll get the drinks."

"Bye." I don't even wait for Jordan to hang up before ending the call. We could easily go back and forth multiple times, but she needs to get back to work, and the hardware store is less than a mile away. We've always joked that we come from a small town, but driving through this so-called downtown area proves we grew up in the suburbs. Well, as much of a suburb as one can get in the foothills. The main street has two regular traffic lights and two four-way stop signs with blinking lights. That's it. No fast food, only a couple restaurants, one grocery store, and the hardware store. It's like something from an old movie. I park in front of JD Hardware, and a woman steps into the open doorway before I can turn off the car. She has to be Joanna Daniels because she favors Jake even though they have different hair colors.

"You must be Taylor," the woman says with a smile.

"That's me. You must be Joanna."

Joanna inclines her head and gestures for me to enter the store. "I just finished getting all the supplies Morgan needs together. I could have brought them by myself, but she told me you were coming."

"It was the least I could do with the offer she made me."

"Still, she didn't have to put you to work before you even signed your contract." Joanna's smile widens, giving me an odd feeling, like she knows something I don't.

"Hopefully, it'll all fit in my car," I say as a way to move the conversation along. I don't mind doing the favor for my new boss, but I hope it won't take all day.

"How are you with taking inventory?"

Joanna doesn't even look my way when she asks the question, just continues toward the counter, and I scowl at her back. It seems an odd change in topic. Is this a test? Does Morgan want Joanna to verify my ability to do additional tasks we haven't yet discussed? No, Morgan doesn't seem the type to try and manipulate others.

"Why do you ask?" I keep my tone as level as possible.

"Morgan has a good eye for people. She also has a big heart. She feels bad that she can't have you start at the house right away for pay, and I've been looking for someone to help around here."

Now that explanation makes sense for the woman I believe Morgan to be. She might not be manipulative, but she would put people together and see what happens. I look Joanna over. She seems pretty straight forward. She dresses plainly enough for a woman who owns a hardware store, and yet something sets her apart. There's both kindness and practicality in the way she makes the statement without being pushy. Joanna needs help at her store. Morgan knows I need steady pay now to get on my feet. The room will help, but it isn't enough without money. Driving back and forth to the city won't be feasible for long with no additional income, so I'll have to quit the hotel job anyway. Though I hate the idea of being given a job out of pity, Joanna is offering something to fill the gap. My mind whirls, and the emotions I thought I'd released resurface.

"What are you looking for, and what's the pay?"

When Joanna's eyebrow lifts, I cringe. The question had come out snarkier than intended.

"I'm sorry. That came out wrong."

"No, I get it. You don't know me from Eve, and I'm offering you a job because someone else told me you need money. It's a pride thing. Morgan's like that too. You should have seen her when she first moved back to Colliers Town. That house was a big ol' mess, and she wouldn't hear about staying with me and barely let us help her get it cleaned up."

For some reason, this new information is surprising. Morgan didn't say much about herself or the history of the house besides what was shared on the website about it originally being a rooming house for mine workers. It explains why Morgan called Joanna to ask her to offer a job rather than just having me sit around the house. Morgan must've known it wouldn't have sat well with me for very long. A new sense of admiration for the woman blooms.

"Don't feel obligated to take the job. It's part time, possibly temporary, unless you wanted to continue."

"No, no. I'm definitely interested. You just caught me off guard, and you're right," I pause for a second. "It's a pride thing. I don't know how much Morgan told you already, but I've been sleeping in my car because I wouldn't even accept my best friend's offer of a room without knowing how long I'd be struggling and unable to pay my own way. It's stupid."

"Nope, not stupid at all. And Morgan didn't tell me much except she likes you, hired you on, is going to let you stay in the house, and that you might want to do some additional work while you wait for the house to open. No details. Morgan's good at keeping other people's stories to herself."

I smile at that. It's just another thing to make me like the woman more. I'm even starting to like Joanna and can see why the two women are friends.

"As for what help I need around here. With the new highway exit opening, I need to get ready for more people moving into the area. More people equals more houses, which means more business. Good for me and Jake...he owns a construction company...but inventory and stocking are my least favorite parts of the job."

At the mention of Jake, I remember the scene Morgan and I encountered in the kitchen. "Yeah, I met Jake today too." Before Joanna can fully smile or say anything more about her twin brother, I finish with a sneering, "and your father."

Joanna's head tilts to the side, and her face falls. If I knew the woman better, or hadn't still been a bit irritated at the audacity of the man, I might've laughed at her confusion. Instead, I squared my shoulders.

"What did my pa do?"

"He called me a pixie before we were even fully introduced, and then he compared me to Tinker Bell, calling me feisty."

The look on Joanna's face makes me pause my rant. It's somewhere in the midst of confusion, incredulity, and laughter, as if Joanna can't figure out which emotion is appropriate to the situation and is trying them all on for size at the same time.

"Joanna? Are you alright?"

"My pa? You're telling me my pa, Garrett Daniels, the most

standoffish man in all of Colliers Town not only said that many words to you, but he made a joke in front of you, a stranger."

Not sure where she's going with this, I eye her warily. Does she think I'm lying? Though Joanna's description of her father doesn't quite match the man I met a couple hours ago, he has to be her father. The twins favor him in height, jawline, and shoulders. Joanna has feminine curves, but she still has the same shoulders as the men in her family. She is both strong and soft at the same time. I think to respond, but Joanna pulls out her cell phone and puts it to her ear.

"Jacob Daniels, what did Pa do to this poor girl?" My eyes grow wide. "He didn't! And you didn't stop him? What the hell, Jake? I almost liked it better before Morgan pulled him out of his silent era."

I swallow, almost embarrassed to be listening in on this family drama. What does Joanna mean by 'silent era'? What did she expect Jacob...Jake...Jacob...shit, which name am I supposed to call him? Anyway, what did Joanna expect him to have done to stop their father from making an ass of himself? Joanna ends the call and looks back at me with that same look of confusion and laughter, though the incredulity has shifted to something else...horror? embarrassment?

"Un-fucking-believable!" is all Joanna says, almost to the air rather than to me. "I'm sorry that my father offended you."

"I'm not. I mean, I wasn't really offended."

"So, you gave the town curmudgeon a dressing down because you weren't offended?"

A laugh escapes before I can stop it. "No, I gave him a dressing down because when I asked what he meant by his offhanded descriptor, his response was 'I didn't realize I'd said that out loud,' and I thought that was a cop out."

Joanna gawks, mouth wide open like a fish. She waves her hand, as if the gesture will conjure words, but none come. Then she starts laughing, a deep belly laugh that has her doubled over against the counter. Her laughter is so loud and unexpected, my stomach flutters making me laugh too. Thank goodness no one walks into the store, or they might have run out to escape the two crazy women. Once Joanna gets control of herself again, she finally finds words that send us both into another round of laughter.

"Oh yeah, you're going to give that old man a run for his money. Please tell me you will take the job, both of them...hell, whatever it takes to keep him on his toes."

I do accept the job, and after packing all of Morgan's items into the car, I reach out and hug Joanna before heading back to Gretna House to move in.

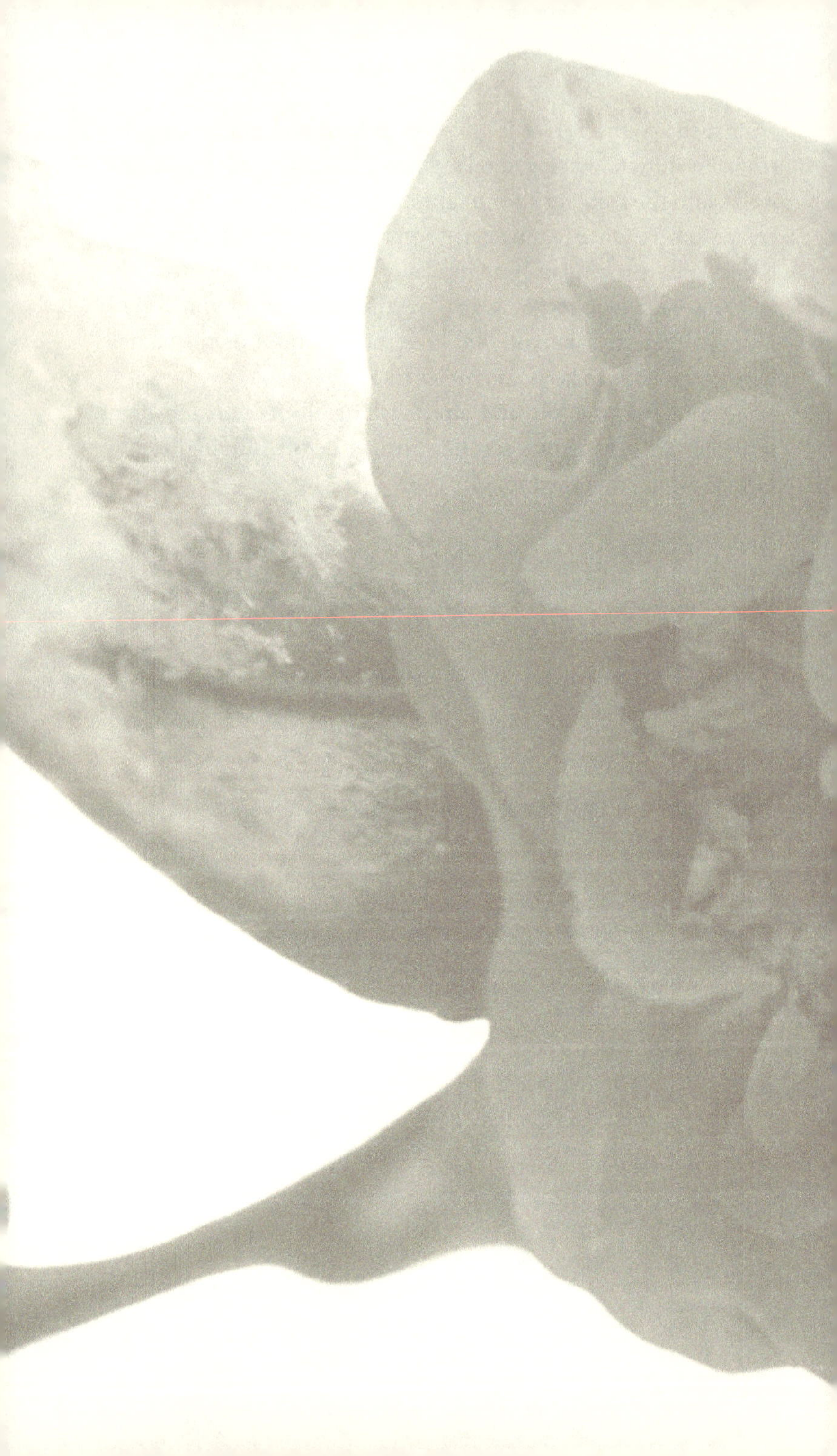

6

GUILT AND REMORSE

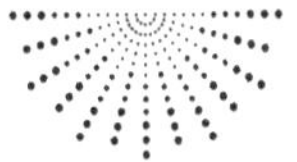

*G*arrett

I walk out of the house scratching my head. What in the hell just happened back there? One moment, I'm washing my hands, and the next, I'm being told off by a little slip of a woman...a woman damn near half my age if not younger. No one ever talks to me like that, not even my late wife. Not that I didn't deserve to be told about myself. It was kind of rude for me to call her a pixie, but dammit, she was wearing all the colors of the rainbow, like she would throw glitter on each of our heads at any moment. And then she got feisty, and that fucked me up even more. She's a spitfire.

Once we're outside by the woodpile and the tools we'd left scattered all over, Jacob spins on his heel. "What was that about, old man? You rarely even speak to people you know."

"What are you talking about? I just said hello to the little woman." I somehow can't bring myself to call her a little girl. She's definitely little, but she carries herself like a self-assured woman. She's a walking contradiction. Jacob crosses his arms, expecting something more, so I finish with a, "Did she not expect to stand out and get attention walking around in all those colors and patterns?"

"Are we back in the 1930s?" Jacob shakes his head with a sigh. "You deserved that talking to, Pa."

I rub my hand behind my neck. There's disappointment in Jacob's eyes, and I hate it. "You're right. I did. I don't know what caused me to say some of that shit aloud, or really at all."

"Well, you better figure it out, old man, so you can get it together because that girl's gonna be around a lot. Morgan not only offered her the job, but she sent her off to meet Joanna about working at the store."

Trying to distract from the lecture he's about to give me, like he's the father, I respond before he can finish his sentence. "Oh boy, kiddo, your ass would be in trouble too if she heard you calling her a girl." My chuckle dies, however, when I realize what he's said. "You've got to be kidding me! I knew there was a reason I didn't like Morgan when y'all were kids. She's gonna be the death of me."

This time it's Jacob's turn to laugh. "It's too late. You already admitted that I was right about Morgan all along. I, for one, am grateful that she brought you back to life."

I nod in agreement and smile. I, too, am grateful to have been pulled from my stupor. It's one thing to grieve the loss of a wife, and I do still miss her. It's another thing to stop living entirely. Guilt eats at me for the years I barely existed for my children when they had lost their mother. They'd not been given the chance to properly mourn their ma because they also had to take care of me and the farm. When I finally woke up from the fog, I took a long walk around the property assessing all I'd lost with my wife. The kids had sold off many of the animals, or they'd died from neglect. The house was barely holding itself together, and the barely was thanks to Jacob. It could not have been easy for them.

"Don't you go getting lost on me again," Jacob said, pulling me from the melancholy always at the fringes of my mind. "I don't want to have to go get Morgan."

"You know, it's a damn shame you have to threaten me with your girlfriend."

"Fiancée."

"Your fiancée," I parrot with a sweep of my hand as if blowing out cigarette smoke. I'd stopped that bad habit decades ago.

Jacob chuckles, and my smile returns. It feels so good to banter with him again. "Let's get this stuff cleaned up and see if we can get Morgan to make dinner," I suggest with a wink.

"Now, that's a plan I can get behind."

We set about wrapping up the extension cords and cleaning off the tools before storing them in Jacob's locked truck boxes. Normally, he would've been working on his company's contracts during the week, but with Morgan being so close to opening the bed and breakfast, he farmed the work out to subcontractors and has been here every day. She'll be opening in two months at half capacity, but that'll give her some income and a chance to work out all the kinks in her business plan. The woman has an eye for the business, and she's an amazing cook to boot. Every time I come over to help, she makes us something for lunch and often invites me to have dinner with them. Will that change when the pixie starts living here? Does Jacob know when she plans to move in? I don't get the chance to ask because Jacob's phone rings.

"What's up, sis?"

I can't quite make out Joanna's words, but I can hear her yelling. When Jacob's eyes lock on mine, I look down with a shake of my head. She must've heard what kind of ass I made of myself. Shit! Just what I need, another woman pissed at me. Here I am a newly single, newly revived man, and three women are pissed at me all in the same day for the same reason. That has to be some kind of damn record.

"Pa took one look at that gir..." Jacob pauses for a moment before he corrects himself, "woman, and called her a damn pixie." I keep my eyes on the ground, but it's to hide the small smile that tugs at the corners of my lips. "What do you mean why didn't I stop him? When was the last time you tried to stop Pa from doing something he set his mind to doing?" My smile falls, and it seems the entire world goes silent for a moment. "Pa, stay with me," Jacob says as he slides the phone back in his pocket before putting his hand on my shoulder. "I didn't mean anything by it. Joanna laughed it off. I'm sorry. I didn't even think. I simply meant that you're a stubborn man."

With a deep breath, I reach up and cover Jacob's hand with mine. "I'm okay, son. I've just had some moments of guilt and remorse. I am good, though. I'm happy to be here and so grateful for both of you."

"I'm not sure you're gonna be grateful for my sister," Jacob interjects with a wicked grin.

My eyes narrow. "Do I even want to know?"

"Ha! You want to be prepared. She is definitely hiring that girl to work at the store too."

"Jesus Christ!" I stomp off toward the house, yelling on the way, "Morgan, I hope you have some coffee in there...and some whiskey too!"

Jacob's laughter follows me as I round the corner to the back porch. As soon as I'm out of view, I let my own smile slip back in. It feels damn good to be alive!

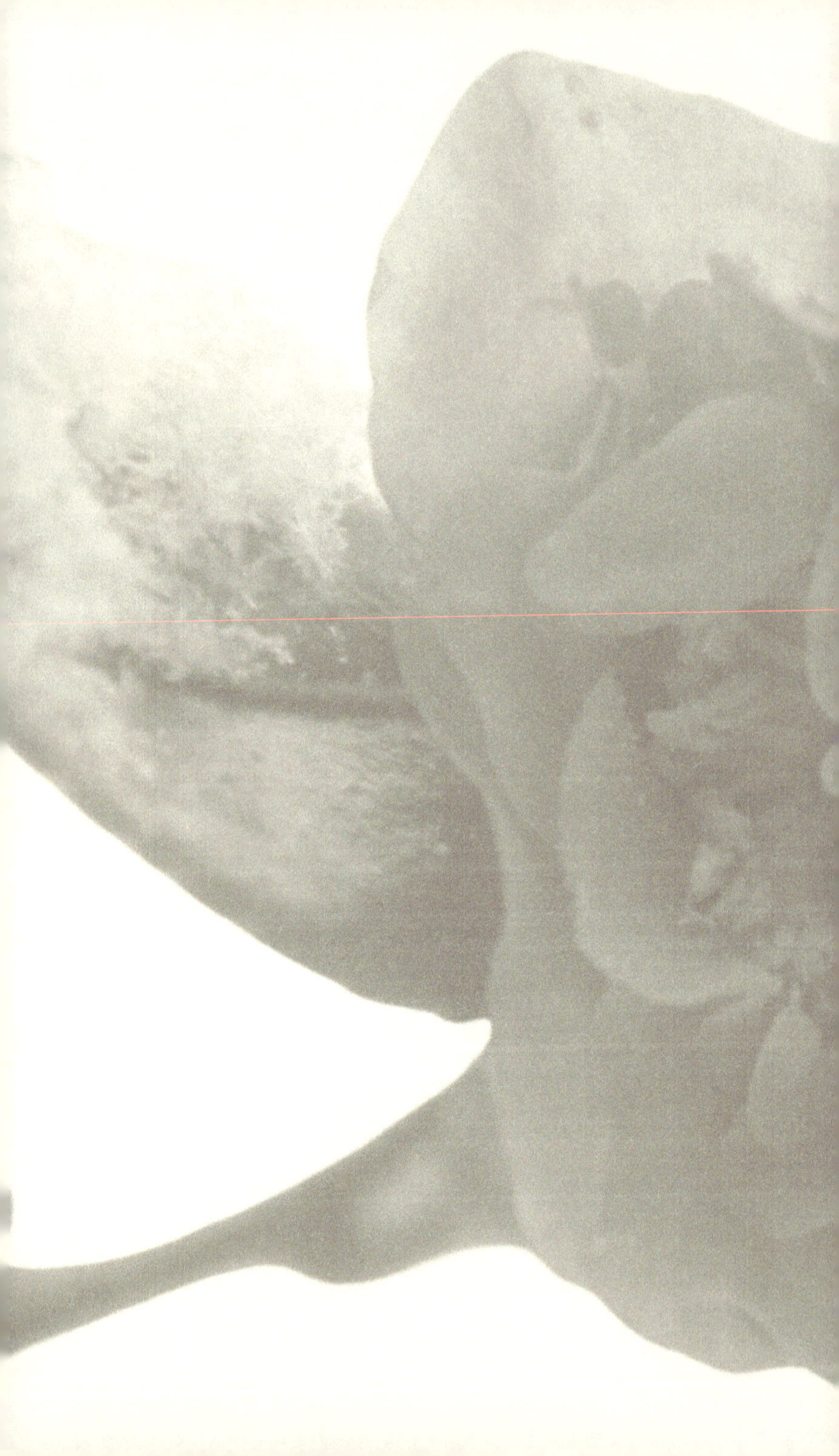

7

IT'S OKAY TO ASK FOR HELP

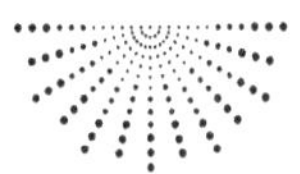

aylor

I'm almost surprised to see Jacob and his father still at the house when I get back. I really don't know anyone's living situation, but for some reason, I didn't expect them to both be sitting at the table eating dinner.

"Welcome back, Taylor. Will you join us for dinner?" Morgan asks from the sink.

"Morgan makes a terrific lasagna," Garrett says, not looking up from his plate.

Jacob grunts in agreement, never leaving his mouth empty long enough to say anything. Morgan turns around and laughs at them both. She holds an empty plate out in my direction, silently asking again. I don't want to take any more advantage of the woman's benevolence than I already am, but then I look at the plates in front of Jacob and Garrett. My churning stomach wins out over my pride, and I nod to Morgan, walking around to take the offered plate that's now full of lasagna, salad, and garlic bread.

"It smells amazing," I say on my way to the empty seat away from Garrett.

He looks my way for less than a second, but it's long enough for me to know he's holding back from saying something. Though everyone else seems surprised at his earlier behavior, I have nothing else to go on but to believe he is a rude, misogynistic, old relic who can't keep his comments to himself.

"You know I don't bite, right?"

And there it is. Morgan's eyes narrow and Jacob's go wide. I just shake my head. I knew it was coming.

"All bark then, huh?"

Okay, maybe it's a little petty to even respond, and probably more so to get snarky with him, but he rubs me the wrong way. He doesn't even look up at my response, and for some reason that irks me more than his comments. I snort a laugh and go back to eating the delicious food, as if to say I won that little tete-a-tete. Really, the meal is the winner. Morgan can cook her ass off! If her breakfasts are anything like this, there is no doubt that there will be many repeat customers after eating Morgan's cooking. I feel eyes boring into me and look up to see Garrett watching from the corner of his eye. I raise a brow, but he says nothing.

When everyone has finished their meal, I rise from the table and take my plate to the sink.

"Leave it. I'll run the dishwasher in a bit."

"Are you sure? I don't mind."

Morgan waves me off. "It's fine. I'm sure you'd rather move into your room than do dishes anyway."

My eyes go wide. There's a difference between Morgan saying she'd have a room ready tonight and finding out that it's ready for me. Tears sting the backs of my eyes when Morgan holds out a key. I take and shove it in my pocket as far as possible, afraid I might lose it, or she might change her mind.

"Thank you. I need to go get all your supplies from the car."

"Do you need some help?" Jacob asks.

"I think I got it," I answer, heading down the hall.

Once outside, I regret having told him no. I forgot that Joanna helped me load the car, and we used a cart to get all the stuff to the curb. Oh well, I'll just make a few trips to get it all inside. After taking a deep breath, I reach for two gallons of paint from behind the front seat, and promptly drop one on the ground when a deep growl and bark come from behind me near my ear...far too close to my ear.

"Shit!" I scream and whirl around, ready to swing the other paint container on whatever creature is about to attack.

"Whoa there, Pixie Girl," Garrett says, grabbing the bucket handle from my grasp before I can hit him with it.

My chest rises and falls as I gulp in deep breaths. "Are you always such an asshole, or is it just for me?"

His smile falls, and the mirth glowing in his eyes fades. "I'm sorry. I thought it would be a funny joke from your response in the kitchen. I was obviously wrong."

His eyes are genuinely apologetic, but I struggle to find forgiveness when my lungs are still threatening to burst from my chest. Instead, I stare at him like he's a lunatic because that's how I feel about him. He claims the behavior was a joke, but I can't find the humor in it. I can, however, feel some strange guilt at breaking his spirit. I'll have to examine that feeling later because it makes no sense. He'd been a jerk earlier in the day, made a smart-ass comment as soon as I'd come back to the house, and now this. I shouldn't feel anything except annoyed at him. Even the memory of his tight ass isn't enough to make dealing with this worth it. I'm so caught up in my confusing thoughts about him that I don't realize he's still standing there staring at me like he's waiting for some kind of response.

"Why are you looking at me like that, Mr. Daniels?"

He shakes his head like he's also been deep in his own thoughts and then blinks a couple times before reaching down to pick up the paint bucket I'd dropped. "Let me help with this stuff." I start to protest, because I'm definitely going to protest, when he turns those apologetic eyes on me again. "It's the least I can do." I throw up my hands and move out of the way when he puts both bucket handles in one fist and reaches into the car for the three plastic bags of smaller items that sit there. "Is there more?" he asks.

"Just those two boxes on that side and then my personal stuff. I can get that."

He looks at me with hardened eyes. He is the one protesting this time. I really don't want his help. I don't want him that close with his woodsy scent, and I surely don't want him stepping into my room upstairs. I'm far too aware of him. Like how the fuck does he smell so good after working outside and building shit all day? It isn't until he disappears inside the front door that I realize I'd been staring at his ass the whole time he walked away. *He's old enough to be your father, possibly your grandfather, T! Get your shit together.* I chide myself before turning away from the house. I run to the other side of the car, determined to carry the last of the items into the house myself before he makes it back. Once again, though, he's right behind me by the time I pull the boxes from the seat.

"I'll take those." His deep timbre runs through me, vibrating my chest.

"Dammit! Stop that!"

He looks down at me, making me feel small, but he doesn't say anything. He simply plucks the boxes from my arms and strides away without a word. What the hell? What is it with him sneaking up on me? What the hell is it with me reacting to his nearness like that? I need some sleep. I need to lock myself away in the room and get some sleep. None of what just happened is making any sense.

I pull two suitcases from the trunk and put them up on the porch. Then, I grab my overnight bag and tub of shoes from the front seat along with my big purse. I'm determined that this time, he will not beat me to the punch. I manage to use my legs to push the suitcases to the bottom of the interior stairs before I climb up with the other items in my hands.

"You almost ready to go, Pa?" Jacob's voice penetrates the closed kitchen door.

"In a minute. Let me finish helping that pixie girl with the rest of her stuff."

"She said she didn't need any help," Jacob counters.

"Yeah, well, she lied. Did you not just see me make two trips back in here with Morgan's order?"

"Sorry, Pa, I was...um..."

"Distracted. Yeah, I could see that."

The sound of water running and dishes clanging in the kitchen conjured an image of Morgan finally filling the dishwasher. I'd place bets that the two of them were taking advantage of having been left alone.

"Now that you're no longer distracted, give me five, and I'll be ready to head home."

"Shit," I whisper and run up the rest of the stairs. Well, I walk as quickly as my legs will allow balancing the tub of shoes with my big bags on each shoulder. Morgan put me in Room One, which was at the far end of the hall on the left. Not that I'm ungrateful, but I definitely wish my door was the one at the top of the stairs right now. Not only was it the biggest room on the second floor, nearly a full suite, but more than that, it was the closest room. No sooner had I gotten my room unlocked and dropped the items I was carrying, heavy footsteps hit the landing. Rolling my eyes and shaking my head, I turn toward the door.

"You really didn't have to do that," I say, my voice holding more exasperation with his stubbornness than anything else. "I could have carried them upstairs once I emptied my hands from the first trip."

"I think the words you were looking for were 'thank you,'" he drawls, and his breath brushes across the top of my head.

I've never thought myself petite, especially since I've always carried extra weight and been larger than most of the girls I knew in both size and height. This man, however, towers over me in an unnerving way. I fight the urge to scowl up at him, but when he doesn't make any move to step back or to let go of my luggage, I push myself to do something. Taking a step back, I look up. His head is tilted to the side, his mouth set in a firm line like he is trying to put together a puzzle that has far too many missing pieces. His brows are drawn together, but when his eyes meet mine, all of his features relax. A smirk replaces the taut line, and his eyes soften in amusement. Though I watch it happen, I'm dumbfounded as to how someone's emotions can shift so suddenly and completely. The man is something else.

"Thank you," I say softly, reaching out for the handles he finally relinquishes. "I do appreciate the help carrying everything in."

He nods in response and turns back down the hall. The room suddenly feels empty, as if he had taken up all the air when he stood in the doorway. What the fuck is happening to me?

"Oh, and, Pixie Girl," he says from the top of the stairs, "there's nothing wrong with accepting help from people."

Grabbing the first thing I can easily pick up, a pillow from the armchair to my left, I run to the railing and throw it down the stairs at him. It hits him square in his retreating shoulders with a satisfying thump. Feeling vindicated, I turn back to my room, close the door, and flop flat onto the bed. I have my own bed to sleep in once again. I have a new job, well, two of them, and a place to stay. Life is good, and Garrett Daniels will not ruin this moment! In all honesty, I don't think he can ruin anything, but I damn sure won't tell him that. Instead, I sit up and get to work unpacking, trying to put the man out of my mind.

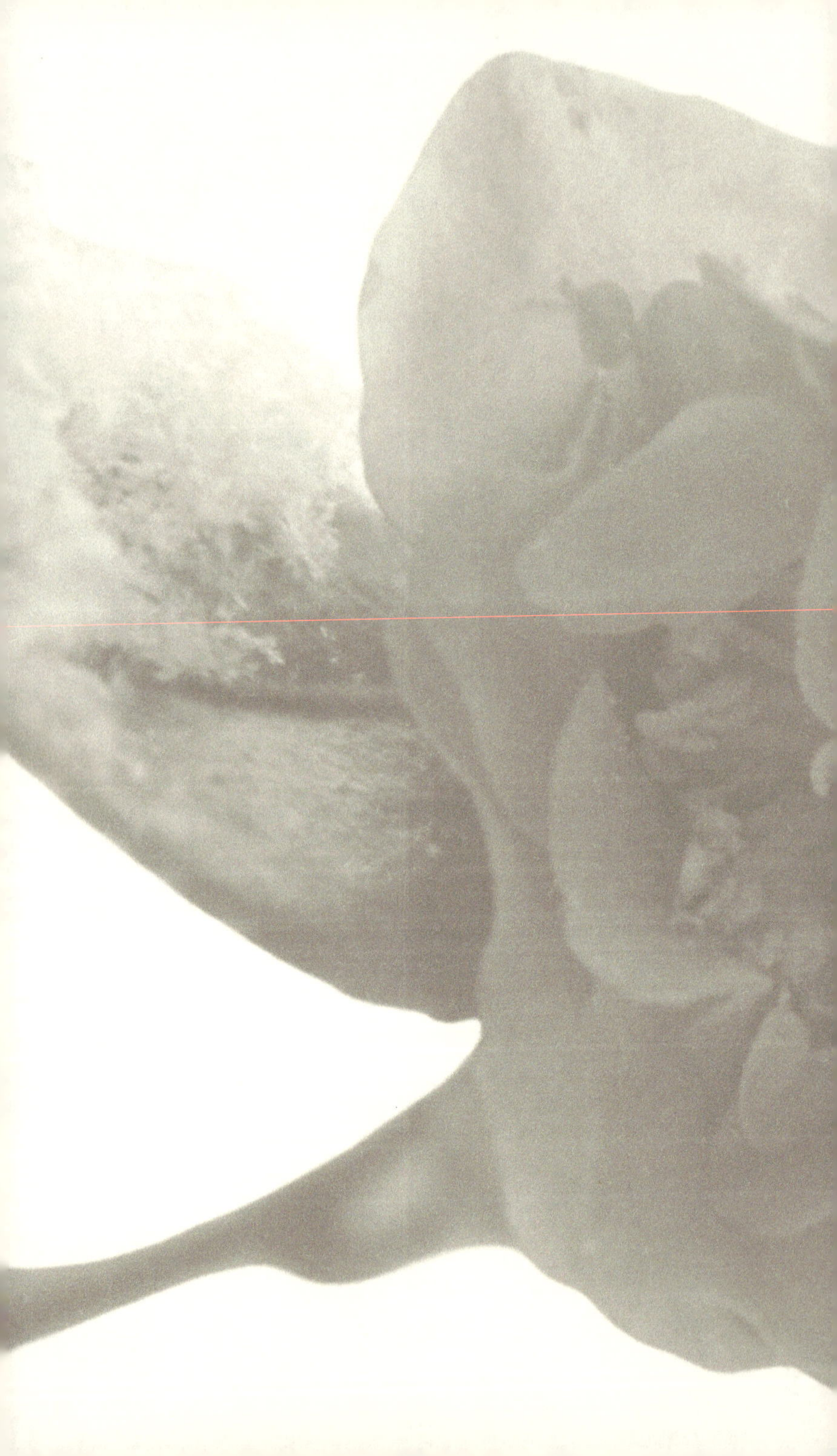

8

WANDERING THOUGHTS

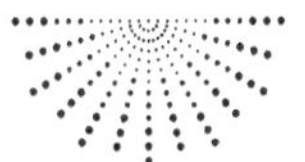

Garrett

I pick the pillow up from the stairs and howl with laughter. Yep, she riles easily, and it's fun to watch. Besides, it's better to be on the receiving end of her reciprocated irritation than whatever that strange thing was that passed between us in the doorway just a couple minutes before. I shake my head, trying to clear the image of her uncertain eyes looking up at me. I'd wanted to cup her cheek. Whether it was comfort or something else I thought to offer, I'm not sure, so I walked off, which might have been a cowardly thing to do. When I turned to find her still staring after me, though, I had to say something, anything to shift the energy. She responded exactly as expected. Of course, I hadn't expected her to throw something at my back, but I smile at the fact that it wasn't something meant to do lasting damage.

I'm still smiling when Jacob and Morgan exit the kitchen and nearly run into me at the bottom of the stairs. "I'm ready to go if you are, son," I say, simultaneously handing Morgan the rogue pillow and kissing her cheek. A laugh escapes when she stands there, mouth open. If I'd been wearing my Stetson, I'd have tipped it at her.

"I'll see you tomorrow, Morgana," Jacob says, oblivious to Morgan's confusion. "I have some things to check on at the office, but I should be here by one-ish."

I stand there watching Jacob say his goodbyes until he pulls Morgan close for a kiss. That's the moment I make my way to the waiting truck. I don't begrudge my son having found the love of his life again, and I damn sure love the fine woman Morgan has grown into. Still, watching them together is a constant reminder of what I lost when my Clara died. Nope, I don't need to watch their moments of intimacy and wallow in my own loss.

"That's a good woman you got there, Jacob," I say when he climbs into the driver's side of the pickup.

"Yeah, she's...well, she's damn near perfect."

I snort a laugh. Even Morgan wouldn't describe herself as perfect, but I understand the sentiment. "I felt the same way about your ma." Jacob glances my way, as we make the bumpy drive off Morgan's property. "We're gonna need to fill in these big ruts before paying patrons start coming, else they'll be ruining their cars on the way in." I hadn't really planned to say that aloud, but I didn't like the look Jacob was giving me.

"Are you alright, pa? You were laughing like a loon when we met you at the bottom of the stairs, and now you seem off again." Jacob continues to give me sideways glances while still watching the road in the shadowy dusk beneath the trees. "Where'd that pillow come from," he asks before turning onto the main road.

The corner of my lip quirks up. "The pixie pinged me in the shoulders with it from the upstairs landing. She's got good aim and a good arm." I'm chuckling by the time I finish that last sentence.

"What in the world is it with you two?"

I fight down the irritation at his question. I don't fucking know. She's different. Different has always been uncomfortable in this town. Somehow, though, she wears her difference like chainmail, and it's fascinating. At the same time, I want to see her without the armor. Is her tongue just as sharp? Her wit just as quick? Is that streak of fierce independence a consequence of wearing the armor or does it go deeper? She's a damn enigma, and yet, she reminds me of Morgan. Knowing my soon-to-be daughter-in law's story doesn't help that comparison feel any less heavy. Did Taylor have to build that chain link by link? Shit. It's not my business.

"Pa?"

We haven't moved from the end of the drive. *Shit.* "She's easy to rile up," I say. It's the truth, at least part of the truth. Hopefully, it's enough to satisfy Jacob's curiosity.

"Who are you, and what have you done with my father?"

I laugh at that. I've been asking myself much the same question. "Would you rather I stayed locked away inside myself hating the world?" Though the question is genuine, I know it will cut. It can't be helped. My thoughts are too all over the place. That girl...no, woman...no, pixie. She raises my hackles and makes me smile and uncomfortable all at the same time. I can't explain that to Jacob though. I know the reputation I have in the town. Hell, Morgan called me on it when she returned. I'd been cold and hard, a curmudgeon, even when my Clara was still alive. I was broken when she left me; truth be told, I haven't even been to her grave since that first year. The kids stopped inviting me.

"Of course not, Pa. It's just strange to see you so open with a stranger, and a woman at that. You're almost playful, and yet judgmental, and yet not. It's weird, and I don't know how...oh never mind. If you're okay, and arguing with Taylor keeps you laughing, then I can't wait to see all the laugh lines you'll have because she doesn't seem the type to back down. Just promise you won't pursue an argument if she does back down. Morgan likes her a lot."

We're nearly to the farm by the time that last sentence takes its place between us. *I like her too,* I think to myself with a grin. I turn to look out the window before Jacob catches my smile and asks more questions.

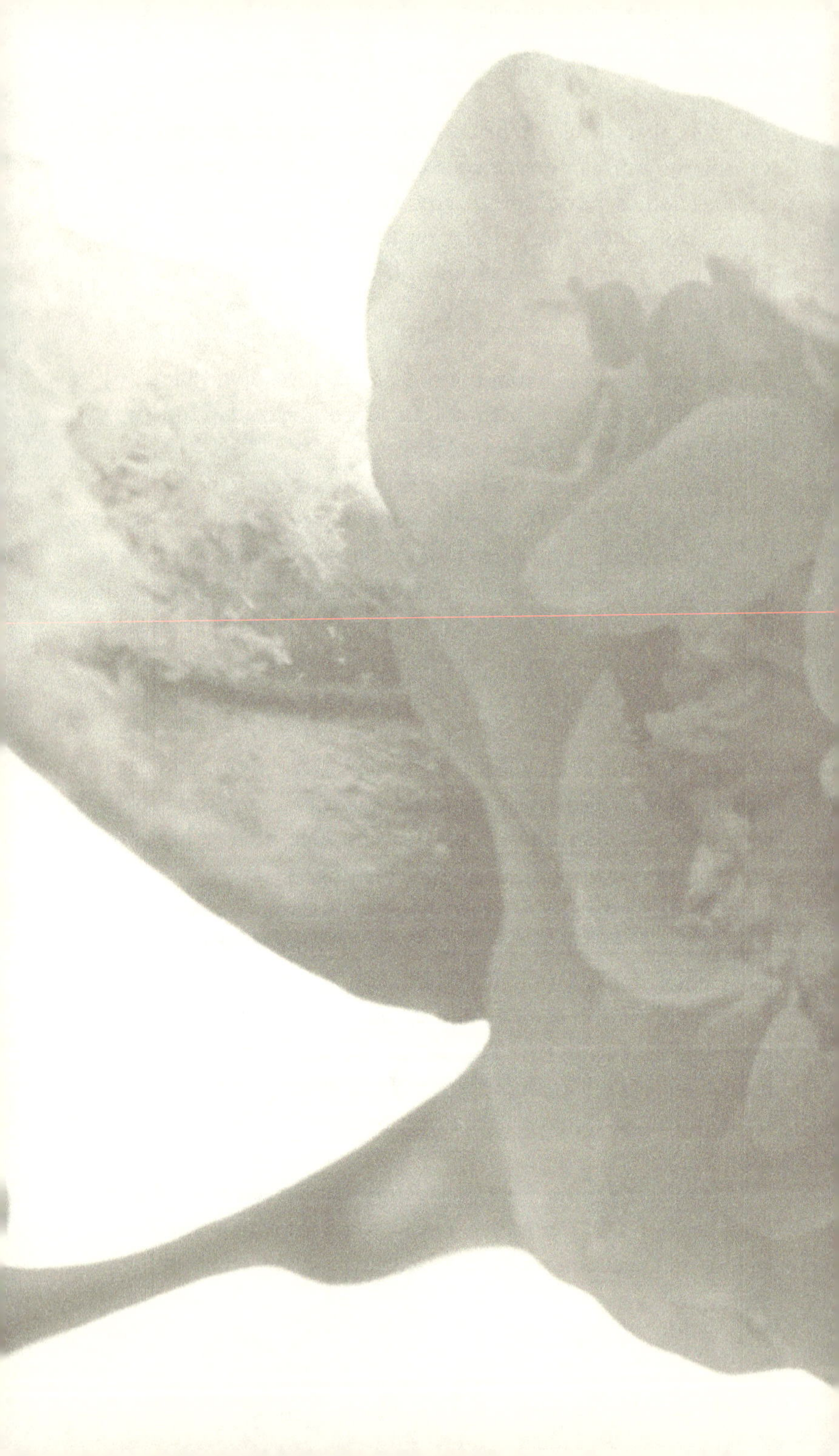

9

TASTE-TESTING DADDY

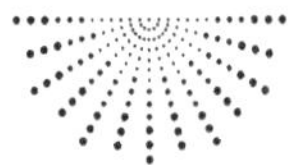

*T*aylor

I wake with a start. The house is silent. With the business opening in less than two weeks, there hasn't been a quiet morning yet. Something is wrong. I jump to my feet and throw my robe over my sleep shorts and tank top. Though they cover all the important bits, they're thin, so I try to be respectful. Upon opening my bedroom door, I'm assaulted by the smell of bacon and coffee. What the hell? Did I miss something? I run back into the room and check my calendar. It's not opening day yet.

The sound of clanging seeps through the closed kitchen door. 'Shit' comes Morgan's voice above the noise. 'Don't use your hand, Morgana. Just put it in your mouth,' Jacob reprimands before she lets another expletive fly. I stand at the bottom of the stairs wondering what in the hell is going on in there but afraid to barge in.

"Think we should check on them?"

My eyes roll, and I hold myself steady, trying to hide the fact he has not only scared the shit out of me again but that he also unsettles me on a cellular level. The smell of sandalwood and pine wafts from him, surrounding me, and I'm suddenly very glad I put my robe on.

"Absolutely not!"

There is no way I want to walk in on my boss and her fiancé. There's even less of a chance I want to do that with Garrett. I look up at the man, and he gives me a conspiratorial wink that has me needing to change my shorts. This man irks my soul, and yet my dumbass body responds to him in ridiculous ways. Just yesterday, I went to spit venom at him for some smartass comment he made in the dining room, but when I saw him in his low-slung jeans and tight-as-sin t-shirt, I drooled instead.

"Jacob, get your hand out of there!"

A loud slap follows her admonishment, and heat floods my cheek. Garret's mouth spreads in a wide grin. He reaches a hand toward the swinging door, and my eyes bulge.

"Coming in!" he yells, and I want to melt into the floor.

"It's about time, old man," Jacob says. "You're late!"

"And the food's getting cold," Morgan adds. "Great taste tester, you are."

"I apologize. I got caught up eavesdropping with the pixie here. There was some concern that something else might be happening in this kitchen."

He pushes the door wide enough that I catch a glimpse of Morgan, her hands firmly entrenched in some kind of dough she's mixing. She has flour everywhere, even in her hair. I take one step into the room and see that Jacob also has flour in his hair. I roll my eyes at Garrett's booming laugh. Morgan turns her face into her elbow, unable to cover her laugh any other way, and Jacob just turns away from me.

"Garrett Daniels, you knew what was happening and let me stand out there like a stalker?" I stand with my hands on my hips, but it is damn near impossible to feel intimidating when the person you're admonishing towers over you by a good foot and a half. "Just for that, you're on clean-up duty."

"You do know you're not the boss, right, Little Pixie?" He leans in and whispers conspiratorially, "But if you ask nicely, I might be convinced."

I wrinkle my nose in disgust, but once again, my body betrays me. Flashes of other things I might convince him to do. *No, no, no. He's old enough to be your father, T!* I once again remind myself of all the reasons I shouldn't be interested in him, not the least of which is how insufferable he is, yet that voice in the back of my head argues, *or you could call him Daddy*. Never gonna happen for so many reasons.

"C'mon, you two. I need to decide on the menu for opening weekend. Get in here out the doorway and make yourselves a plate of everything."

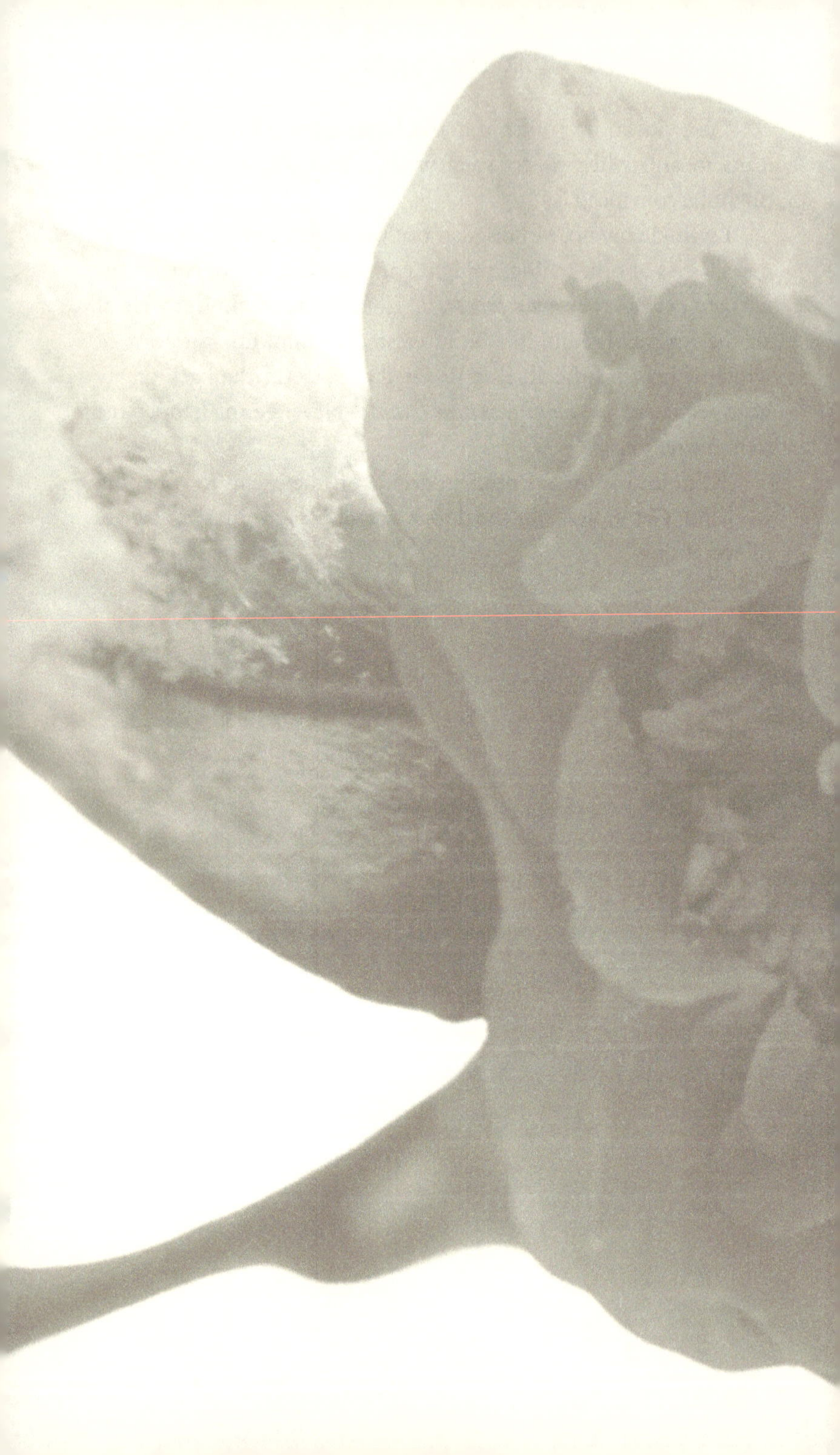

10

RUNNING ME RAGGED

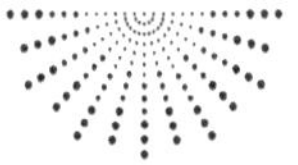

Garrett

I hear her puttering around in the storeroom. It's hard not to when she's so quirky and clumsy, and distracting. Yep, that's what she is, a delightfully obstinate distraction. Ever since that damn pixie came to town, I'm acutely aware of her. When she's at the house, I have to force myself to work outside or be on a different floor just to get anything done. I've come to the store on days I know she's with Morgan to try and not be caught up in the web of her brightness. I'm no good when she's around, and yet I want all of her attention. Like right now, it's taking all my willpower to stay here in this office and not stalk out there to watch what she's doing.

I turn back to the contraption of a computer Joanna insists on using to keep the books, and I can't make head nor tails of it. She's been out sick with the flu for nearly two weeks, and I hate to leave her a mess to clean up when she gets back. I'm sure I left her a big enough mess when she took over the business years ago. Why couldn't she just keep the simple paper trail we'd used for years? If it ain't broke, don't fix it, I say. The bell for the front door chimes, giving me an excuse to get out of this chair.

Taylor's voice echoes through the store as she greets the customer. I hang back just inside the doorway. She's got it covered, but I can't throw away the opportunity to watch her spread sunshine all over the place.

"Well, welcome to Cole County...JD is my boss, Joanna Daniels...We have everything you need to build, remodel, and decorate your home, or home away from home."

She rattles the pitch off like it's second nature, like she's been here her whole life and not just three months. She could sell me anything. Of course, I'd have to give her a hard time before I handed over my credit card, but I'd definitely be making a purchase if she offered.

"No, sir, I am not for sale," she says with a chuckle, but I feel the change in her demeanor. The laugh is tight, closed off. I can't hear what the man is saying, but I push off from where I've been leaning on the boxes alongside the doorway, ready to pounce when her all-business voice kicks in. "Do I look like I have a barcode on my forehead? Like you could just scan me and get a price? Go ahead and take your overpriced audacity out of here before my six-and-a-half-foot tall cowboy escorts you out."

Her cowboy? I'm frozen in my tracks for a moment, and yet my mind is running sprints. Did she just claim me? Was she even talking about me? Maybe she's just blustering to throw the man off. She doesn't need my help, not really, but the moment his voice raises, I step into the doorway with as intimidating a look as I can muster considering the raging hard-on I'm sporting. That dressing down was already damn sexy, especially since it wasn't directed at me, and then that simply two letter word 'my.' When my shadow crosses his field of vision, the man's entire face drains of color. Without a word, he turns and exits the store. She doesn't bother to turn around.

"Did you do all Joanna's dates like that, Cowpoke Daddy?"

Laughter bursts from my chest, nearly knocking me into the

doorjamb. I grab ahold of the wood to steady myself as the absurdity of her statement washes over me.

"Joanna never called me Daddy, cowpoke or otherwise," I say between deep breaths while trying to compose myself. She starts to turn in my direction but stops herself, and I can see her cheeks flush red. "Besides, all the idiots who tried sniffing around already knew who was protecting her."

"How would Joanna feel knowing you're chasing off the customers?" she asks, obviously trying to deflect from the effect my words have had on her. Now, I could tell her that the intent behind those words was no innuendo, but something about seeing her flustered eggs me on. She's all sunshine until she sees me, and then she's all spitfire. I want to see what happens if she ever just lets herself go. What would it take to see the woman underneath? Which side would dominate? Would she be run just as ragged as she runs me?

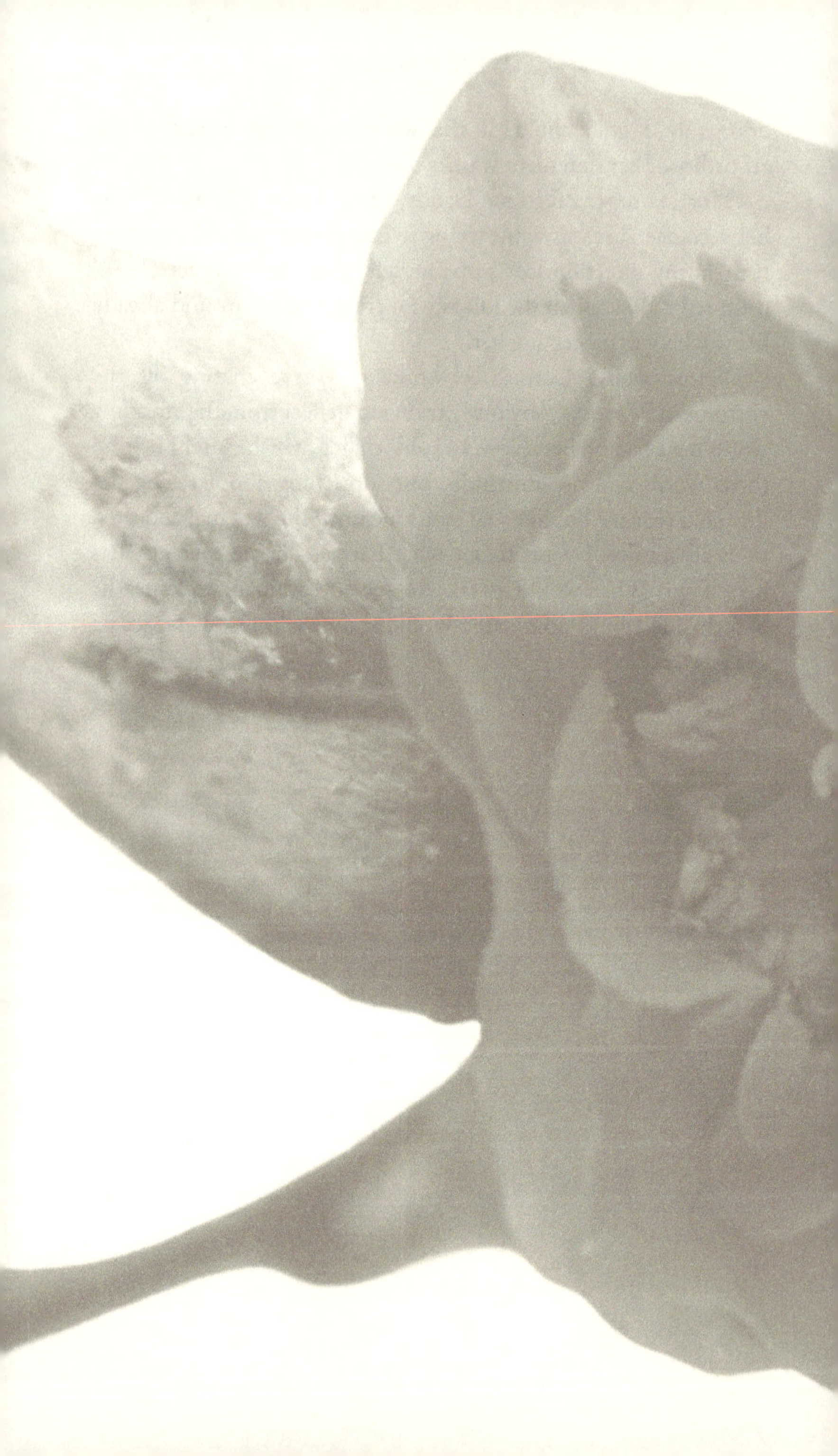

11

JOANNA'S DREAM

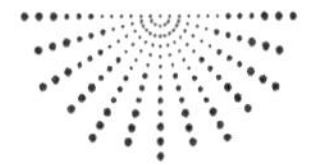

*T*aylor

Three months. That's how long I've been at Gretna House. That's how long I've been helping Joanna in the shop. That's how long I've known Garrett Daniels. "What the fuck, T?" I ask aloud to the storeroom at the back of JD's Hardware. Why am I measuring time by how long I've known that man? He's infuriating and frustrating and fascinating. He's also old enough to be my grandfather. Not quite, but still. A few weeks ago, I told Jordan that Garrett gives off total Daddy vibes, and she's been giving me hell for it ever since. I should be repulsed by the idea, yet, the more time I spend around him, even at the periphery, watching him interact with everyone else, I just want to get closer. "Dumbass!"

"What was that?" Joanna asks from the next aisle.

We're working on preparing orders for season changes. Joanna starts ordering her fall stock in the late spring, so we're counting and projecting what she'll need. There are seeds for fall vegetables, different types of shovels to get through the harder-packed soil, and Halloween decorations the locals will start gathering come August. The latter includes dozens of hay bales the residents will put in their front yards with scarecrows and bundles of dried cornstalks.

"Oh nothing, just talking to myself."

"You must've needed a stern talking to," Joanna responds with a laugh. "I give myself those types of talks all the damn time. Lately, it's been a question of 'what the fuck am I doing with my life?'"

I stop what I'm doing at Joanna's words. I've noticed her becoming more solemn and almost melancholy these past six weeks, but I've been afraid to say anything. I'm still relatively new, and Joanna has Morgan to vent to if needed. Still, I won't ignore the open door. I walk around to the next aisle.

"Are you alright?"

Joanna jumps, obviously surprised to find me watching her. "Yeah, I'm fine," she responds quickly with just a little sniffle.

"You're not, but I won't pry. I know we don't know each other very well, but I want you to know that I can be a good listener."

We lock eyes, and Joanna's are rimmed red with tears she's managed to keep silent. I hold in a gasp before quickly closing the distance and wrapping her in a tight hug. Her body remains stiff, like she's fighting the emotions and trying to push away the comfort I'm offering. We stay in that position for what has to be five full minutes before she relaxes and hugs me back.

"Thank you."

I look into Joanna's eyes, giving her a quiet smile. The tears are gone, probably shed all over my shoulder, but I don't mind. If it makes her feel better, a wet shoulder is a price I'm willing to pay.

"Do you want to talk about it?"

She lets me go completely and walks a few steps away before speaking, and once she gets going, it's like the floodgates open. She tells me all about her farce of a marriage, her mother's death, and Jacob's heartbreak. "I've never been anywhere else and never on my own." Tears run down her face, but she doesn't try to wipe them away. I stay quiet, letting her get it all out. "I feel stuck. Now that Jacob and Morgan are moving forward with their lives and dad is out of his stupor, I feel stuck and purposeless. Who the fuck is Joanna Daniels anyway?"

I take in everything she says, knowing what it's like to feel responsible for loved ones. I know what it's like to try and meet unrealistic, and sometimes unfair, expectations. I also know how important it is to figure out who we are without all those obligations. That's what I'm trying to do now at twenty-six. I'd probably be as lost as Joanna if, at thirty-four, I was still in my parents' house, taking care of everyone else, and withering away under my stepfather's reign. Thankfully, Garrett Daniels doesn't appear to be anything like the monster my mother married.

He's kind, though cold. Helpful yet harsh. Playful but petty. He's a walking contradiction. I can't imagine him despondent. I try to picture him as Joanna described him in his grief, and there's nothing of the man I've seen these past six weeks in that image.

"Have you talked with your family about how you feel?"

I ask the question before my brain registers how inappropriate it is. Of course, she hasn't. Hell, I never talked with my family either. I just got to the point where I couldn't take the situation anymore and left with whatever would fit in my car. Joanna's life isn't quite as dire, but I won't pretend to say her feelings aren't as strong or valid. When she doesn't answer right away, I try to clarify.

"I'm sorry, that was insensitive of me. I know I never talked to my family when I was ready to leave. I was simply thinking about how close you were to Jacob and Morgan. Parents are a little different. My best friend knew everything I was thinking and planning."

Joanna shakes her head and purses her lips. I'm not sure if the look of irritation is at me for asking the question, the actual situation, or at herself.

"No. I've wanted to talk to Morgan about it, but my brother is always there, or we're both busy with our businesses. She's so happy to be back that I also feel bad for my desire to leave."

"Do you think she would be happy to know you're miserable?" It's a genuine question and one I'd asked myself a million times about Jordan before I decided to share my darkest fears. We both go silent for a moment, stuck in our own ruminations.

"So..." I'm not sure how to ask the question formulating in my mind. Joanna turns back toward me and raises a questioning brow. "I was just curious..." I pause again. I'm not trying to push the woman into a decision she isn't ready to make, but Joanna looks so unhappy. "If you were to leave Cole County, where do you think you'd like to go?" There, that question is hopefully more inquisitive than directive. Really, I've wanted to ask what plans she's putting in place and what I can do to help.

Joanna's head tilts to the side in contemplation. "Another great question. I don't know that I have any true destination in mind. I want to see places and meet people. I don't want to be stuck in one place."

I nod in understanding. If not for my younger siblings, I'd have probably roamed for a while myself, though living in my car hadn't been as much fun as the nomadic life seems in books. "Do you know anything about horses?" A thought percolates in my mind.

"Oh yeah. My parents always had horses, but we sold them all off when my mother passed, except Jacob's old mare. Pa wasn't able to care for them, and my brother and I were too busy with the businesses."

My smile grows. I need to call Jordan and verify some info before saying anything, but a plan is forming. I will not let this beautiful woman waste away here if she has dreams of something more. No one deserves to be miserable simply because they dedicated years of their life to others.

"I need to get back to Gretna House. Are you gonna be okay?"

Joanna snorts out an ironic laugh, and I almost trip over the paint cans on the floor behind me. She barks out a genuine laugh and grasps my hand as I windmill my arms to steady myself.

"What in the heck, Joanna? What was that snort for? You damn near caused me to break my own neck here."

By this point, Joanna has somewhat gotten her laughter in check and immediately covers her mouth to hide the continued giggles. I glare at her, trying to keep the corners of my own lips from pulling up.

"I still find it ridiculous that Morgan named that house after her mean, old grandmother, and you calling it by the new name without sneering made me laugh. I don't think I could use that woman's name without a sneer."

"I'm sure there's a story in there somewhere. Maybe one day you'll share."

"It's not my story to share, but since my best friend is an open book, I'm sure she'll tell you enough that you'll be able to piece the story together. Anyway, thank you for listening. I feel better. Go and get that house ready for its first holiday weekend.

I turn toward the front door, grab my jacket from the hook on the wall, and wave goodbye before leaving the storeroom.

Taylor

Jordan picks up the call on the first ring. I'm so surprised I nearly choke on the soda I'd just sipped thinking I had a few more seconds.

"Are you alright?" Jordan asks, concern obvious in her voice.

"Of course. Why?"

"You never call without texting first. That's some shit I do, not you."

I laugh. "Yeah, I'm good. I just had something on my mind, and I needed to ask you about it. You got a minute?"

"Yeah, my class doesn't start for another 20 minutes. What's up?"

"Do you remember telling me that Junior said they were in need of another horse handler? I can't remember what they call them." I'm not sure what I'll say if Jordan asks why I want to know, but I have to ask anyway.

"Yeah, he said they needed a new horseman and groom. Why?"

"Do you think they'd consider a horsewoman?"

"They have women on their team. Again...why?"

"I might know someone. I just didn't want to reach out to Junior without double checking with you first. That's all."

"Wait, you know someone who might want to travel all over the country smelling like horses for months at a time?"

Sarcasm oozes through the question. "I know all kinds of people, J." Jordan scoffs. "I do. Anyway, that's all I wanted. Have fun in class." I hang up the phone before Jordan can ask any more questions. Though my best friend doesn't know Joanna personally, and she wouldn't say anything even if she did, it still feels weird to give away the secret that Joanna is wanting to leave town. Nope, I'll keep that secret until there's an actual plan in place.

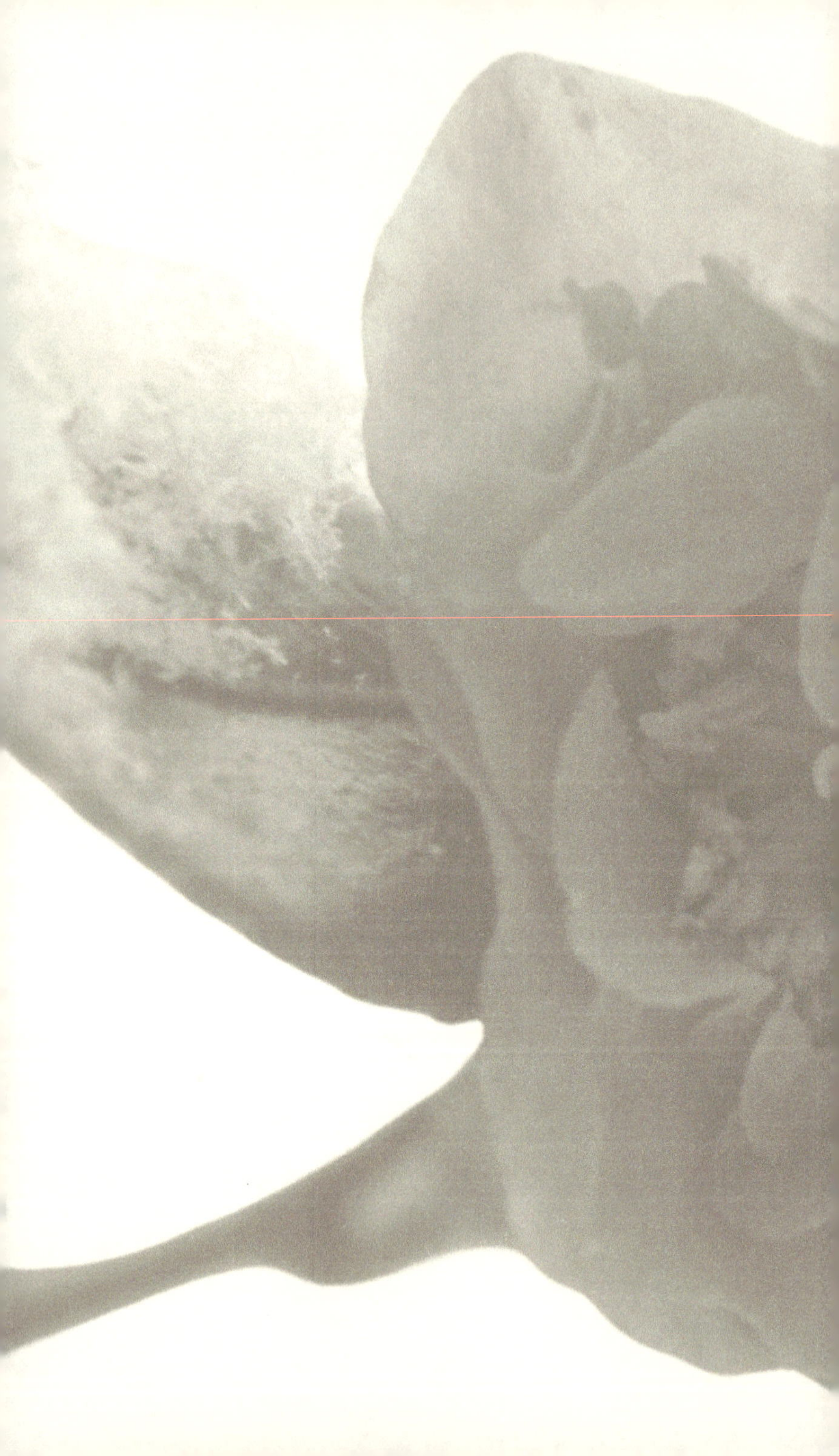

STABILITY MAKES ME NERVOUS

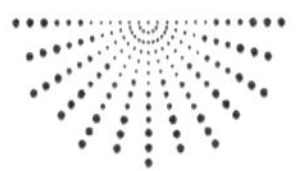

Garrett

"Every time you have that cat that ate the canary look, it never bodes well for me." My tone is light, but my nerves are shot. There has been so much going on these past five or so months, and the busyness has helped keep the demons at bay, but now that Gretna House is up and running, Joanna is healthy and back at the store, and Jacob's back to his construction business full time, I have far too much time on my hands, too many idle minutes for my mind to wander.

Lately, I find myself seeking out my favorite pixie when I need to get out of my own head. Though I try to play it cool, I'm sure she's started to notice. Hence the shit-eating grin she's giving me right now.

"I'm just so happy to see you, Cowpoke." She sweeps out of the dining room and wraps her arms around my waist.

I glare down at her, thrown off by her behavior, my body's response to her being pressed against me, and the smell of her hair that teases my senses. I put my arms around her shoulders, pulling her closer on instinct, as I look through the door, trying to see what might have caused this whatever it is to happen.

"You're scaring me, Pix," I whisper against her hair.

She makes a giggling sound, but her body is stiff. "Just play along," she whispers back before pulling herself free and slapping my chest. "Stop that! Act your age," she says aloud with a wink before turning back to the room. "Breakfast is almost over, and then you can help me clean up. Morgan's busy in the kitchen."

I eye her suspiciously before catching the way she looks to the side. There's someone in the room she's putting this display on for. I start following her in when Morgan's voice comes from behind the kitchen door.

"Poppa Daniels, come grab a plate."

My gaze is locked on Taylor when I answer Morgan's call. "Be there in a bit, the pixie needs my help with something."

"Take this plate, old man," Morgan says, having pushed the door open before I can take another step.

I smile knowingly. Of course, she already had my plate ready. She gives Taylor a quizzical look, and I watch her shrug in response out the corner of my eye. Morgan's mouth does its little quirk when she's trying to solve a problem that she's not yet sure is a problem before she, too, shrugs and returns to the kitchen.

In the doorway of the dining room, I sweep my eyes across the room. There's one couple in the back corner, a family of four at a high top straight ahead, and one guy at the counter against the left-side wall. He must be the one making her uncomfortable.

"Do you care where I sit, Pix?"

"Anywhere against the wall is good. I'm about to turn over all these tables."

A smirk comes over my face as I walk behind the guy. He's sitting there trying to ignore me while scrolling through photos on his phone. When I plop myself down on the stool just two spots from him, I make sure to give him a curt good morning. He looks toward me, eyes shifting between me and his phone before he replies weakly.

"You here for business or pleasure? Come with friends? Family?"

"What's with the third degree, old man?" he asks, and my lip quirks up before I stuff a bite of pancake in my mouth, chewing slowly.

"Just making casual breakfast conversation since we're the only two people here alone."

"The hostess is here alone, and I was having a nice conversation with her before you came in."

"Interesting," I say, once again popping a bite of food in my mouth.

The guy turns his legs toward me, brows furrowed. "What is that supposed to mean?" I shrug and take another bite. "Dude, what is your problem?"

I turn my head to look past him. Pixie's there biting the cap of her pen watching us. "I hope you're checking out this morning." He sits up straight, taken aback by my statement, but I don't give him a chance to respond. "I don't think the owner would want you sticking around if she knew you were harassing her employee." I lean closer to him and drop my volume, so only he can hear. "And, anyone who makes that beautiful pixie run into my arms is two steps from having his legs broken because she can't stand me." Taking my last bite of bacon, I wish him a good day and get up to help reset the dining room for tomorrow.

My dishes are barely in the cart before he's packed up his belonging and left. I watch him head out to his car, occasionally looking back toward the house. Bold of him to think he's worth chasing.

"I don't know what you said, and don't get any ideas that I owe you, but thanks. The guy was creepy. It's to be expected in this business, but still, glad you were here, and I didn't have to talk myself to death to get him to leave. Hopefully, he won't be a repeat customer."

"Oh, I doubt he'll come back," I say. "You have a way of making a man feel real welcome."

She looks into my eyes, and I can't pull my gaze away. We simply stare at each other for mere moments, or maybe it's minutes before she blinks and breaks the connection.

"Ok, Cowpoke, back to work! You promised to help me clean up, and I'm holding you to it."

I laugh at her need to boss me around before I grab a rag and start wiping down the tables she's already stripped of their linen.

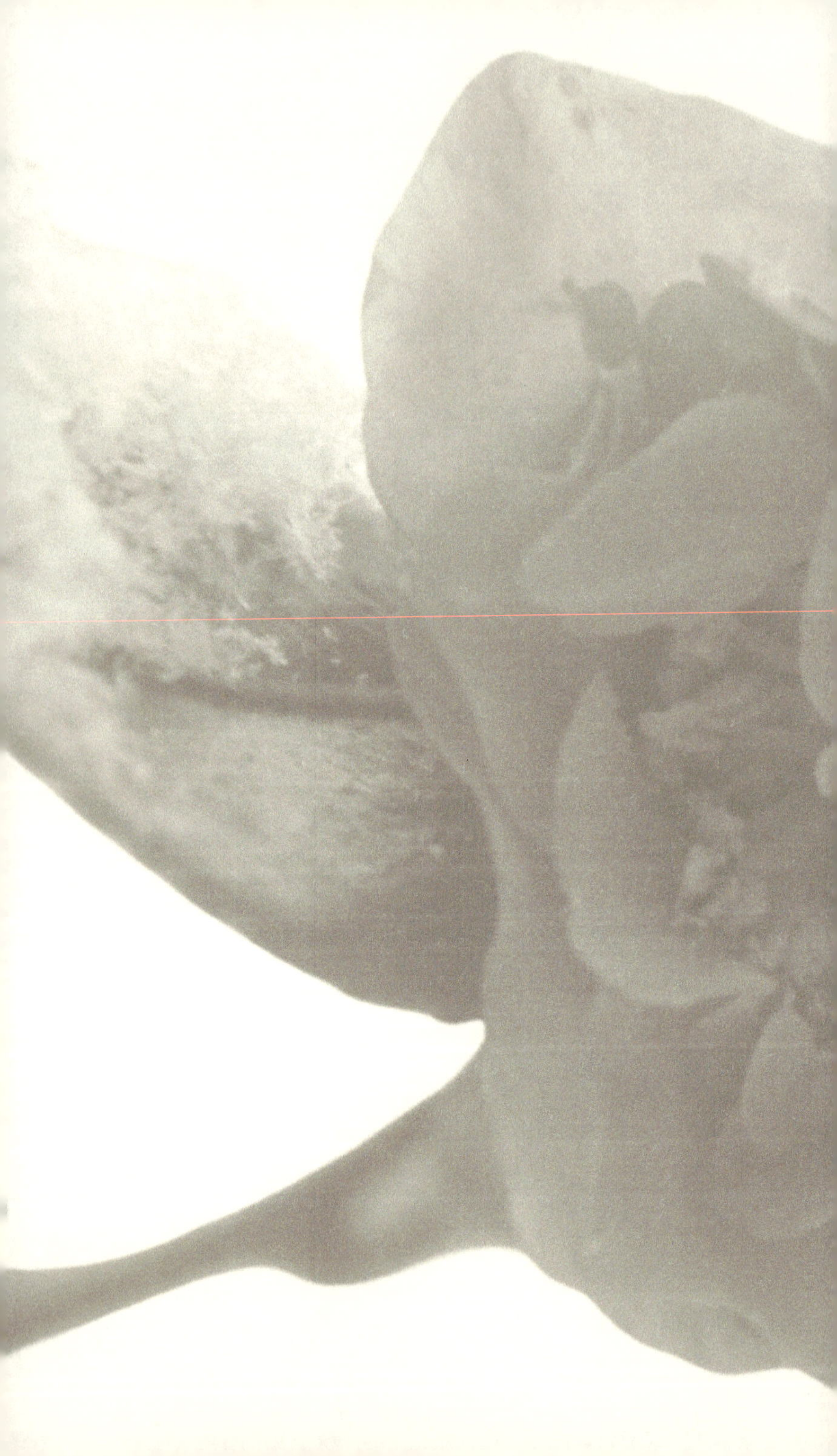

13

THE SHIT HITS THE
PROVERBIAL FAN

aylor

"When were you going to tell me you planned to join the fucking circus?"

Garrett's voice bellows through the storeroom as he stomps toward the back office. I've never heard him yell before. Hell, he's never even raised his voice toward Joanna in the six months I've been around. She seems to be the one who keeps him settled. I guess, then, it shouldn't be surprising he's upset about her potentially going away.

"Good morning to you too, Pa," Joanna's sarcastic voice retorts from the back office as I make my way to peep around the end of the aisle I've been working in.

"I had to hear that shit from your brother? I told him he was full of shit, that you wouldn't even consider such a thing." He takes a deep breath and lowers his voice to the point I can't hear him.

"I'm not joining the circus, old man. I'm not a fucking clown, and I'm too damn old to swing from a trapeze."

This must be a day of firsts. Joanna has never before cussed at her dad that I've seen. I'm not usually nosy, but I am curious as to how she'll handle the old man.

"Sorry, Pa."

"So, it's not a joke? You're thinking of leaving."

"Have a seat," she says softly.

A sudden pain grips my chest at the sadness in Garrett's voice. I'm listening in to stand up for Joanna should she need it, but I feel for him. They must've moved to the small loveseat at the far side of the office because I can no longer hear what they're saying. I shuffle closer to the open office door, trying to either catch sight of them or get within earshot. I accidentally trip on a rough patch in the concrete and fall against the door frame. Both of their heads shoot up, their eyes wide. "Is everything ok?" I ask, my voice unsure.

"We're fine," Joanna responds, her brows drawn down in confusion.

I look back and forth between the two of them. Joanna wears a smile beneath the question she's shooting my way. Garret is completely stiff, yet his eyes are sad, almost broken. I long to reassure him, though I can't say why. I shouldn't feel anything for him. I'm here to protect Joanna from being railroaded into staying. Still, I don't want him hurt by it.

"Please excuse us," he finally says, and I notice the lack of gruffness in his voice. Again, my chest tightens. I'm used to him bantering back and forth with her. I can't bring myself to look away from him, uncertainty freezing my muscles. Will he break down? Will his anger get the better of him? He's so hard to read, and I'm worried about Joanna. At least that's what I keep telling myself. Then Joanna nods in agreement that it's safe for me to leave. I give them a slight smile and close the door behind me.

I go back to the paint aisle. Inventory is a pain in the ass because most of the extra empty buckets, rollers, and stirrers are on the higher shelves, and my short ass can't reach, or even see them, without climbing. I start stacking empty 5-gallon pails and flipping them over. I don't know where the step stool is, but even that thing doesn't quite let me reach beyond the second shelf. As I move my makeshift set of stairs into place, my thoughts trail back to Garrett's look of brokenness. Even now, the urge to comfort him is tearing me apart. If that is how he looked for all those years after his wife passed, I understand Joanna staying around to take care of him.

He'll need someone to take care of him in her absence, my brain offers. I try to imagine who that might be. Jacob isn't really the caretaker type. He'll get Garrett out of the house and put him to work, but the only person that man takes care of is Morgan. *We can do it*, my heart interjects as I take two steps up toward the second shelf. "Hell no!" I say aloud to the empty storeroom with a vigorous shake of my head. I miss the next step up and screech, cartwheeling my arms and trying to catch my balance on one foot. When I try to put my second foot on the small surface, it slips, and I reach out, grabbing for the shelving unit. I grab at the bottom of the third shelf, thinking I can make the hop onto the second shelf when it gives loose, dropping a few inches. I drop with it, hitting the floor.

The last thing I remember is a door crashing open, and footsteps heading in my direction.

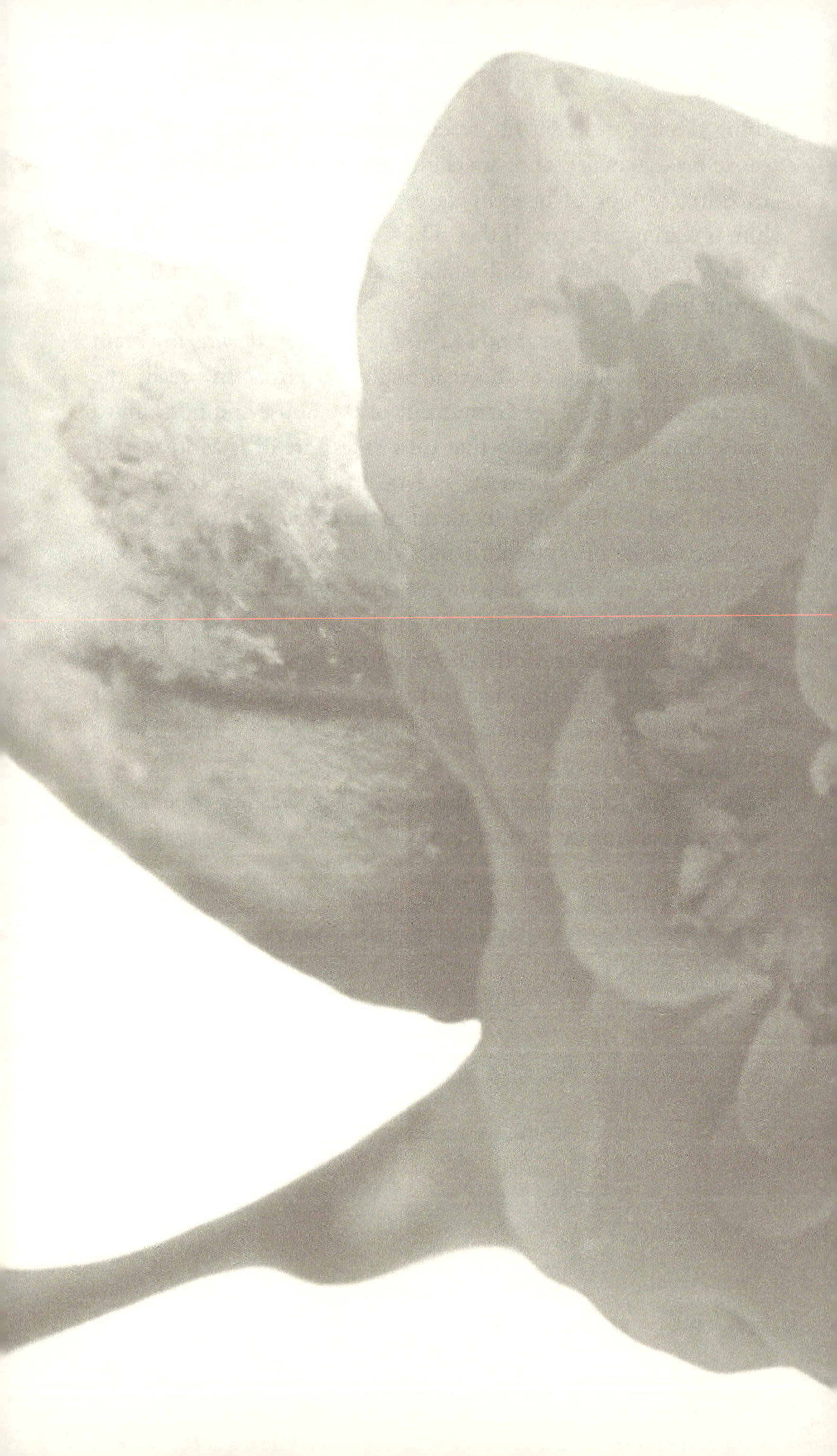

14

THE BROKEN SHELF

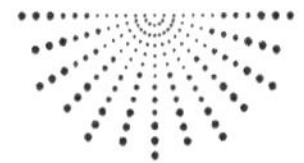

*G*arrett

There's a pile of empty paint buckets strewn across the concrete floor in the far corner near the last aisle of the storeroom.

"Taylor?" Joanna calls.

I don't wait for a response, just continue my sprint to the aisle. A soft moan drifts through the storeroom before I can turn the corner. *Shit, she's hurt!* I don't even slow down to move the buckets, just kick them out of the way.

"Call 911," I yell back to Joanna.

"What? Is she okay?"

"I'm not sure yet, but call anyway."

Joanna's footsteps take off in the opposite direction, and I search the floor to find Taylor with a couple buckets thrown over her legs and a few empty boxes around her. Thank goodness, they're empty. I throw everything off her, and kneel down next to her chest. The steady rise and fall of her breaths is like music to my ears. I look her over for obvious signs of blood or broken bones. Her head is on the concrete floor, so I don't move her just in case she'd hit it hard when she fell. I look around at the shelves trying to figure out what exactly happened. One of the third-level shelves dangles precariously low in the front. Had she been climbing the shelving unit? No, she's too smart for that. Maybe a bolt snapped. I haven't checked any of the shelves for needed maintenance since they were put in. Dammit, I'll never forgive myself if she's really hurt because of something that could have been prevented.

"Pixie Girl," I say while grasping her hand. I soak in the warmth of her skin, grateful that she hasn't gone into shock, but now I need her to wake up. She moans lightly and tries to turn her head toward me. I brush her short hair off her forehead where it's fallen almost into her eyes. "C'mon, stubborn one, open your eyes and look at me." She makes a sound that resembles a snort, and it's all I can do not to chuckle aloud.

"An ambulance is on the way, Pa. Is she alright?" Joanna asks from the end of the aisle.

"Seems to have knocked herself out good, but I think she'll be fine. Looks like a bolt might have busted up there." I tip my head back toward the broken shelf.

"Oh no!" Joanna's hands fly to her mouth. I know the moment guilt sets in by the sad shift in her eyes.

"I should've done better maintenance checks on these things. We put them up almost 25 years ago, and I never looked at them again other than to put stuff on them. Don't take on my failure. We'll get Jacob to come in and check them all for any needed upkeep and to fix the broken one. The important thing is that Taylor is fine."

"Oh, so you do know my name," says a weak voice that makes my heart jump.

Her eyes are still closed, but there's a smirk on her lips. "Of course, I do, Pixie Girl." She wrinkles her nose, and my smile explodes.

"It's bright as hell in here," she says, squeezing her eyes tight. "I've tried to open them, but it hurts. My head hurts." She tries to pull her hand from mine and shifts her legs. "Shit, everything hurts. What happened?"

"Looks like you pissed off the gods of empty boxes and paint buckets," I say, holding one of the boxes over her head to block the bright overhead lights.

Her eyes fly open, but it takes a moment or two before she focuses on my face. "You're a jerk, you know that?"

"So I've been told."

Joanna, who's been arranging the fallen buckets out of the way for when the paramedics show up, comes to kneel on Taylor's other side. "How are you feeling?"

Taylor jerks her head toward Joanna's voice, and her eyes immediately roll back, closing. I cringe. She likely has a concussion, and they'll definitely be taking her to the hospital to get checked out. I put a hand to her cheek and grip her other hand tighter.

"C'mon, Pixie Girl, wake back up. You gotta stay with us here. You can sleep later." She gives one of those soft groans again, and my insides tie in knots. I hate that she's hurt. "Joanna, open up one of those boxes there, and set it up to shield her eyes from the lights. We need to keep her awake. Also, call your brother, and tell him to get over here to fix this shit!" The longer she remains silent with her eyes closed, the louder my voice raises. "Oh, and make sure the front door is open, so the medics can get in. Where in the hell are they?"

"Why are you yelling? Your voice is too deep for all that."

I let out a breath and looked down to find her eyes fixed on me. "Welcome back," I say on a sigh.

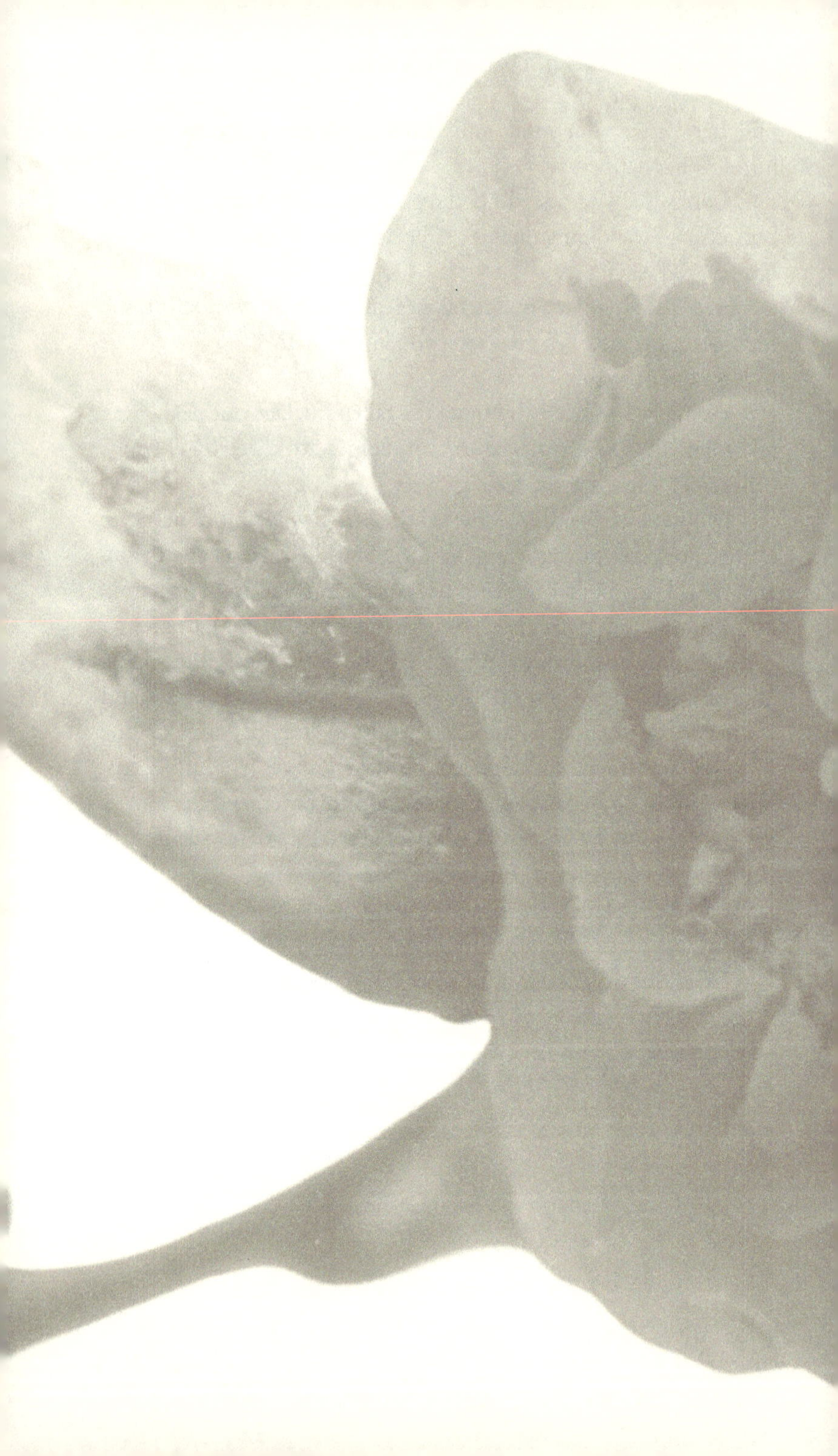

15

DON'T LEAVE ME ALONE

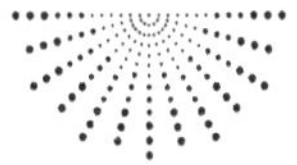

Taylor

I'm not sure about this feeling in the pit of my stomach at finding Garrett watching over me. Though it's hard to maintain focus at first, I want to drown in those midnight blue eyes. They hold so much emotion—worry, guilt, and something else I can't quite read. I'd happily wake to that ruggedly handsome face every time, though, especially to find his hand on my cheek. It's so warm that I keep snuggling into it. Shit, I shouldn't be enjoying his closeness so much. I need to get up and move away from him.

"Lay still, Pixie Girl. You likely have a concussion. Just hang tight until the paramedics get here."

I try to roll my eyes and feel that rush of dizziness again. A groan of frustration escapes. I hate being unable to move and him shaking his head at me when I flop back down from the eye roll pisses me off. "You're the worst," I say when he chuckles.

"I know. I'll be back to my charming self once you're better," he retorts with a wink.

I groan again, this time completely at him.

"I think she's going to be just fine," Joanna says from where she stands somewhere near my feet.

Joanna isn't alone. Two paramedics flank her, and Garrett moves out of their way. I immediately miss his touch and nearly reach for him, but the medic grabs my arm to connect the blood pressure cuff.

"I want you to look straight ahead," one of the medics says, pulling my attention from Garrett. "How many fingers am I holding up?" He then proceeds to hold up various fingers at different locations around his head for me to count. The constant movement of my eyes is making my head hurt again just when it had finally started to calm down.

The other paramedic, talks through starting an IV and giving me fluids while the one with all the fingers places a vise around my head and neck. Ok, maybe it isn't a vise, but it damn sure feels like it. I close my eyes again. The thing is so bulky that I can't look at anything besides the lights above me anyway.

"Don't go to sleep on us, Taylor. Stay awake just a bit longer."

"I'm not sleeping. The lights hurt my eyes and my head."

"We're going to get you into the ambulance, and then we'll gather some information from you if you're able to answer."

"Okay."

Everything else is a blur with my eyes closed. They jostle me around a bit, roll me from side to side, and then I'm levitated when the stretcher is lifted to its full height. As we start moving, I hear Joanna and Garrett arguing. Their voices seem so far away, but the storeroom isn't that big. I doubt they'd have both left me alone there, so they couldn't be far.

"I'll go with her."

"I'm going. You wait for your brother."

"Don't you think I should be the one going with her? I'm her boss."

"Until you leave town. Then, I am, it would seem."

"What in the heck is wrong with you, Pa?"

"You and your brother get this place into shape. Make sure you check all the shelves, not just the one that fell. I'm going, and that's that."

I cringe at them fighting over me. I should've paid better attention when I leaned against the shelving unit to rest after having emptied all those boxes. Shit, I've left one hell of a mess for them to clean up. The medics lift me up into the ambulance, and are getting ready to close the doors when Garrett asks them to wait.

"Sir, are you family?"

"No, I'm the co-owner of this store and her boss. Her family isn't here in Cole County, so I'm going with her."

I open my eyes, trying to look down toward where the two men are talking. The female medic is at my side moving things around, but I can't see her any better than I see them because of this damn thing on my neck.

"Let him come, please. It's alright. I'd feel better not to go alone."

The woman's face leans over mine. "Are you sure? We could make him follow in his own vehicle."

"No, it's alright. I'd like him to be here."

"Let him up, Charles. She asked for him to ride along."

They are silent for a moment before someone grunts, and Garrett's calloused hand closes around mine. Though I can't see him, his presence helps me relax. My eyes fall closed again until the medic begins asking for personal information. Most of the questions are simple and don't cause me to think too hard, but then she asks about next of kin. I don't want them to contact my parents; I don't want anything to do with them.

"We need to put down someone for your next of kin, Taylor."

"Can't she just give you an emergency contact?" Garrett asks, and I squeeze his hand in thanks.

"We will gladly take down an emergency contact, but we really need someone who can make emergency medical decisions should something happen. I don't foresee that, as you've been able to stay conscious for us and answer questions. It's really a precautionary measure."

"All my numbers are in my cell."

"I have it here, pixie girl. Do you want to give me the code?"

"Just let me touch the button."

I unlock the phone and tell him to give the medic Jordan's number as my emergency contact. Reluctantly, I have him share my mother's number as well. For the first time, I wish I wasn't the eldest child and that one of my siblings could take that call. Oh well, hopefully, they won't need to call anyone at all. We'll get to the hospital, figure out that I just need some time to work through the dizziness, and then I'll be fine to go back home to Gretna House. I'm so sleepy, but nerves and the constant bouncing around of the ambulance makes it near impossible to relax into the slumber I crave. At some point, Garrett takes my hand again without me realizing until the ambulance parks, and he lets me go. His absence is more jarring than his presence.

They pull me out of the ambulance. Next thing I know, there are bright lights everywhere, and I hear Garrett arguing about being able to sit with me.

"I'm not leaving her."

"Sir, only family is allowed back here with the patients."

The medic looks at me over the collar. "Sorry. I was afraid that was going to be an issue."

"I don't want to be here alone," I say vehemently.

I've never come to the emergency room alone before, never even visited a doctor alone before. I hadn't been allowed to, and the few times I should've gone, I hadn't been taken because too many questions would've been asked. There's no way I want to be here alone now. The medics finish getting me moved to a gurney, so they can leave when the female medic says, "Hey, that's her boyfriend. She's asking for him." Heat rises up my cheeks at the statement. What will Garrett say if he overhears that? I do want him here. He's the closest thing I have to a friend in this place, but to call him my boyfriend. Will they even believe the lie after looking at the two of us?

"Why would you do that, Maggie?" the male paramedic asks.

"Look, Ced, she's scared to be here. What harm could come from him holding her hand while the doctors and nurses do their job? He kept her calm in the ambulance. She could use some of that calm here."

The medic comes up and places her hand on my shoulder. "It's going to be alright. You should be out of here in no time."

"Thank you."

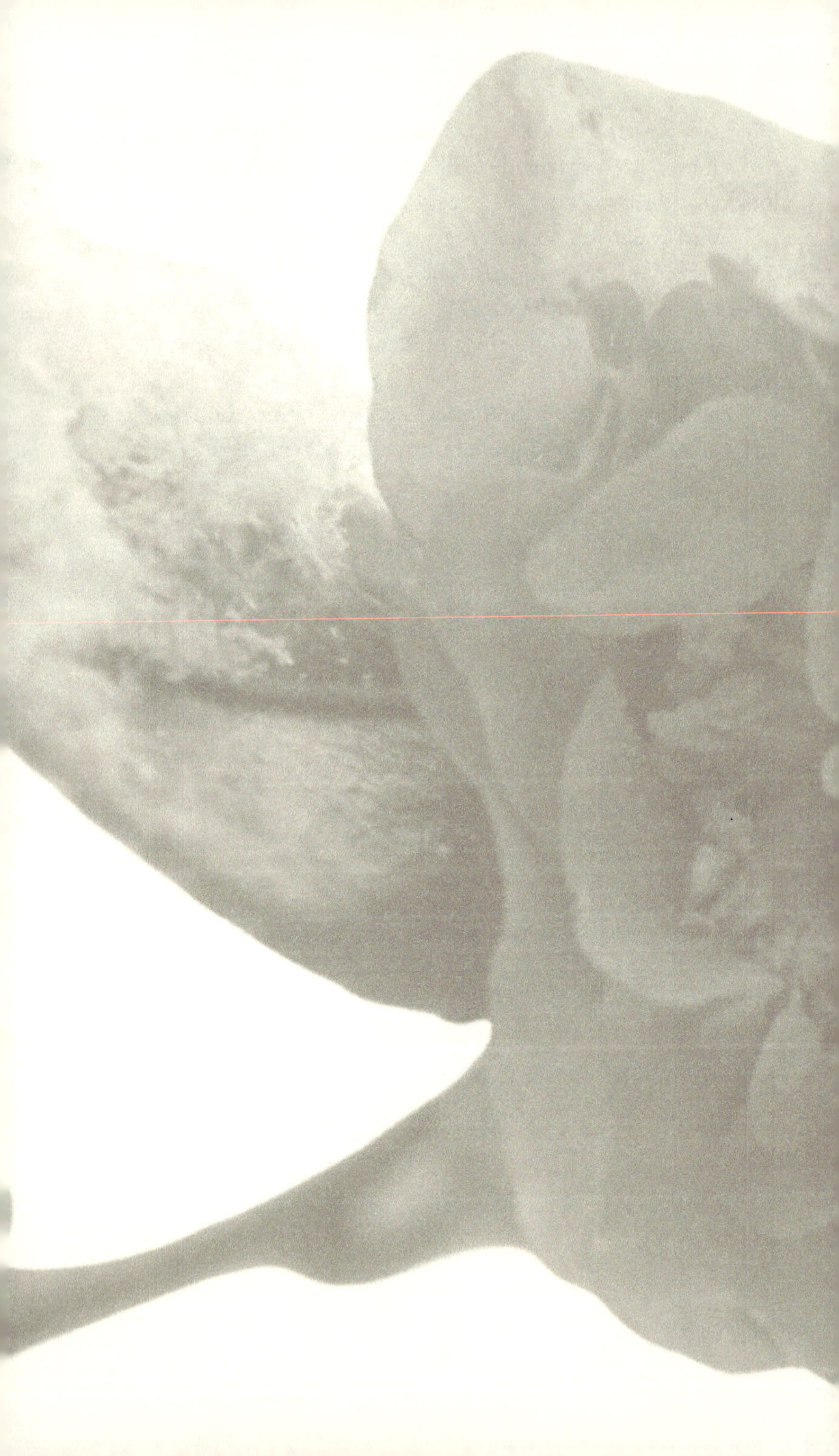

I'M THE BOYFRIEND

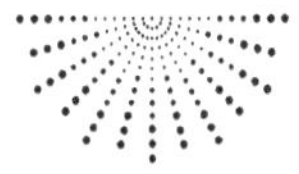

*G*arrett

"Garrett Daniels?"

As soon as I slump into the waiting room chair, someone calls my name. I'd done everything in my power to stay with Taylor save start a fight with the attendant and security that insisted I wait out here. I hadn't given anyone my name, though, at least not my full name. Well, I can't remember giving anyone my name. I'd have said anything to not leave her back there alone. Why is that? She's being taken care of by medical personnel. She should be fine. In fact, she should be better than fine without me back there shooting her blood pressure up like I seem to do regularly. Still, something eats at me about not being there to hold her hand.

"Garrett Daniels?" The deep voice calls again.

Jumping to my feet, I approach the nurse at the doors separating the ER from the waiting room.

"I'm Garrett Daniels."

The nurse is a couple inches shorter than my nearly six foot three inches and yet still manages to look me up and down. In any other place at any other time, I would've called the other man out.

"Is Taylor alright?"

"I'm sorry," the nurse says, though his tone isn't the least bit remorseful. "When the medic said the patient was asking for her boyfriend, I assumed..."

My eyes go wide and then narrow in the span of a heartbeat. I'd be lying if I said my heart didn't flutter a bit at being called her boyfriend. I know it's a ludicrous thought, but it makes me feel younger than my fifty years. Yep, that's the part that gave me a thrill...at least before this young kid has to go and remind me of my age, the little shit.

Stepping in close to the man, I mutter loud enough for only him to hear, "You know what happens when you assume, right? Now let me back inside to my girl before you make more of an ass of yourself."

He lets out a deep breath when I back away toward the ER doors. The young man blinks a few times and finally puts his badge to the button on the wall. To his credit, he doesn't apologize. I'm not ready to let him off the hook, though, so as we walk toward the bay Taylor was put in, I say, "I've been told I wasn't very nice when I was younger, kind of a hard ass and mean for no reason. Yep, I was more likely to kick a man's ass for looking at me funny. Maturity and a good woman will do things to you." With a wink, I step inside the curtain.

Somehow, my pixie is still cute as a button, even with that thick neck brace on. Wait...my pixie? Where the fuck did that come from? Before my mind can wander in that direction, Taylor opens her eyes, and a smile lights her face. I rub the back of my neck and return the smile.

"Hey there, Pixie Girl."

"Hi yourself, Cowpoke."

I raise a brow, and her smile grows. "They told me you were asking for your boyfriend, but I couldn't find him."

Red creeps into her cheeks. "Yeah, um, about that. The medic..."

Taylor stiffens in the bed when a man's voice filters through the curtains blocking her bay. The hair on the back of my neck stands at her response, and I looked between her and the opening in the curtain.

"Pix, are you alright?" I walk closer to her bed to stand next to her.

"Where's my daughter?" the voice asks again, louder this time.

"Sir, what is your name, and who is your daughter?"

Taylor grabs my hand. She's shaking her head back and forth when I look down at her, all the brightness of moments before having faded from her face. I open my mouth to ask what's happening when the curtain opens. A man around my age with salt and pepper hair walks in. He's dressed like Mr. Rogers, complete with the out-of-place sweater vest, considering we're still experiencing the late-August heat. I eye him skeptically, though the man doesn't even look my way. When Taylor squeezes my hand, and I hear her ragged breaths, my eyes narrow to slits. The man's face softens when he looks at Taylor, but his eyes don't match the facade. What in the hell is going on here?

"Hey there, pretty girl. How're you feeling?"

He has a slight drawl, one that pretense tries to hide. I've met many men like him. They want to feel like they're better than everyone else in the area by losing or pretending not to have an accent. Pretentious bastards. There's something more to this one, though. Something is off in the way Taylor's acting.

"Why are you here?" she asks, her voice cracking, pulling my attention to her face. Disgust reads in the way her nose is scrunched, but her eyes hold something else entirely.

"Now don't act like that, Taylor. Of course, we would come check on you when the hospital called your mother."

"Where is mom?"

"She, regretfully, couldn't come. She had to stay with the little ones. She's had to be stuck at home a lot since you left."

She winces, and I place my free hand on the top of her head. I'm ready to take this guy outside if he keeps upsetting her.

"Who's this?" the man asks, his voice taking on a serious, almost possessive tone.

"Forgive me if I don't shake your hand. The name's Garrett, and I'm the boyfriend."

Taylor sucks in a breath, but I keep my eyes locked on the man standing at the foot of her bed. The man's eyebrows raise before a harder edge takes over his features. I'm not sure if he doesn't like the idea of her having a boyfriend, or if he just doesn't believe the statement. There's probably a bit of both.

"Well, Garrett," the man finally says after clearing his throat, "thank you for being here with our little girl. She has family here now, so you are free to leave. I'll take her home when they release her."

Taylor squeezes my hand again, and I can feel the slight shake of her head under my other palm. Even without her response, I have no intentions of leaving her alone with the man. Something is off about him.

"I'm not leaving her," I say, my tone icy.

The man's lips purse, and he looks like he's going to blow a gasket, but then he takes a deep breath and turns his attention back to Taylor. "At least give me a few moments alone with Taylor to talk about the family. I'm sure she'd like updates on her mother and her siblings while we wait for the doctor."

I ball the fist that isn't clutching Taylor's hand like a vise. I'm ready to make it so this guy can't say anything to her or anyone else for that matter.

"It's ok, Cowpoke," Taylor says, "I'll be fine."

I turn to look at her. She has to be kidding. She's not fine. Nothing about this situation is fine. I give her a pleading look, though I'm not sure what I'm pleading for. For her to not send me outside? For her to give me permission to beat the hell out of this dude? When she nods, I do the only thing I can think will let them both know I'm here for her. I lean down with the intent to whisper in her ear, but her eyes are so full of fear, and her lips are parted. I kiss her. It's soft at first, more like a peck. Then she runs her free hand through my hair, and I'm lost. Everything falls away. The hospital with all its movement and beeping. The asshat who has to be staring at us wide-eyed. The whole world just ceases to exist.

The man clears his throat. "Don't you think that's enough of a public display?" he asks, venom dripping from his lips. At least that's what I imagine when I look at the man to see him nearly foaming at the mouth in anger.

"I'll be right outside the curtain, Pixie Girl," I say when she still hasn't released my hair. When she does let me go, I give her a wink and walk around the bed, keeping the man in my view the entire time. I look at Taylor and gesture that I'll be right there if she needs me. She gives me a sad smile, and I close the curtain.

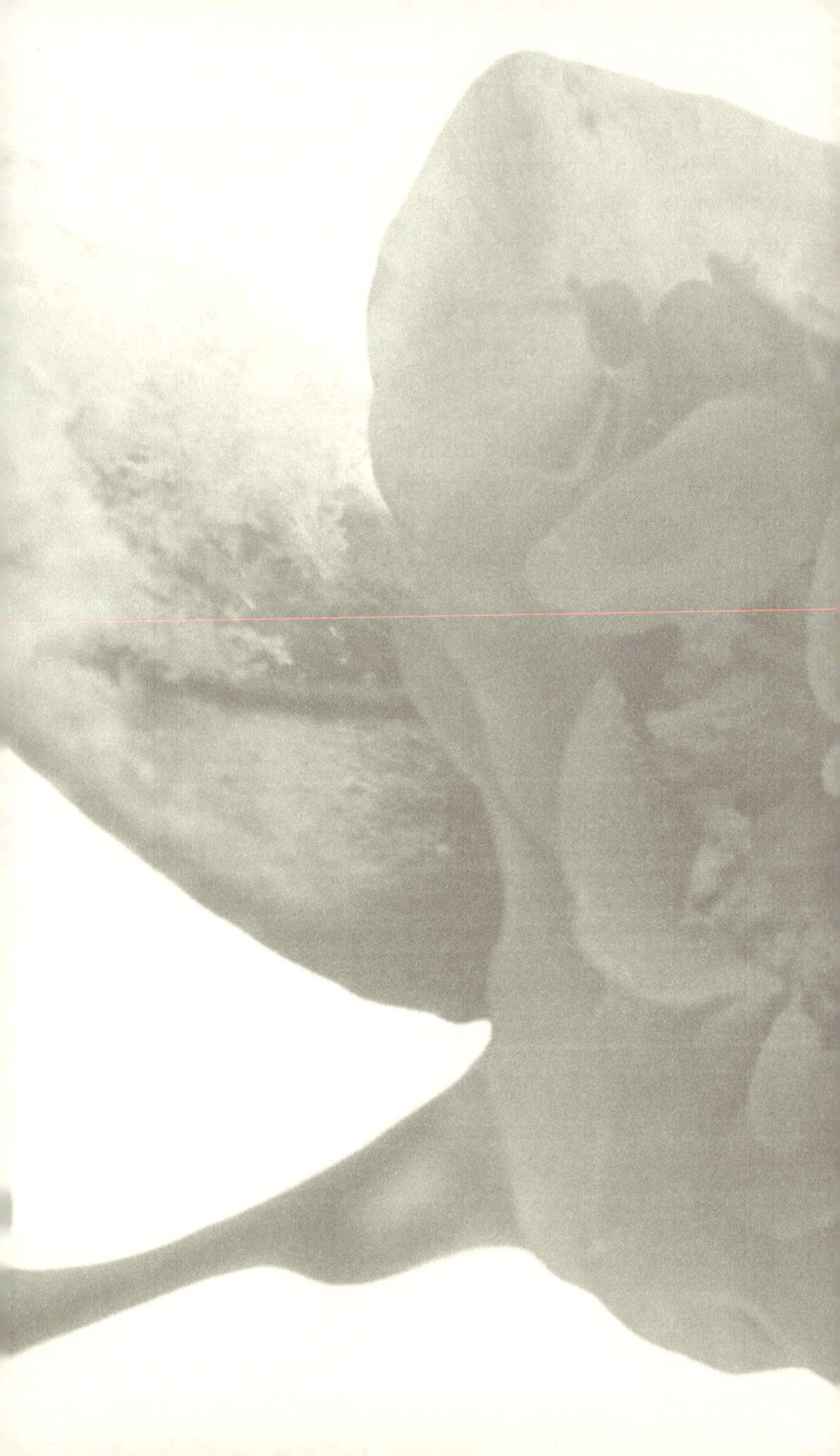

ALL HELL BREAKS LOOSE

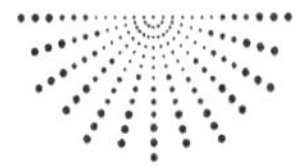

Taylor

My lips tingle, and my mind is awash in chaos. Garrett is kissing me. He's done it for my stepfather's benefit. I know that, but still, his lips are on mine. And it's better than all the times I've fantasized. He is all strong muscle, but his lips are soft. When he pulls away, I want him back, and it's all I can do to let go of his hair instead of yanking his mouth back to mine. I turn my attention from where Garrett has closed the curtain behind himself to glare at my stepfather. There's fire in his eyes. I've seen his fire many times over the years, different types. This is anger, and it's directed at me. Without thinking, I flinch, and he smiles sardonically.

"We've missed you," he says with a sickeningly sweet tone that hides the malice in his sneer. "You shouldn't have run away. Your sisters need you."

"I'm 26 years old. I did not run away. I moved out."

His smile grows more dangerous, and I have to will myself not to cower. This man has tormented me for long enough. I'm also not alone with him...not really. Garrett, my cowpoke, will swoop in and rescue me if I call for him. I won't call, though. I need to be strong. I need Phillip to know that he's no longer in charge of me; he no longer has any power over me.

"Why are you really here, Phillip?"

"What, no 'dad'?"

"You're not my father. I don't live with you anymore, and you don't deserve that name."

"Didn't I take care of you and your mother when your father disappeared? Didn't I help rear you? Didn't I take care of you like you were my own?"

"More like that you owned me." My eyes burn and my nostrils flare, but I blink back the tears threatening to spill.

"Oh, pretty girl, you had things all wrong. I didn't own you when you came willingly. If I'd have owned you, you'd have come kicking and screaming."

Embarrassment at the truth of his words roils in my chest, and heat creeps up my neck. His gaze locks on mine, and he takes a step around the bed. My heartbeat increases and my breathing becomes more labored. Why am I alone with him again? Why is he here?

"Please leave," I managed to squeak out between breaths.

He chuckles. "I told your mom and sisters that I would bring you home. You don't want to disappoint them all again. You don't want to disappoint me, right?" He reaches his hand up, like he's going to pat my hair, and I scream, trying to roll out of the bed away from him, but I'm caught in the blanket, my hand still connected to the IV drip, and the side of the bed is up. I'm trapped.

"Don't touch me! Don't ever touch me again!"

Then all hell broke loose.

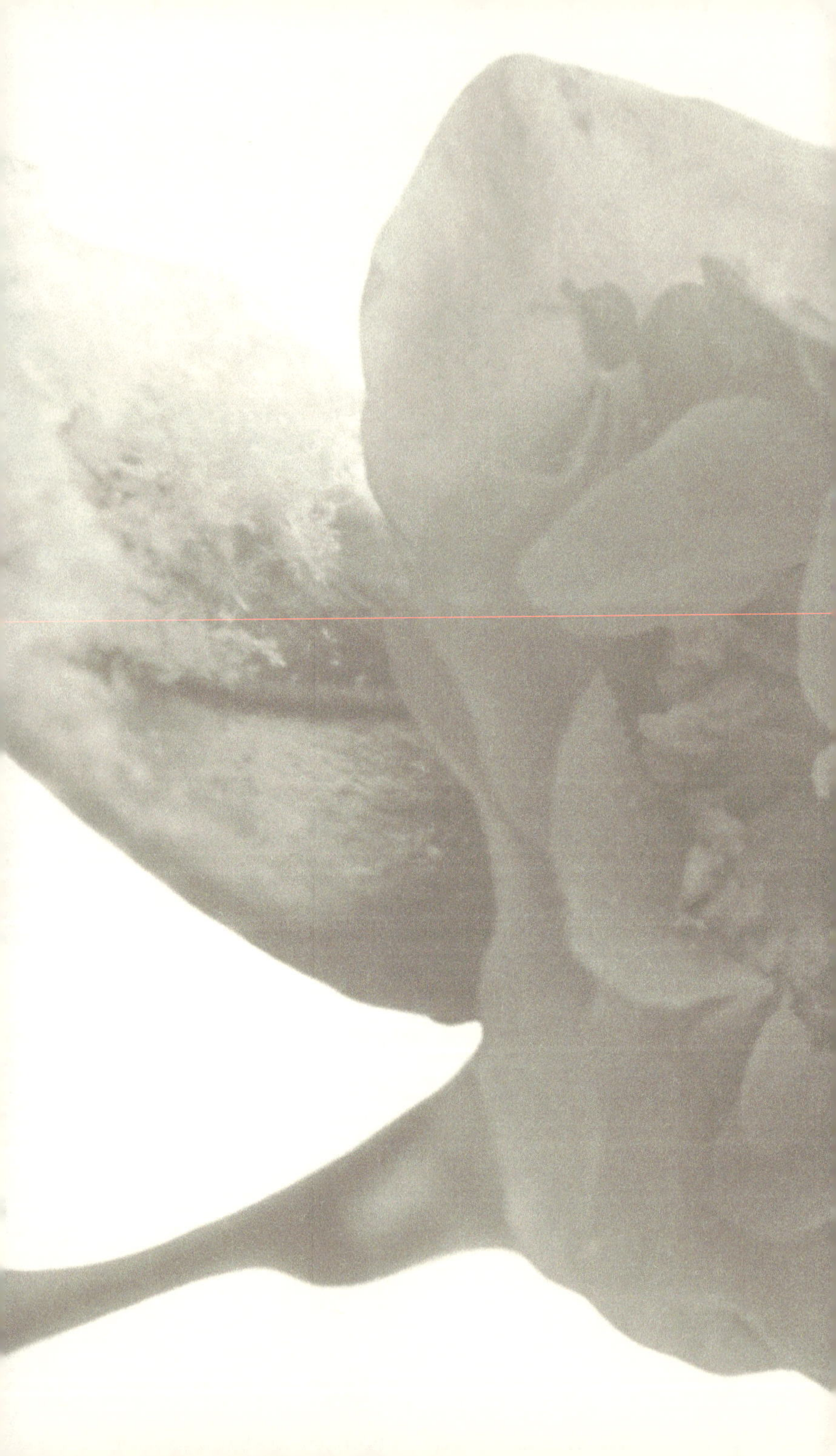

SAFE IN MY ARMS

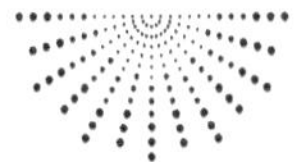

Garrett

Taylor's scream sends chills through me, and I jump up from the chair I've pulled to right outside of her bay. When I see her trying to get away from the man by jumping out of the bed and getting stuck, I freeze trying to figure out what's happening. Her words, though. The fear in her voice. My god, she sounds like a small child, not the feisty woman I've known these past 6 months. Rage kicks in, and I turn from her to the man at the side of the bed.

Moments later, the bay is abuzz with doctors, nurses, and security. I'm seated on the bed, and Taylor is in my lap with her face turned in toward my chest. I have little recollection of what happened between Taylor's initial scream and the moment I cradled her in my arms. I watch the flurry of activity within the ER bay, but I'm not really here. I'm disconnected somehow, like there's a movie playing, and we sit in the middle of the scene. The medical staff works on the man whose body is in a bloody heap on the floor while security stands to the side, hands on their tasers, staring at the couple on the bed, staring at us, Taylor and me. Are we a couple? She sure feels good in my arms. It sure feels good to watch them pick up the unconscious man from the floor and plop him onto a gurney.

"Pa," Jacob's voice comes from the hall, pulling me back into myself.

"Taylor." That's Morgan.

Joanna can't be far behind those two. She's likely been here almost as long as I have. When the gurney exits the bay, a faint "Holy shit," drifts through the curtain. That's my Joanna. Taylor lifts her head from my chest. Her eyes are swollen from crying, but they no longer hold the fear I'd seen in them earlier. I couldn't deal with that again. She'll have nothing to fear if I have anything to say about it.

"It's ok, Pixie Girl. You're safe. He's gone. It's just us here, well, and security. Oh, and I'm sure you heard the others coming to check on us." I chuckle quietly. The whole situation seems surreal, but when she lets out a laugh, I just pull her in tighter again.

"Hey, I can't breathe here, Cowpoke," she says, still laughing. When she slaps at my chest playfully, I loosen my grip.

"Are you two alright?" Joanna asks, as the three of them push through the curtain, but they stop short when they see security standing to the side of the bed.

The energy of the room shifts when they notice Taylor wrapped in my arms. She must notice the change as well because she once again lifts her head and tries to extricate herself from my lap. I reluctantly let her go, so she can sit next to me. She looks into my eyes, wariness haunting her features, but I smile reassuringly and stand to let her get back into the bed.

"We're fine, still waiting for the doctor to come back with the final diagnosis, though Taylor seems okay now." I reach out and take her hand.

"Mr. Daniels, we need to get your statement," the taller security officer states, "and we'd prefer to do that before we have to call the police."

"And we need to get Ms. Wright's statement as well," the other chimes in.

"So, ask your questions, gentlemen, and get it over with," I say nonplussed.

Joanna crosses her arms, and I close my eyes before I roll them at her. Her judgment is neither needed nor warranted. I did what I had to do, and I will not regret it. The officers give me an exasperated look, like they've been asking me questions all night and I've refused to answer. They've not said more than five words to me before now. If they weren't the ones wearing tasers, I'd have thought they were afraid of me or something.

"Protocol says we must get your statements separately."

"Fuck protocol. The last time I left her alone in this bay..." My fists clench, and Taylor puts her free hand on top of where our other ones are joined, rubbing her thumb across my knuckles in a way that calms me.

"We'll stay with her, Pa," Jacob says. "We'll make sure she's safe."

I look at my son. I know Jacob can protect her, and I should trust him, yet the very idea of letting Taylor's hand go nearly has me trembling. I turn uncertain eyes to her, and she smiles. Other than her laugh earlier, which was likely more a response to the ridiculous situation we're in than genuine mirth, this is the first real smile I've seen on her face all day. It bolsters me, and when she whispers that she'll be fine, I relent.

As I stand to leave, though, her voice draws the attention of everyone. "Joanna, please go with your dad. I'll feel better knowing he's not alone either."

My heart flip flops in my chest, and emotions I don't feel worthy of threaten to overwhelm me. I've not felt so raw in years, not since my Clara got sick. Not since she'd begged our children to look after me. I'm afraid to look into Taylor's eyes, afraid she'll see the tumult alive in me. Unable to find words, I turn and leave the bay past the taller of the two officers who holds the curtain open for Joanna and me.

bay past the taller of the two officers who holds the curtain open for Joanna and me.

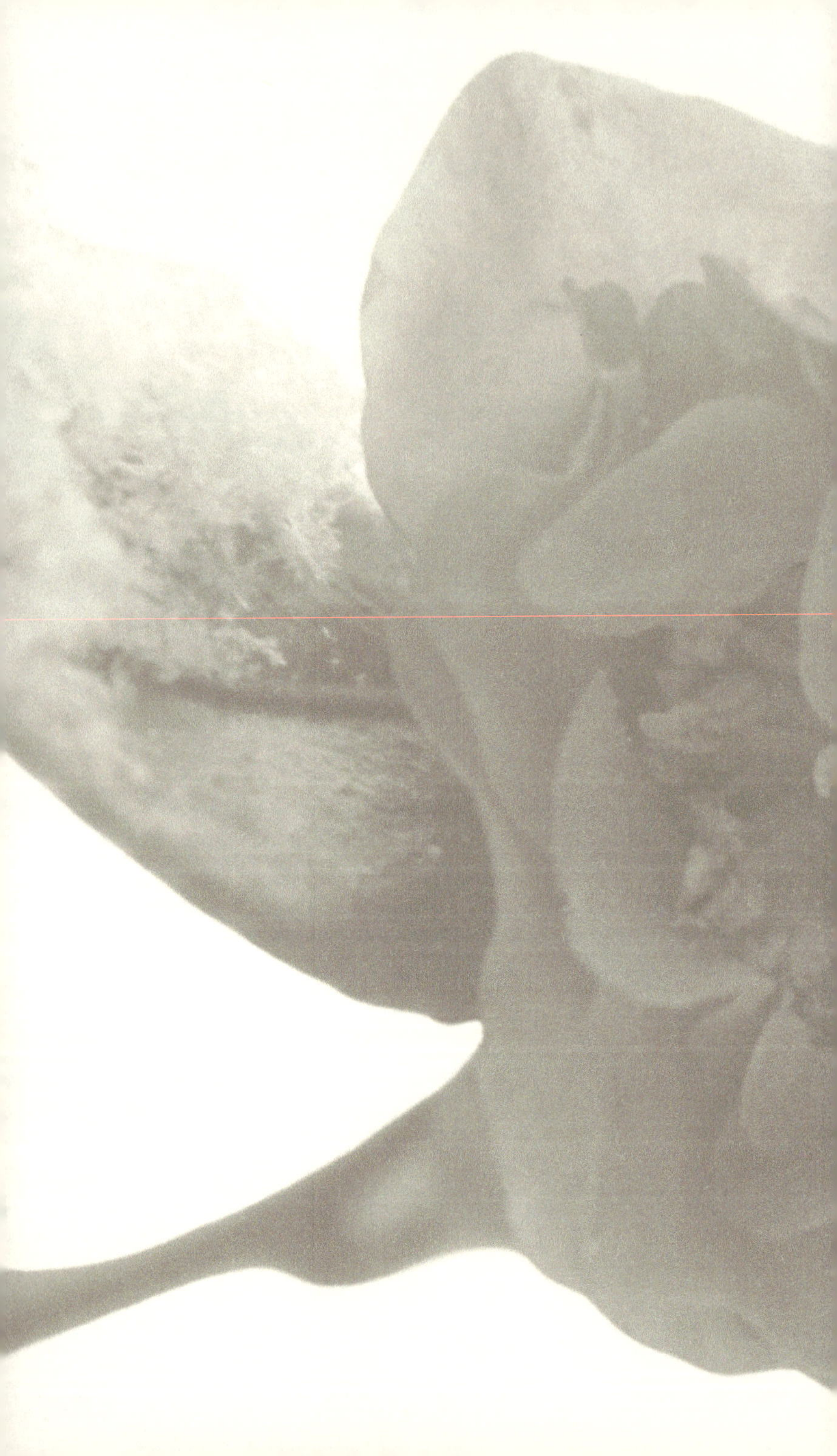

HIDING THE BROKEN PARTS

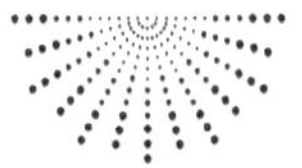

Taylor

"Are you avoiding me, Pix? You've not done that in at least a good month. Ignore me? Yes. Outright avoid me? Nah."

I look up from where I've been adjusting the new linen in the dining room. My breath catches at the sight of him, all god-like in the mid-morning light that streams through the new arched window. When I'm finally able to take in air, ready to deliver a snarky retort, he licks his bottom lip, and I'm transfixed on the tip of his tongue. I've relived the feel of his tongue entwined with mine a million times in my dreams this past week. The memory is like a siren's song pulling me into a daydream of him wrapped around me. His woodsy scent enveloping me until I'm delirious with need.

"Earth to Taylor. Come in, Taylor. Are you there?"

I blink a few times, a gasp leaving my lips when I realize he's now standing next to me. His scent wraps me in a cocoon, and I take in a deep breath. The smile he wears at his own little joke morphs into more of a smirk, taunting me.

"You're in my bubble, Cowpoke."

His knowing smile deepens, and he takes two steps back with a mock bow. On instinct, I take a step toward him, and a chuckle leaves his lips. I snap the towel I've been holding to wipe down the silverware at him, and he grabs it, pulling me against him.

"Oops...sorry to burst your bubble, Pixie Girl."

"You're just full of dad jokes today, aren't you? Is this my punishment for avoiding you?" I say the last part while making air quotes as I take a step back from him.

I don't look into his eyes. I might not be able to break away if I do. He doesn't get the memo, and brings his eyes level with mine, which makes him hunch over awkwardly, like one might do with a child, and it's all I can do to contain a laugh.

"Maybe. If that's what you consider punishment." His brows lift suggestively, and my breath hitches, all thoughts of laughing gone, replaced by other, more distracting thoughts.

"How can I help you, Mr. Daniels?"

"Are we really back to that?"

"Only when you're being difficult."

He places a hand over his chest. "Me? Never. I have to run to the orchard for Morgan and wondered if you might want to join me."

"Apple picking? Count me in!" I blurt before I can stop myself.

"Great!"

His genuine smile has me returning it and kicking myself at the same time. I do not need to spend time alone with this man. I already can't keep my thoughts together when I'm around him. Still, I'm excited to go to the orchard and pick apples. I finish polishing the silverware on the table, drop my towel on the table near the dining room door, and grab my jacket.

"How are you doing?" Garrett asks as soon as we get out onto the main road.

"I'm good," I say out of habit without even looking in his direction.

He turns his head slightly, and I can see his scowl in my

peripheral vision. He's not buying it. I know he has questions about everything that happened in the hospital, but I'm not sure I want to talk about it. I've not told anyone the whole story besides the therapist I've only recently started seeing again.

"I'm okay, really. I'm..."

"You know you don't have to pretend with me, Taylor. You don't have to hide from me either. I know you can't be completely okay after what happened."

I take in a deep breath and let out a sigh. "I'm not...well, I wouldn't say I'm completely okay, but I've been worse. I'm functioning, able to work, and talking with my therapist is helping some." He lets out a snort before playing it off with a cough. "Don't believe in therapy, Mr. Daniels?"

"It's not that I don't believe in it. I think it helps some people believe they're getting better or coping better. I just..."

Though he doesn't look at me, I can almost feel the plea his silence is making. "You wish I'd talk to you?"

A breath whooshes from him on that last word, like he's been holding it. "I know you don't owe me anything, so please don't think that. It's your story to tell or not to tell. It's just that when you went silent with me...Did I do something wrong?"

We've stopped at a stop sign, and he turns to look directly at me. I reach out and put my hand on his where it's sitting atop his water bottle in the console. The plastic crinkles under the weight of our hands and the way his fingers have tightened around it.

"You did nothing wrong, Garrett. I have nothing but gratitude for everything you did that day. You didn't have to do any of it. It's not like we were anything but antagonistic to each other leading up to it. And the way you were feeling about Joanna's plan to leave Colliers Town, I wouldn't have been surprised if you didn't want to stay away from everyone." I slide my fingers between his, prying them from the bottle while still holding his gaze. "But you didn't stay away. You stayed with me. When I was scared and alone, you were there." I turn his hand, grabbing it between both of mine. "When I needed a hero, you rescued me. When..."

"I thought maybe you were mad or uncomfortable because of the kiss," he says, interrupting.

A laugh bellows out of me. I am definitely not upset about that kiss. I hate the situation that prompted it. I'm angry that the perfect moment was overshadowed by Phillip's presence and actions. I'm frustrated at the incessant need to pull out my vibrator every single time his lips come to mind, but..."No, I'm neither mad nor uncomfortable because of the kiss," I finally say.

His shoulders visibly relax, like he's been holding himself ready for an argument. "Then why avoid me?"

I don't let his hand go, but I turn myself to again face forward. "Fear. Fear that you would look at me like the broken woman I am. Fear that our banter would turn to something sad and guarded. I don't even really know why or how it started, but I look forward to our back and forth. I didn't want to see that change once you knew about Phillip...about me. Please know that no matter what he said, or what you heard him say, I didn't want any of it, ever."

Garrett pulls the car over onto the side of the road and turns the ignition off. He links his fingers with mine. "I know what it's like to feel broken. I'm sure you've heard the tragic story of mean ol' Mr. Daniels whose wife died, and he became a hermit dependent on his children." I start to shake my head in disagreement, but he cuts me off. "It's true. All of it. I loved my Rosie. She took such good care of us. To show my appreciation, I did everything I could to make sure she and our children were taken care of in turn. I opened the store, so I could stay close to home to help and have something to leave to Jacob and Joanna. I kept an eye on their schooling and their friends. When neither of my children found their long-term happiness, I felt like a failure, and then when Rosie got sick, I just kind of gave up. It took Morgan coming back after all those years missing to get all of us back on track in some way."

I wipe away a tear because I feel like she's also helped me get back on track. "You had to want to make that shift as well. It wasn't just her appearance. You did the work." I look at him with a tight-lipped smile.

It takes a few long moments before he looks up into my eyes, his breath unsteady. "And then this little spitfire of woman with short-cropped, pink-streaked hair, wearing colorful clothes and clown shoes showed up, and I said, "Garrett, you better get your shit together because your ass is delusional right now if you're imagining Tinker Bell walking through the house." He gives me a wink, and I chuckle. "You're not broken, Pixie Girl. You've just been through some shit. I mean, I don't know. Maybe you were at one point, and maybe it feels like some of those scars were torn open again last week, but you're not broken. You're a breath of fresh air in this old stagnant town."

"Awww, I think that's the sweetest thing you've ever said to me, Cowpoke."

"It's your damn pixie dust making me soft!"

Without another word, as if nothing had happened, he hit the ignition and got us back on the road toward the orchard. The radio plays, but I don't pay it much attention. Instead, I watch his profile, a myriad of emotions playing across his face. His brows drop. His smile broadens. He even bites his lower lip at one point, and my thighs squeeze together of their own volition. I don't want to interrupt his thoughts, but I'd sure like to know what he's thinking.

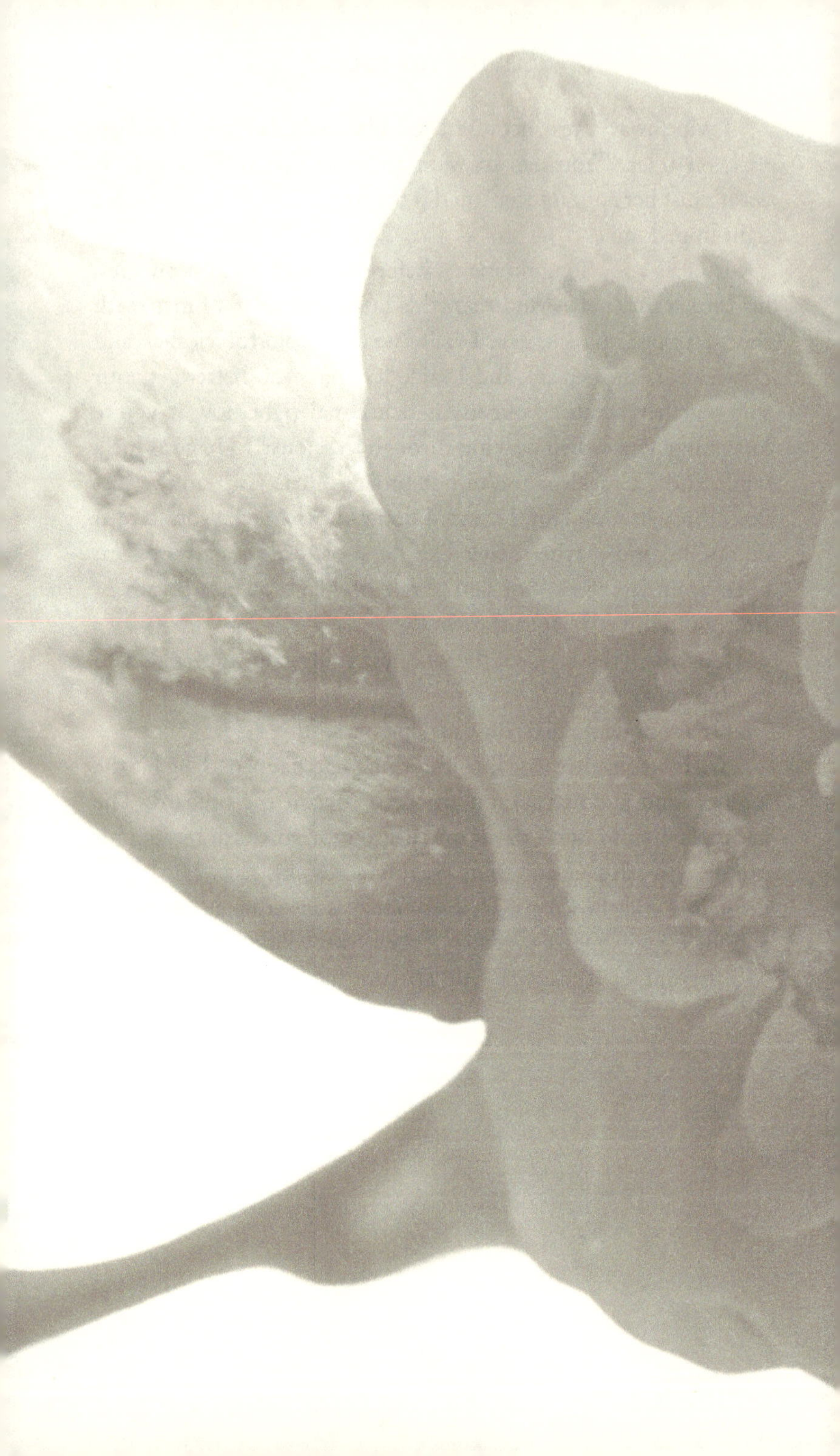

FIRST OF MANY FIRSTS

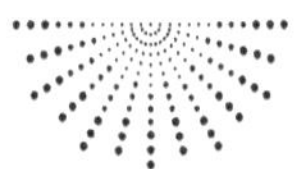

arrett

Did I really just say that corny shit? Her pixie dust making me soft...Ha! There ain't shit about that pixie that makes me soft. If anything, the essence of her makes me hard in ways I shouldn't be feeling. I'm no better than her stepfather if I can't keep my thoughts off of how many times I jerk off thinking about her. She's younger than my damn daughter for Christ's sake! But, even with all the vulnerability she's shown this past week, hell, just today, she's still all woman. I've not known her as anything but the woman next to me.

I turn my eyes and catch her watching me. She doesn't seem to notice that I've seen her. A smile plays across my face. She feels something too...she has to. I'm not going to push her. I'm happy with how things are and how they've always been between us, but it makes me feel good to know she feels something.

The largest orchard in Cole County is only about a 30-minute drive from Colliers Town, and it's absolutely beautiful this time of year. The apples are ripe for picking, and the trees have begun wearing their fall colors. Though there's an open market closer to the street, I prefer to pick my own, and since I've known the owner my entire life, I get that benefit.

I chance a glance at Taylor watching the trees as we make our way up the drive. "There are so many," she says.

"Trees?" I ask. "This is an orchard after all." My tone is as sarcastic as I can make it. She wants banter, I got plenty.

"Smart ass!"

"You're gonna have to do better than that, Pixie Girl."

"Or I could just leave you here to argue with yourself, Cowpoke."

"Nah, you wouldn't do that. Who's going to carry all the apples Morgan asked for?"

She turns toward me with an expression that speaks volumes about who will be carrying what when we leave here.

I lead the way toward the barn where Jared has baskets set out for those of us locals who like to wander the endless rows. I grab two, handing one to her. Her eyes grow wide with excitement, and I realize I've never seen this emotion from her before. My breath catches as I try to hold onto this moment before I ask, "Have you never been apple picking before?"

"No," she says with a shake of her head. "I was always labeled as clumsy, so I wasn't even brought out to places like this where I might try to climb a tree and fall. At least..." she trails off and her countenance darkens. "No. Let's just leave it at that."

Though I want to know what she was going to say, I don't push her to share. We're in public, though there's no one else near us. Instead, I ask, "What are some other things you never got to do because of your so-called clumsiness."

She turns a contemplative smile my way. "Great question. I've never been to the fair or swimming or horseback riding. I'm actually kind of jealous about Joanna going to work with and ride horses."

"Don't tell me you want to leave too," I say, my words more

abrupt, more pained than I had intended. We're supposed to be keeping it light.

"Oh, heck no, I just got here, and I'm happy. I just think I'd love to work with the beautiful animals."

"Did she tell you we use to own and board horses at the farm?" My voice softens. "We only have Jake's old mare left, but I'd like to open up the boarding again one day. Maybe you can come over and spend time with the mare. She's not good for riding anymore, but she's super sweet."

"I'd love that!"

I love the idea of her coming to the farm, of sharing another first with her. "C'mon, let's go get us some apples."

*T*aylor

The smell of freshly picked apples fills the car from where we sat the bushels on the backseat. My heart is so full as I take in the sweet scent and think about the man sitting next to me. Garrett Daniels is nothing like I expected him to be when we first met. He was gruff and rude as hell that first day, but these past few months have taught me there's so much more to him. He's still brusque at times and intimidating in the way a tall, burly, and intense man can be.

I squeeze my eyes closed in the same way I squeeze my thighs to keep myself from sighing with need. The man is a walking enigma and too damn sexy for everyone's good. *But he's off limits*, I remind myself. He's my boss's future father-in-law, for fuck's sake, and he's old enough to be my father. A shudder runs up my spine as Phillip's face pops into my head.

"What're you over there ruminating about?"

His deep drawl pulls me from the dark place my stupid brain was wanting to go. How the hell can I be sitting next to this wonderful man, thinking about him, and then boom, the moment ruined with thoughts of a monster. It makes no sense, and though Garrett tried to tell me earlier that I'm not broken, how is this not a sign of someone who's been completely shattered?

"Taylor. Stop whatever you're doing and get back in this car with me." His voice is soft, making the ridiculous command even funnier, and laughter bubbles out of me. The car slows slightly as he turns his head to fully look in my direction. His brows knit together, like he's trying to put a puzzle together, and he knows there are pieces missing.

I take a deep breath and let it out with a sigh. "I'm here...in the car...with you," I say, pausing each phrase. When his brow raises, I finish off with a quick, "Promise," holding up my left pinky. Surprisingly, he wraps his own around mine, and warmth trickles from my fingers all the way up my arm. When he pulls his hand away, I want to whine. Instead, I put a smile on my face. "Thank you for bringing me out here today. I loved every minute of it, even if you did make me carry my own apples."

Garrett barks out a laugh. "I didn't... No, I couldn't make you do anything. You're too damn stubborn for that. Still, I'm glad you had a good time and didn't hurt yourself."

"Huh?" My chin tilts up. "Hurt myself? Carrying a basket of apples?"

His hands grip the steering wheel tighter than necessary. "You said you'd never been because you were clumsy and likely to hurt yourself."

"Oh," I let out on a breath. He's right. I did say that. The lie had slid from my lips so easily after years of practice. It wasn't even necessary anymore, and yet, I hadn't stopped myself from saying it.

"I've watched you climb ladders, hang over banisters, and paint thirteen-foot ceilings. I'm guessing your lack of experiences has nothing to do with clumsiness." I shake my head, but he doesn't even turn my way to see, just continues driving in silence for several minutes before speaking again. "You don't have to make up stories, Taylor. Not with me. I see you, the person you are right now. There ain't shit clumsy about you."

A tear slides down my cheek, and I quickly whisk it away. While Jordan has always been the person I could confide in who did everything to protect me emotionally, with Garrett, I actually feel seen. Not only that. I feel safe for the first time in forever.

"Well, nothing clumsy except the way you try to pretend you're not the least bit intimidated by me. I mean, I am the big and scary Garrett Daniels. Don't worry, most people can't hide their nerves around me."

He turns and winks before turning up the radio and letting the sounds of classic rock blast through the speakers. I pull my lips together and snort a laugh out of my nose. He's right. It's getting harder and harder to hide the way he makes me feel.

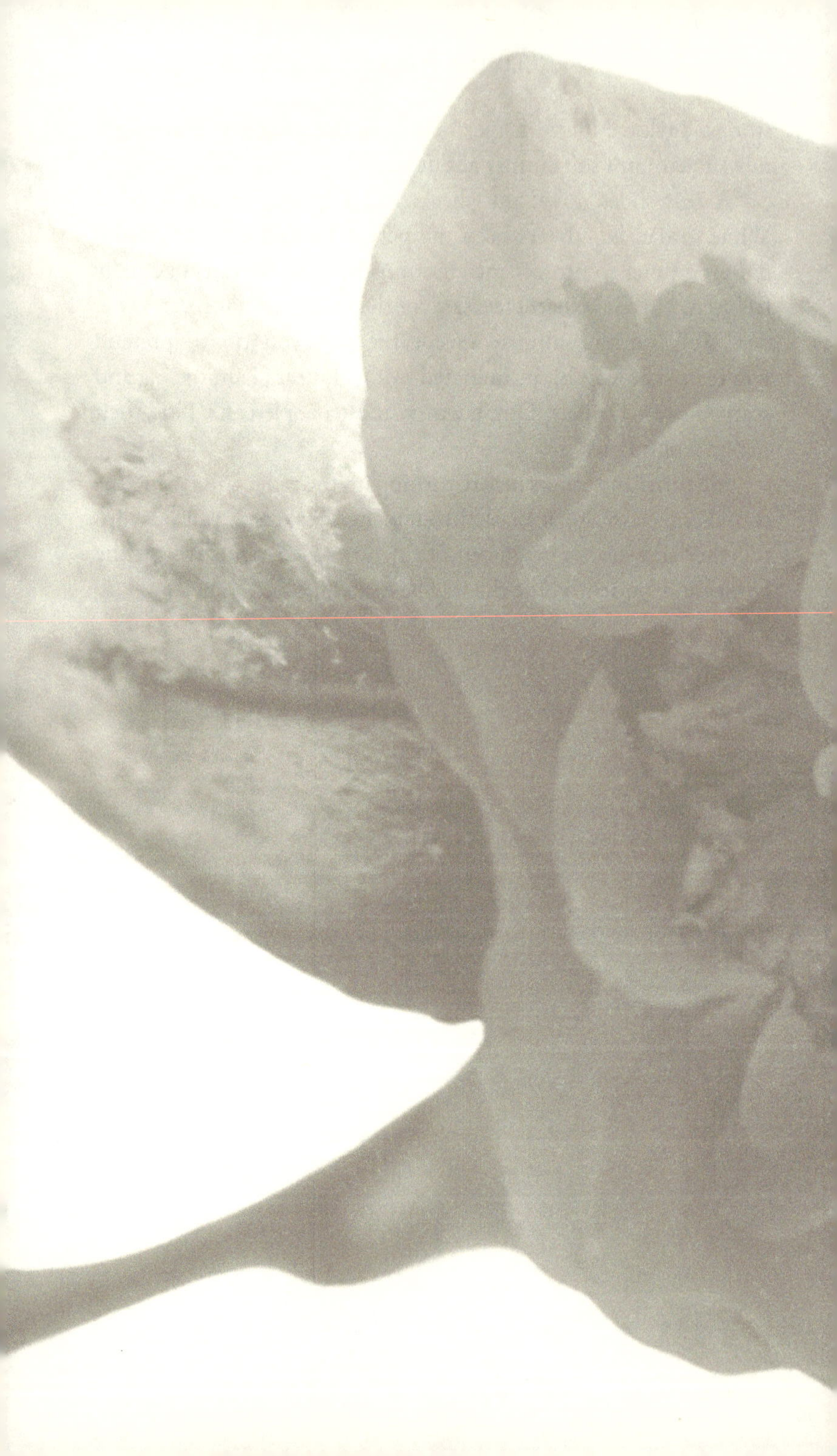

WHERE'S TAYLOR?

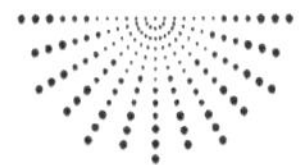

G arrett

"Hey there, Mr. Daniels. Looks like we have a nearly full house this weekend, and a snowstorm's threatening to come down from the mountains."

"Seriously. Still with the Mr. Daniels? How many times do I have to ask you to call me Garrett? Hell, you'll be my daughter-in-law soon enough, just call me Dad, for Heaven's sake."

"Okay, Mr. Da...d," Morgan says with a smirk. I roll my eyes, eliciting a chuckle from her. "Any chance you could help me this weekend with the guests?"

"Where's Taylor? She not working?" I can't keep the worry from my tone. It isn't like Morgan and Taylor can't run this place on their own. The two of them are a well-oiled machine. Now that Morgan has hired two housekeepers, they are nearly ready to open the additional rooms Jacob and I recently finished renovating. "What about your new hires?"

"Say you don't want to help without saying you don't want to help, Dad." her tone drips sarcasm, and I scowl.

"That's not what I was saying at all. It was more concern, but in my way of being concerned." She laughs again, causing a more dramatic eye roll.

"Seriously, though, I gave Taylor the weekend off to spend with her best friend. Today, Judy, the younger housekeeper, called in afraid that the storm would keep her from getting back up the mountain to her children. If I had realized a storm was coming, I'd have asked Taylor to wait until next weekend."

My mind immediately wonders what Taylor and her friend have planned. From the brief conversations we've had the past few days, she's still trying to process everything with her stepfather through the help of a therapist. Though I don't believe in that hocus pocus therapy stuff, she says it's helping, and that's enough for me. Between her statement and those of others nearby in the ER who heard her screams, hospital security called the cops. They arrested Phillip Truman, handcuffing him to his gurney before he even had a chance to wake up from the pummeling I'd given him. Taylor's touch was the only thing that stopped me from killing the man that day. Of course, there will still be investigations, court, the whole nine yards, but for now, she deserves a weekend away.

"So, can you help your favorite future daughter-in-law out?"

Morgan's question pulls me from my thoughts. Of course, I'l help. I just have to give her shit first. I'll do whatever it takes to keep Morgan happy and around because her being around makes Jacob happy. I'm just about to tell her so when Jacob comes busting through the kitchen door.

"Has anyone heard from Taylor?"

My heart stops. Jacob has his phone clutched in his hand, concern etched on his face.

"She's supposedly on vacation with her friend," I say, trying to hide my rapid breathing.

Jacob shakes his head, and Morgan puts a hand on his arm. "Jordan just called. She hasn't heard from Taylor for a few hours, and whenever she'd tries calling, the phone goes straight to voicemail."

"I thought they were traveling together," Morgan says, and something in her worried tone makes my hackles rise.

"Where were they going?"

My son and Morgan both look at me, their brows furrowing in unison.

"She didn't talk to you about it?" Jacob asks in an almost mystified tone. What the fuck is going on here?

"No. Was she supposed to?"

"Based on your dad's response to my asking for help this weekend, I'm guessing she did not."

"You two just seemed so chummy the past week, or maybe since the hospital," Jacob says, his tone quieting, "I assumed..."

I look back and forth between the two of them. "Where were they going?" I ask again, maybe a little harsher than necessary from the stricken look on Morgan's face.

"I overheard her telling Morgan that she just wanted to get away from everything for a couple days to clear her head, so I...um...offered the cabin."

"The cabin?" My heart pounds in my chest. "My hunting cabin?" My fists clench. He cannot be saying he sent her up to that fire hazard, drafty-ass, lean-to of a cabin.

Jacob puts up his hands. "I've been working on it, Pa. I've sealed it up real good, put in a wood-burning stove. There's a fridge, a bed, and running water."

My eyes bulge. When? How? I have so many questions going through my head, but he cuts me off.

"Morgan and I have been up there a couple times. I would not have taken her if it wasn't safe, and I damn sure wouldn't have offered it to Taylor if it was uninhabitable, Pa."

I know he's right. I know he isn't that reckless. I'm just in shock about the whole thing. And, I'm worried about Taylor.

"None of that changes the fact that Jordan is worried about Taylor, so they're not together," Morgan says, bringing the conversation back around to what really matters.

"Call Jordan back and put her on speaker," I tell Jacob.

The phone barely rings once before a frazzled female voice says, "Any word from her?"

"Jordan, this is Garrett Daniels."

"The old cowpoke with hot daddy vibes?" she asks, and my face heats.

Morgan covers her mouth, but her shoulders shake with stifled laughter. Jacob's mouth hits the floor. I roll my eyes and wave them both off.

"Um," I start, not knowing what to say in response. I clear my throat. "Can you tell us what the plan was, so we can try and figure out where she might be?"

"Yeah, sure, sorry. I've just heard a lot about you." The corners of my mouth ticks upward, and I turn my face away, so Morgan and Jacob can't see. Jordan takes a deep breath, and then she tells us everything Taylor had planned in one long sentence without taking breaths. "I was about to head that way myself when I heard on the radio that many of the roads to and up the mountain are becoming dangerous. I don't know the way well enough." The last part came out on a sob, and my chest tightens with the same discomfort. Taylor's out there somewhere on her way to or up the mountain without any way of letting us know if she makes it safely.

"I'll find her," I say, holding my hand out for the key to Jacob's truck.

He hangs up the phone and pulls his keys out. "I'll come with you."

"No need in both of us getting out there and stuck together. You stay here with Morgan. Is the old satellite phone still up there?"

I'm already walking toward the door. I'll need to stop by the house for a couple warm blankets in case she's been stuck out in the cold for a while. I'll also need a coat. I don't know if Taylor even has a warm coat upstairs in her closet, so I'll just grab one of

Joanna's for her. I pull open the front door to find an unknown car parking in front of the house. I turn around to let Morgan know that her first guests have arrived, and she is standing directly behind me. I hadn't even heard them following me, but she and Jacob are staring like I've lost my mind. They can think whatever they want; I will not leave Taylor up there on the mountain alone, and if she didn't make it to the cabin, I will find her.

"I'll text you as soon as I locate her. If I don't have a signal, I will call from the satellite phone." I put a hand on Morgan's shoulder. "That pixie is too stubborn to give up. She'll be fine."

Though I say the words with as much conviction as possible, I have to force myself to believe their truth. She has to be fine. I can't imagine this place without her light and her snark and her scent and the taste of her lips. Though I only had them once, I've relived that moment so many times since that day. No, I refuse to believe that anything bad has happened. She's simply hunkered down in the cabin without a signal. Maybe Jacob forgot to tell her about the satellite phone or how it works. If there's firewood and matches for the stove, she's fine. Maybe the storm hasn't even hit up there yet. There are so many possibilities, and I'm going to hold onto them all.

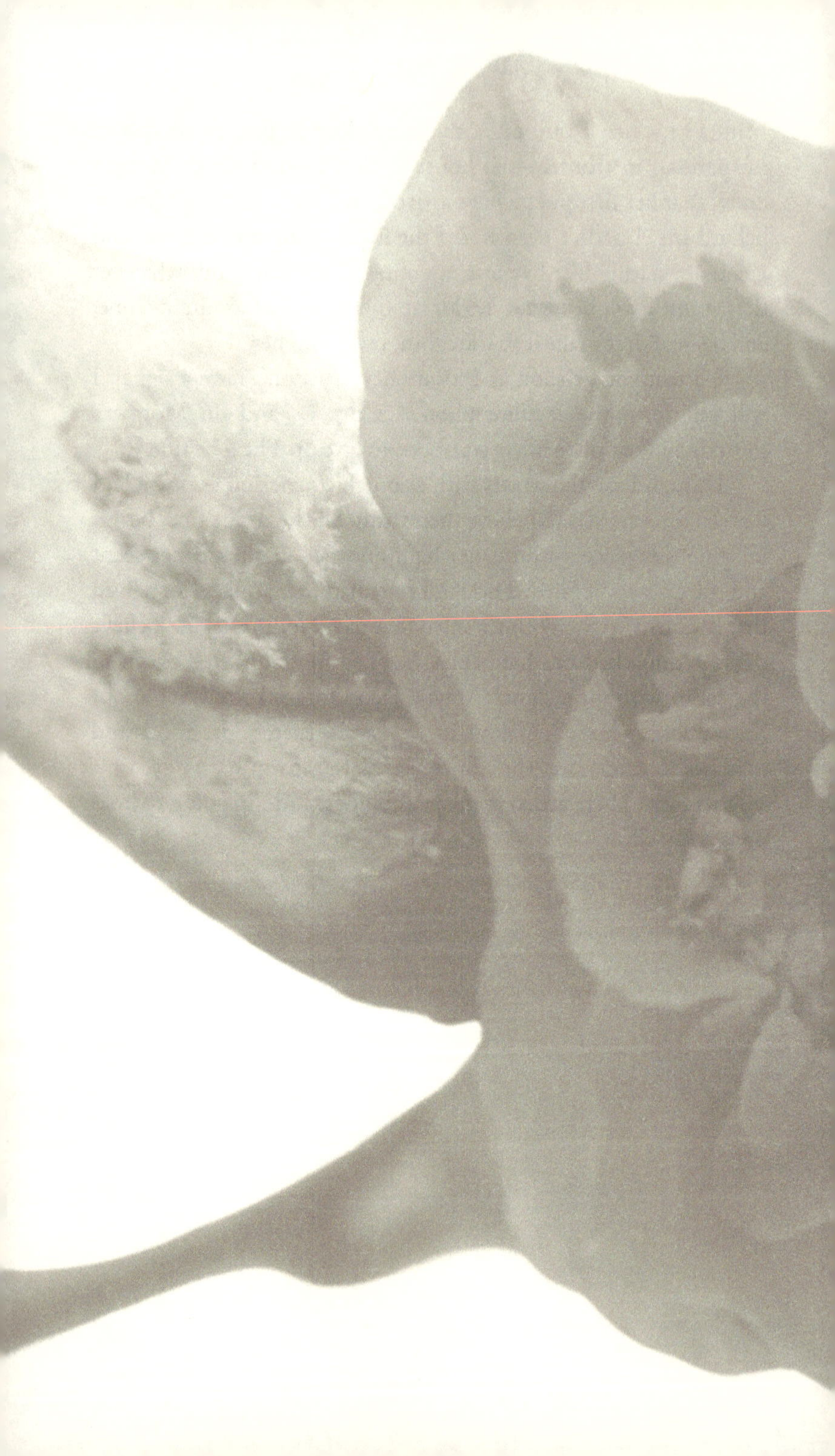

THE SNOW WINS

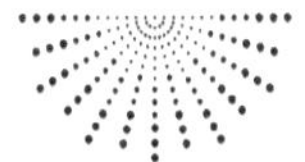

Garrett

The temperature indicator on the dash screams the reality I've been trying to ignore for the past forty-five minutes; it's thirty degrees colder up here on the mountain than it was when I left Colliers Town. According to the weather app, the temperature is dropping quickly, and the snow has already started around the other side of the mountain. I take the Slate Ridge exit. After a quick detour to make sure Taylor hadn't pulled off to get gas or snacks, I continue my climb. The four-lane highway quickly narrows to two lanes as it curves around the mountain away from the last tourist retreat. Hopefully, she'd already turned on her GPS, so she wouldn't miss the mountain pass that leads up rather than around in another ten miles. There's a sign, but it's not large, and who knows how detailed my son was in his directions to the cabin.

Five miles before the turn, flakes hit the windshield. Another two miles, and the sides of the road are covered in a thin white blanket. Every nerve ending screams for me to pick up the pace, but I know how treacherous these mountain roads can be at the beginning of a snowstorm when icy cold precipitation hits much warmer pavement as the temperature drops. I can't help Taylor if I slide off the road and down into a ravine. I maintain my safe speed as the snow thickens. When I get to the point that the road is covered in white, I'm not sure whether I should be relieved or concerned that no other tires have marred the pristine landscape. Even when I turn up the pass and then onto the drive toward our remote cabin, I still see nothing that says anyone has been this way recently.

I slow down as I traverse the narrow drive. There's no ravine here, but it is possible to slide off into a ditch, and I'd rather not have to hike the remaining miles up in the thick snowfall. The flakes falling now are much bigger, and the drumming of my fingers on the steering wheel reaches a crescendo when I come around a sharp curve and catch sight of a blue vehicle half on and half off the drive. Slamming the truck in park, I jump out. I don't even bother to grab a coat.

"Taylor!" I yell her name, as I run toward her Honda. It's already covered in so much snow, I'm lucky to have caught any blue at all. The doors are all locked, and when I clean the snow from the driver-side window, it's obvious the car is empty. She's not here. I yell her name a few more times and then hurry back to the truck. There are no footprints leading in any direction that I can find. Hopefully, she hiked back up to the cabin. Since the car is facing down the mountain, I assume she got worried about the snow or the fact that she had no signal and thought to go back home. I take a deep breath and put the truck back in drive, carefully skirting around the Honda and continuing my way to the cabin.

The remainder of the drive consists of me scanning left and right for any sign of her along the side of the drive while calling her name every couple hundred feet. I watch the covered path in front for footprints. When I round the final curve and see the cabin standing strong against the sea of white, the breath whooshes from my lungs as if it's been stuck for hours. Thin wisps of smoke trickle from the chimney. As soon as I put the truck in park,

Taylor opens the door, and I have to fight back tears as relief washes over me.

I jump down from the truck and stalk toward her. I need to see her up close, need to hear her breath and feel her warmth. I need to know she's really alright and not my imagination playing tricks on me.

"Garrett?" Her voice is a whisper, like she's surprised to see me. That's one need met, but I don't stop my approach, simply slow my steps. She comes fully into view as I climb onto the porch, and my heartbeat calms. That's two needs met. She says my name again, and I wrap her up in my arms. Her arms slide around my neck, and she's so warm my knees nearly buckle under me.

"What're you doing here, Cowpoke?" Her words come out on a sob.

I pull back from her to look into her eyes. They're shiny with unshed tears, and when one swells to roll down her cheek, I wipe it away. "Are you okay?" I ask, looking her up and down. When she shivers, I rub my hands along her arms. "Let's go inside before you freeze," I offer. She doesn't move right away, just stares at me.

"I didn't bring a coat," she says without breaking our gaze.

"I brought you one," I say, caressing her cheek. Her breath catches, and her eyes flutter.

My eyes graze over her face and land on her lips. She pulls one of them between her teeth, and I suck in a breath.

"I was so worried about you," I say, trying to give myself a moment to breathe. When she frowns, I want to take it all back, and then she starts to apologize. I put my thumb over her lips to stop her. "Don't. Jordan called Jacob, and we were all worried. I," I pause, not sure how to say what I'm feeling, what I'm thinking.

"You?"

I smile. "I told them you were too stubborn to not be okay." I look from her to inside the cabin. "It appears I was right," I say with a shrug. She giggles, and my heart flutters. "But then I found your car off the drive, and I don't think my heart beat again, or maybe I didn't breathe again, until you stepped out on this porch and said my name." Instinctively, I wrap her in my arms again to reassure myself that she's really here, safe and sound. "I need to call Jacob and let everyone know I found you."

"There's no signal up here. That's why I was trying to get down the mountain." She grabs my arms and looks up at me with worry in her eyes. "Jordan. I wanted to warn Jordan. Is she alright?"

I chuckle. "Jordan's fine. She called Jacob worried when she couldn't get ahold of you and had heard that the storm was making the roads dangerous. She never even left home."

"Thank goodness," she says, resting her forehead on my chest and melting into my arms.

"Let's go inside," I say again and start walking her backward toward the door.

"Garrett," she says, her voice breathy, "I...I...god...yeah," she nods her head, "let's go inside."

With that, she let's go of me and turns back into the house. Suddenly, the cold closes in, and I quickly follow, shutting the door behind me. I make my way to the stove, stoke the fire and add another log, all the while trying to ignore the need to pull her back into my arms.

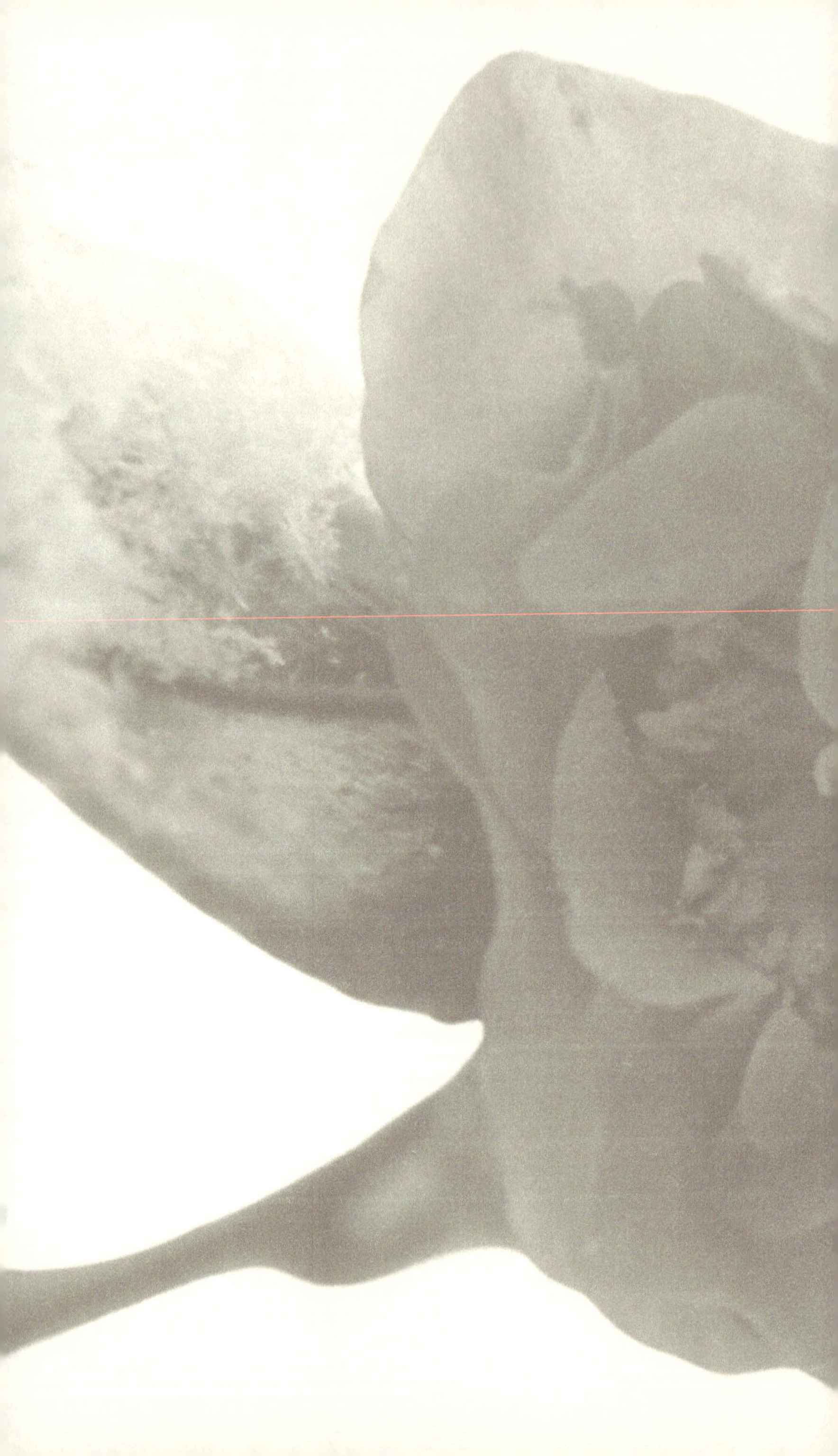

AMBROSIA WITH A SIDE
OF TRAUMA RESPONSE

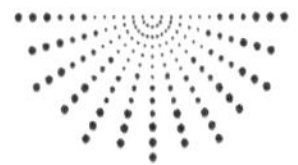

Garrett

"Have you eaten anything?" Taylor asks, looking at me from the small kitchen area Jacob had created.

He really did a fabulous job upgrading this small hunter's cabin into something livable. It's like a tiny vacation house. There's a kitchen area separated from the living space by an island with two bar stools. There are new appliances that Morgan must've helped pick out because they are her style. Though the living area is rather small, there's enough space for a queen-size bed and two comfortable looking armchairs with ottomans. I couldn't help but notice there is not a couch. The wood-burning stove puts out plenty of heat for the small cabin, and I'm ready to peel off my shirt shortly after arriving. I don't out of fear of how Taylor will feel, but I surely want to.

"No. I was supposed to have dinner with Morgan and Jacob when he told me you were missing..."

I start to say more, but her eyes turn sad, and her bottom lip puffs out. I walk to her, taking her face in my hands before she can apologize, or worse start crying. She stares up at me, eyes glassy with unshed tears. They pull me into their depths like a siren's song, and I lean down to kiss each lid.

"Don't apologize. You didn't know it would snow. Be grateful Jordan had the good sense not to come up here herself."

"But you risked your life, and now you're stuck up here with me. I know that's not how..."

I don't let her finish. My mouth lands on hers. I have no idea how to say what I'm feeling, how I felt when she went missing, or how I've been feeling the past few weeks. Instead, I kiss her to quiet those insecurities, but when she opens her mouth to me, her tongue flitting along the tip of mine, I pour all of my emotions into that kiss. God, she tastes divine, just like how I remembered her from our short kiss in the emergency room. There's healing ambrosia and redemption on her lips. I feel renewed, whole again, for the first time in years.

"I'd have searched for you everywhere," I say between heavy breaths as I trail kisses along her jaw line to her ear. When I take the bit of flesh between my teeth, she releases a heavy sigh. I run my tongue down her neck, and she whimpers making my erection press painfully against the zipper of my jeans. Fuck, this pixie is going to make me lose myself like a teenager. I nip the skin right where her neck and shoulder meet. She digs her nails into my arms before running her hands up and into my hair. I've never been so glad to be overdue a haircut with the way she's grasping it. I let my hands roam down her sides as I bring my mouth back to hers. Her breathing is erratic, and her eyes are closed. When I slide my hands up under her shirt, her body stiffens.

Pulling my hands away and releasing her mouth completely, I look down into her face. Her eyes are wide open, confusion and pain, no, fear, no...I can't quite read her. "What's wrong, Pixie Girl?" Her chin quivers, and she grasps my shirt like she's trying to hold herself in the present. "Hey, talk to me." I grab her hand lightly and give a slight tug toward the armchairs. I don't dare head toward the bed. When I sit on the chair, I gesture for her to sit on the ottoman in front of me. Thankfully, she takes a seat facing me, her knees between mine. I'm careful to keep my legs wide and my hands pressed on my thighs. Something spooked her, and I don't want to cause any more pain.

"I'm so..."

I shake my head. "You never have to apologize to me, Pix. If I did something wrong, I'd rather you tell me than to see that look of fear on your face. I don't want you to ever fear me. If you don't want me to touch you, I won't. I also won't lie and say that I don't want to. I've wanted to damn near since we met and you told me off." I chuckle at the memory, and she cracks a sheepish smile. "If I was wrong in thinking you felt similarly, I'm sorry." I want to reach out and grab her hand to show my sincerity, but I don't.

She pulls her lip between her teeth, and I struggle to keep my gaze on her eyes and not down at those soft lips. My cock is still screaming for release, the fucker. I try hard not to let my internal conflict show.

"I do," she finally says. When she doesn't continue, I give her a small smile of encouragement. "I do have similar feelings. I'd been telling myself it was just a silly crush on an older man with total daddy vibes..."

I can't help but laugh out loud, catching her off guard. Her head cocks to the side in confusion, and I laugh harder, holding up a finger until I can catch my breath.

"Did you say that to Jordan?" I finally ask, a huge smile on my face.

The blush that creeps into her cheeks at my question speaks before she can even open her mouth. She looks down demurely, and I chuckle again, putting my index finger under her chin to lift her face to mine. My lips purse to the side, waiting for an answer. It's a challenge, and I can tell by the way she squares her shoulders that she recognizes it as such. That's my pixie. I so like her with a little fire in her eyes.

"I may have said something like that to her a time or two, why?"

I consider letting her figure it out on her own, but I'm so happy to see the life and energy in her eyes that I want to keep the conversation going. "I called her back to find out where you were the last time she spoke with you, and she asked if I fit that description. Talk about being caught off guard," I say with a raised brow.

She blushes again and shrugs. "Oopsi." We both chuckle.

"Now, finish what you were saying. Tell me what happened a few moments ago. Help me know what not to do."

She swallows before taking a deep breath and letting it out. "You didn't do anything wrong. I was saying that I thought I was just having a one-sided crush until you kissed me in front of Phillip. Stupid me thought his name at the same time your hands touched my sides, and I froze..."

"You were picturing what he had done," I say, finishing her sentence. She nodded.

"There's not much he hadn't done. I don't want to live my life afraid of being touched when I want it." Tears, once again, well in her eyes.

Anger churns inside me, the look on Taylor's face, though, tells me that my anger won't be appreciated right now. I don't know what all Phillip did to her, but she doesn't need a reminder of him. She needs tender acceptance. She needs to be in control.

"Did he ever let you be in charge?"

"Hell no. He'd threaten, coerce, manipulate. I don't know how much you heard him say there in the hospital, but when he said I came willingly, it was only when he'd threaten to get one of my sisters."

My fists clench. I should've killed that motherfucker. I should've pulled his fucking head off. I picture his bloody body on the floor with his head on top of the bedside table. Taylor's hands on my cheeks bring me back to the present.

"Hey, where'd you go just now?" she asks.

I shake my head. "You don't want to know."

"I'm...I...You're probably right. How about some dinner?"

I know that's her way of trying to lighten the mood, change the subject, and somehow deflect from what was happening between us. Thankfully, I actually am hungry, and not just for her.

$\mathcal{T}$aylor

I breathe a sigh of relief when he moves his leg and lets me up to fix us something for dinner. I've never been more grateful to have gone shopping before in my life. I need a moment to breathe. I want to climb this man every which way but Sunday, but I'm afraid of freezing up again the next time he touches me. The frustration has tears burning my eyes and an ache between my legs that I just can't relieve. Fuck!

"Whoa there, Pixie Girl." Garrett says from behind me, his smooth voice like a melody that sings straight to my core. He grabs the skillet from my hand before I can slam it down on the stove. "What did these pans do to you?"

"What do you mean?" I ask, feigning confusion to hide my embarrassment. I didn't realize how much I'd been banging everything around. He reaches his arms around my sides, not touching but hemming me in, and heat pools in my center. Damn, this man makes even the simplest tasks hot.

"How can I help?" he asks, his arms still extended on either side of my torso.

I'm overwhelmed by his presence, his scent, his heat. My entire body is on fire, and the inside of this cabin is far too warm for all these clothes. I have never been so aware of a man, never so attracted to one before. Anger at Phillip boils up. He's the reason I can't just act on my desires. He's the reason I'm broken. My fists clench, and I squeeze my eyes shut to fight back the tears of anger and frustration.

"Hey, where did you go just now?" His breath is on my ear, and my head lolls back against his chest involuntarily. He runs his nose down my neck, barely touching my skin, and I shudder.

"You don't want to know," I say on a breathy whisper. He chuckles, and I smile.

"Do you have any idea what that smart mouth does to me, my little pixie?"

I don't know, but I want to. Damn, how I want to know. He still hasn't touched me, not really, not with anything more than his breath, and I'm damn near panting with need.

"Cowpoke," I say with as much faux exasperation as I can muster, "you are making it hard to cook."

He immediately steps back, and my breaths come a little easier, but my body is still on fire. I can feel him watching me from where he's leaned against the cabinets behind me. This tiny kitchen doesn't leave much room when a tall-ass cowboy and my big ass are both in here at the same time. I don't dare look at him. Instead, I poke my head into the fridge rummaging for something to add to these simple grilled cheese sandwiches I'm about to make. I find the container of pulled pork I'd picked up back in Slate Ridge and quickly heat it in the microwave. Thank goodness, Jacob and Morgan did such a thorough job on the remodel. This place has damn near everything we need for a snowed-in weekend. That thought gives me pause. Oh shit, I'm snowed in with Garrett Daniels. Like, legitimately stuck up here. One bed, one shower, no doors, except for the bathroom. Shit, I'm in trouble.

"Don't start throwing things around again, Pixie, else we'll starve before we can get off this mountain." The mirth in his voice has me cutting my eyes toward him, and he winks at me. Fucking winks!

"Keep distracting me, and I'll burn your sandwich."

He laughs aloud. "You're not that mean, or that naughty."

"I can be both," I say before I can stop myself. Fuck, this man does things to me. I turn fully away from him again.

I barely get the sandwiches flipped when he's once again at my ear. "You let me know whenever you want punished for being naughty." When he walks away, I catch the twitch he does, as he readjusts himself in his pants. Thank goodness I'm not the only one affected by this closeness, this banter, this desire that has my panties drenched.

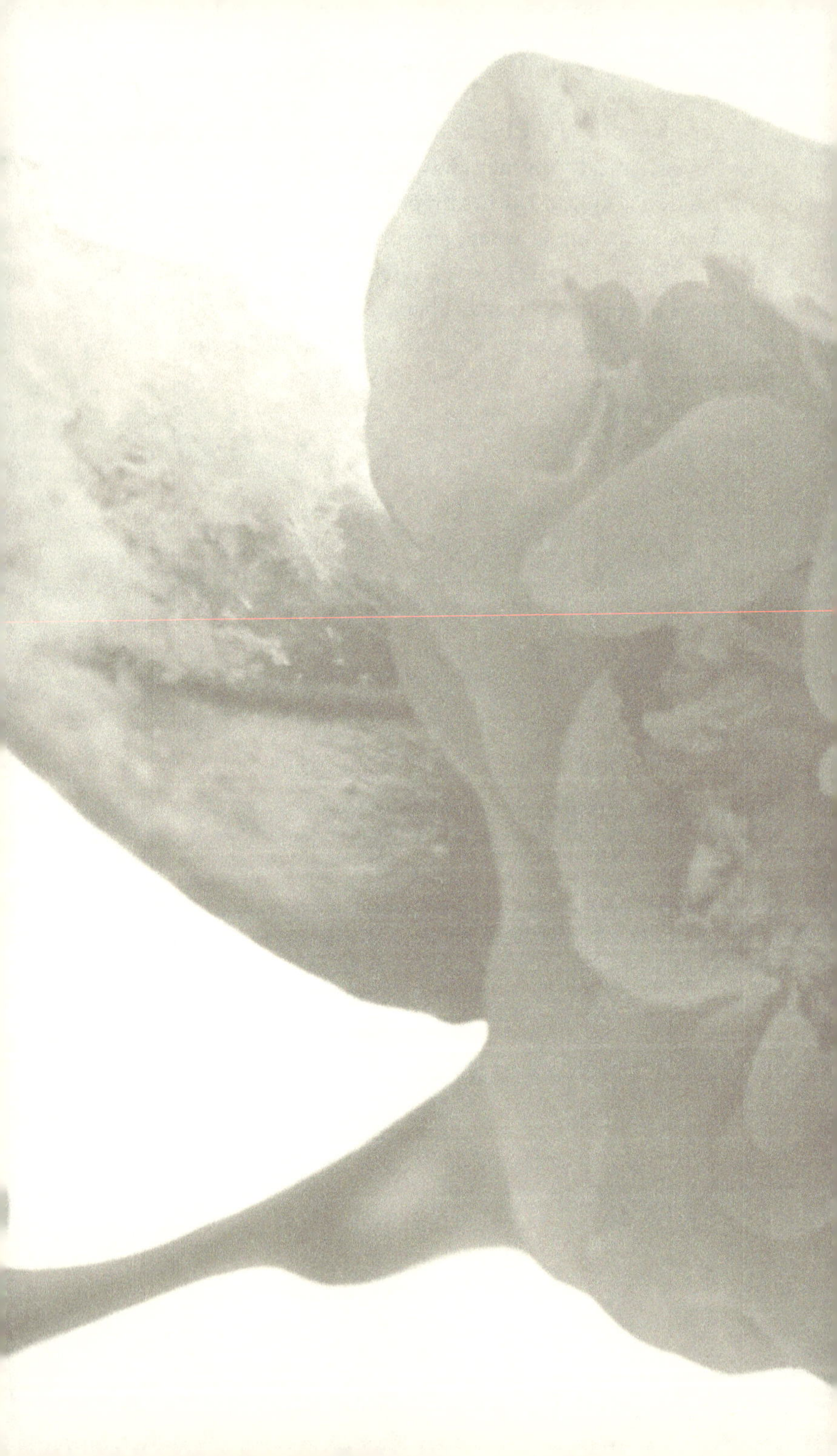

IF THAT'S WHAT YOU NEED

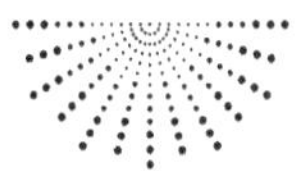

Taylor

We eat dinner in relative silence, neither of us taking the first step into whatever comes next. Hell, I've masturbated to thoughts of this man so many times over the past months that I know I'm going to hell for sinning. If not for fear of embarrassing myself by freezing up on him again, I'd reach over and run my hand up his leg. My fingers itch to feel the tight muscles of his thighs, his abdomen, his chest. If I wasn't afraid of crying in the middle of a moan, I'd unbutton his jeans and slide them off his hips to take him in my mouth.

I've read enough romance novels and seen enough porn shorts to know that men respond differently, and I'm dying to hear Garrett's response. Will his moans be deep or higher pitched? Will he growl? Will he say my name? I'm lost in my fantasies when Garrett does say my name.

"If you stare at me any harder, Pix, I might spontaneously combust." His voice is hoarse, and when I look up at him, his pupils dilate. I open my mouth to say something, but no words come out. His gaze drops to my lips, and I pull one between my teeth, wishing he was the one biting on it. "Woman, you're making it very hard not to kiss you again. I'm trying to be a gentleman."

I smirk and stand to walk around him, grabbing our plates to take them to the kitchen. When I get to his other side, he puts his arm around my waist and pulls me into him. He takes the plates from my hand and puts them back on the island. "They'll hold," he says, his voice gruffer than I've heard before. I put my hands on his chest and run my fingers over the ridges of his pec. I can feel the toned muscle through his shirt. His body is tight, and I remember the first time Morgan told me he was Jacob's father. I couldn't believe it, and I still find it hard to believe this man is nearly twice my age. He's absolute perfection wrapped in a gruff attitude and a heart of gold. And, he wants me.

"Pix..." I stand on tiptoe, bite my lip, and then touch my lips to his. He lets out a groan, and I close my eyes, savoring that response. I want to hear him moan my name. I want to control all of his responses.

I step away from him, and he reaches for me. I shake my finger in front of him. "Earlier, you asked if I'd ever been given the chance to be in charge..." His eyes close for a second, and I hold my breath. Was he regretting putting the thought in my head? Before my anxiety can take hold, he opens his eyes, and there's nothing but heat in them. I want to melt for him. "Would you let me?" The question comes out quieter than I wanted, less assertive and more unsure. Shit, how can I take charge of this situation if I can't even ask him to let me. His response is an immediate 'yes,' and I lock my eyes on his. He nods. I don't want either one of us to change our minds, so I grab his hand and pull him back to the chairs, pushing him back onto one.

Watching him closely, I sit back on the ottoman where I was during our conversation earlier. "I want," I begin, and he raises an eyebrow waiting for me to continue. "I want to see you."

He smirks. "How much of me?"

I bite my lip. "All of you," I say on a whisper.

"Tell me what to do, Pixie."

My heart is beating out of my chest when I say, "Take off your shirt." I asked to be in charge, but I'm not sure how to actually take charge. I'm certainly not innocent, but this desire I have is far beyond anything I've felt before. I want this man, and I want him to want me. I don't want to fuck this up. Then he pulls his shirt over his head, and all coherent thought leaves my mind. When he lifts his hips and slides his jeans down his legs, my mouth goes dry. He's all lean muscle, hard everywhere I'm soft.

I think back to my first impression of his ass in Morgan's kitchen and the number of times I wished he wasn't so damn attractive. I never wanted to want him, or any man, for that matter, especially not one old enough to be my dad. I was certain Phillip had killed any chance for that, but here Garrett is making me squeeze my legs together to alleviate the tingling between them.

His eyes bore into mine, desire clearly written on his face, but also control. I'm supposed to be the one taking charge, but this man is in complete control of himself, and I'm over here struggling to breathe. The only thing I can think is that I'm so glad to still be fully dressed, and that I'd worn pants rather than a dress. They're leggings, but still, they cover all the bits of me that want to be touched by him. I need to get the upper hand in this seduction, or it's all going to fall to shit.

Before he can tuck his thumbs into the waistband of his briefs, I reach out my cool fingers and run them along his clavicle. He hitches a slight breath but still maintains that air of patience, like he's waiting for the moment to pounce. That's not what I want. I want him begging for me. I want him just as wound up as I am. I want to decide when he gets to touch me, if I let him touch me. Fuck, I want him to touch me.

I run my fingers down his chest, feeling the ripple of his muscles with each inch. When I rub around his nipples, they tighten, and he licks his bottom lip. Good. I continue to trail my nails down to his abs, and they tighten under my touch. As impossible as it seems, his eyes dilate more until they're nothing but black holes pulling me into their depths. His hands grab my knees and slowly slide up my thighs. The heat from his hands permeates the thin fabric, scorching my skin. I stifle a moan and grab his hands to place them on the arm rests of his chair.

"Keep them there, Cowpoke. Don't move them until I say you can." That one brow draws up in defiant challenge, and I raise both of mine in a silent dare. When he nods in acquiescence, I stand from the ottoman and straddle his legs.

The room is beginning to cool, but rather than ruining the momentum by stoking the fire with an added log, I choose to feel his heat against my body. With my hands on his chest, I push him to lean against the back of the chair and settle myself on his lap completely. His head drops back and my core pulses with the knowledge of his arousal. He's so hard under me that I'm once again happy I'm wearing pants. I lean forward and kiss his neck, running my tongue up to his chin where I nip through his low-cut beard. His skin is as delicious as his lips. A low moan, nearly a growl, comes from his throat as I run my hands up into his hair and curl my fingers tightly around the soft waves. My hips rock back and forth at his response, and he bites his lip.

Releasing his hair, I put my hands on either side of his face, pulling it down until he's looking at me. His eyelids are low, and his unsteady breathing gives away the fact that he is steadily losing the control he's been fighting so desperately to hold.

"Look at me. Don't take your eyes off of my face. I want to know you're here with me."

"Oh, Pixie Girl, I am one hundred percent here with you."

I kiss his soft lips, sucking each one into my mouth and nipping at it with my teeth. My heart is banging in my chest, and the pulsations in my vagina are matching the beat. Though I initially started rocking my hips to break him, rubbing against his erection is doing things to my body I've only dreamt of feeling with someone. I try to distract myself by kissing him, by nibbling at his skin, by observing his response to my actions, but I'm losing all sense of where I want this to go. It's like my core knows what it wants and is straining to reach it.

Our eyes lock, and his nostrils flare. "Pixie." The word is a wish.

"Tell me, cowpoke. Tell me what you're feeling right now."

"I feel you rubbing against my cock, making me crazy with that steady rocking. It feels so fucking good, but I'm not sure how much more I can take. It's been a long time, and your wetness seeping onto my skin is going to make me finish before you let me get started."

He lifts his hands from where they've been gripping the arm rests at my shocked expression. I wanted him to lose control, but I didn't actually think it would be this easy. Suddenly, I want more from him. I stop moving and look down at his hands before raising my brow at him. His hands once again grip the chair. I smile and reward him with a searing kiss that leaves both of us panting.

Without a word, I stand, and he groans in protest. "If I could give you one small gift right now, what would you like?" I nearly slap my hands over my mouth once the words are out. Where did that come from? My chest tightens at the devious look on his face, and the anticipation of his answer has me holding my breath.

"Let me taste you."

My eyes go wide. I wasn't expecting that answer. I thought he'd want me to take off some article of clothing. Shit! How can I fulfill my implicit promise without giving myself over to him. He watches me expectantly, a smirk on his lips the longer I stand there unmoving.

Slowly, seductively, at least I hope it's seductive, I smile at him and run my hands over my breasts, my eyes nearly crossing when I lightly pinch my nipples through the cloth of my shirt and bra. I let out a deep breath, and he licks his lips. I slide my left hand into the waistband of my leggings. He can't see, but I have no panties on. He isn't wrong about feeling my wetness, though. The crotch of my pants is soaked, and when I run my fingers along my slit to press onto my clit, I can't help but let out a moan. His expression is feral, and his grip on the chair is lethal. I have no doubt he wishes it was his hands on me right now. I swirl my fingers around a few times, my eyes never leaving his. He tries hard to maintain eye contact, but every move of my hand catches his attention. it's like he's at a tennis match, except his eyes go up and down rather than side to side.

The stimulation of my fingers and the hunger in his eyes is almost too much. My breathing is shaky, and my knees threaten to buckle. His mouth is wide open. I slide my hand from my pants and hold my fingers out in front of his mouth. He leans his head forward and takes in a long, deep breath through his nose before sticking out his tongue and locking his lips around my fingers. The sound he lets go from his throat is nearly my undoing.

"Taylor, fuck," he grounds out, elongating the last syllable like it's his last breath as he licks my fingers clean. "Let me put my mouth on you. No hands needed. Let me give you what you're obviously denying yourself. Please. Let me swallow your orgasm. Shit, sit on my face, if that's what you need to do to feel in control."

Oh my god. His words, and the desperation in his voice, has me dripping. I have never been so wet, so close to coming without steadily rubbing my clit for a long time. He's going to make me come without touching me. And why am I denying myself. What is my goal here? I know that a big part is wanting to make sure everything that happens to me is because I want it to. There's no fucking denying I want him. Shit, I want him to do everything he just said because it sounds so damn hot. But I want more. I want to know for sure that he won't force himself on me as soon as I'm vulnerable. Fully clothed, I have a chance to say no. Naked, I have nothing to fight with. Though he's not responsible for the broken pieces Phillip caused, for some reason, I want Garrett to be the glue that holds me together. I want him to deny himself until I'm good.

"Not yet," I say with a shake of my head to emphasize my

resolve that is tenuous at best. I drop to my knees in front of him. "Keep your eyes on me."

I lean forward, and his intake of breath is audible. With a smirk he can't see, I swirl my tongue around his belly button. His stomach muscles ripple. Reaching up, I graze my nails down his torso until my fingertips slip inside the waistband of his briefs. "I think it's time these come off," I say, pulling them down and trying not to gape at the size of his cock. I knew he wasn't small from the way his erection felt as I rubbed myself along it through our clothes, but seeing it is a totally different thing. He's, well, he's definitely not small. Nope, not small. Nope, not gaping. Nope, not at all. Shit!

"Do you approve?"

The question is so ridiculous, I have to keep myself from laughing at my own naive embarrassment. Instead, I put on the calmest look I can muster and then scrunch my nose up at him, making him chuckle.

"Remember what I said. Keep your eyes on me."

I don't give him time to control the laughter. Instead, I watch the sudden change in his expression when I slide my hand up the length of him from base to tip. When I wrap my hand around the head, and squeeze tightly just under the tip, his lips tighten. I'm pleasantly surprised when he manages to keep his eyes open and locked on mine. Slowly, I lick my lips, wetting them before running the tip of my tongue along the same path my hands took. A long drawn out "fuuuuuuuuck" escapes his lips, but his eyes remain steadfast. I smile internally and lick around the head of his cock before sliding the large bulb into my mouth, closing as tightly as I can around the tip, just like I had squeezed with my fingers. Keeping my eyes locked with his, I swirl my tongue around the tip, lapping up the precum.

"Pixie, I...shit."

I flutter my lashes at him and slowly work his length into my mouth. I'm not sure I'll be able to accommodate the entire thing, but I'm willing to try. The crazed look on his face, and the ecstasy in his voice drives me to make him say my name again, my real name. Though I've gotten used to his nickname for me, I want him to want Taylor, the woman. The woman who is beyond the point of needing him. I love the feel of his thickness in my mouth, and when he touches the back of my throat, I moan. His moan, as I relax my throat and take the head even further has me dripping down my thighs and through my pants. When I pull him out of my mouth with a pop, he is slack-jawed.

"Don't come until I say you can."

"I don't know if I can hold it. I told you..."

"You have one job, old man. Hold back for me."

It takes all my strength to hold back the tears and keep my lip from quivering at the vulnerability in that request. I need this from him. I need him not to let me down. I lost my faith a long time ago, but I send up a silent prayer.

"If that's what you need..."

I don't wait for him to finish the sentence. I know in my heart he's agreed. I grip the base of his cock tightly and swallow his cock in one swift motion. I allow myself a few moments of unfettered ferocity, impaling my throat with his cock before pulling it up to lick and suck on his balls. He's whimpering, and the sound turns me on so bad. I let him go and stand up to remove my pants. Without giving him a chance to think, move, or react, I climb up onto the chair and do exactly what he'd asked of me before. I put my pussy in his face and grind against his mouth. After just a few seconds, he opens his lips, and his tongue slides between my lips to find my swollen clit. I gasp at the sensation. He circles the bud, and every nerve-ending in my body responds. My hair stands on end. My fingers clench. My thighs tighten on the sides of his head. My core tightens at the feel of his moan, and when he pulls my clit into his mouth and sucks on it, I scream out his name over and over with each wave. There may have been a few expletives thrown in there, but I lost track of everything that wasn't my orgasm. My entire body shudders at each spasm, and he does exactly as promised. He sucks up every drop.

My weight collapses on him as my knees give out, and I lean my head on the back of the chair. I'm likely breaking his neck or suffocating his ass, but I can't function enough to try and shift my weight. At some point, his hands came up around my ass, and he picks me up. He actually picks my ass up, my legs still wrapped around his neck, and lays me on the bed. My body is putty in his hands. When my breathing calms, I whisper a quick "Thank you" and let my eyes close. He climbs up next to me and wraps his arms around my body, pulling me close. His cock is still hard as a rock against my hip, but he doesn't complain, doesn't say a word, just holds me. A tear slips from my eye, and I hope he doesn't see it.

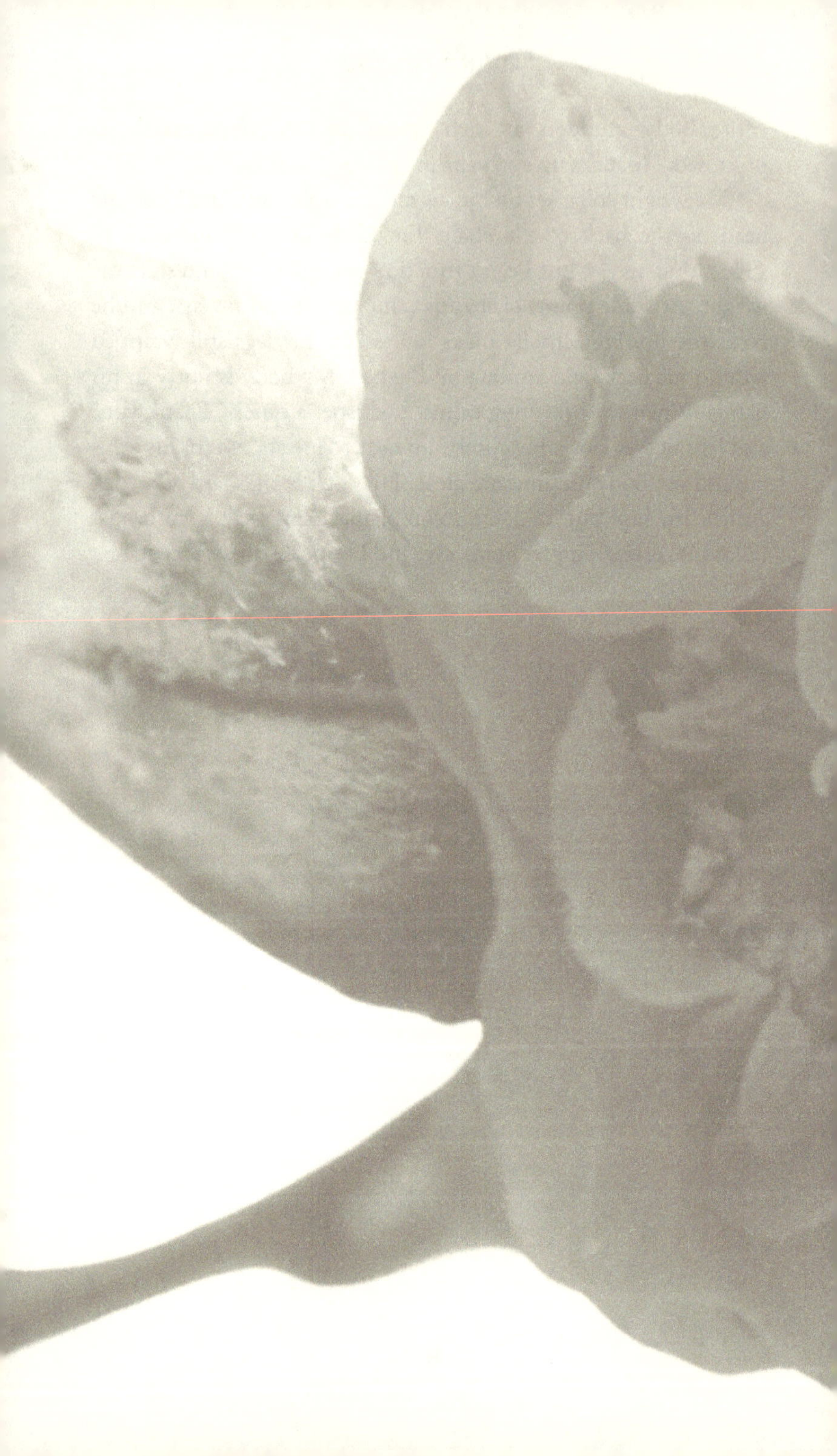

WAKE-UP CALL

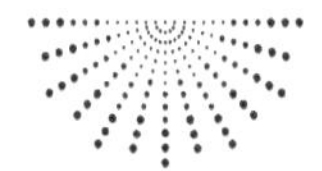

Garrett

I don't know how long I hold her against me. The smell of her arousal, of her orgasm, lingers, and I can still taste her on my lips. It's nearly impossible to not take care of my own aching need, but she needs me to give without taking. I can do that. Hell, I've been alone for so many years now, what's a few more hours, days, weeks going to hurt. Whatever it takes. I want this luscious and feisty pixie for more than relieving the raging hard-on she's created. Truth be told, I have one nearly every time she's near. Over the past months, she's grown to be an important figure in my life. I look for her every time I walk into the store, and I listen for her laughter each time I help out at the house. I'd be lying if I said I don't visit both places more often than necessary just to be near her. She is a light, and I need her like breathing. My final thought before I, too, drift off to sleep is about how she'll handle tonight's activities in the light of day.

My dreams are anything but holy. Her naked body is pressed against mine. Her hands trail along my shoulders, her nails bite into my skin as she drags them down my back. Her lips trail kisses down my neck to my chest, and she laps at my nipples, the tiny nubs standing taut at her ministrations. She milks moans from my throat by grazing her teeth over my nipples and sucking them into her mouth. Her fucking hot mouth that continues its trail down my stomach. Her tongue rims my belly button, and I hold my breath in anticipation of her going lower. It's been so damn long, and my fantasies about her have become almost more than I can take. Every night, I take my cock into my own hands with visions of her face and her laughter swimming through my head. And then I dream about her, like I am now, and I have to stroke myself to sleep just to get some peace.

This, however, is not peaceful. This is torture. I feel her in my dream, knowing I can't touch her. I can't run my fingers through her hair and pull it tight, leading her mouth to where it's needed. The most exquisite torture is when she finally kisses the head of my cock, her warm lips caressing it like she's done the rest of my body. She takes her sweet time. Then she licks the head, swirling her tongue around it like an ice cream cone before blowing cool air across the tip. My body shudders, and I'm jolted awake.

My cock is enveloped in the sweetest heat. Taylor's mouth is on me, working up and down my shaft until she has it wet enough to press to the back of her throat, and I let out a full moan. Her name a gasp. "Fuck, baby, yes, like that." I lift my hand, ready to set it on the top of her head, and I catch myself, using my fingers to swipe hair from her face. She looks up at me, her eyes ablaze with lust. I don't know what I expected to happen when she awoke, but this was not it, and I am not at all complaining. Fuck, her mouth feels so damn good. She works my shaft up and down with her hand, sucking hard on the bulb until I'm panting. "Taylor, shit, baby, don't stop!" I can't control the words dripping from my tongue as she takes all conscious thought from my brain.

Just as I get close to coming, my breathing erratic, and my heartbeat pounding in my ears, she stops. Her eyes are bright, and her smile is so wide, I can see damn near all her teeth. "You're having fun edging me, aren't you?" Her lids close slightly, and she looks down. "Don't play coy with me, my naughty little pixie." Her grin returns.

"I woke up to a gift," she says. "He was standing at attention, calling my name. I couldn't just leave him there without saying hello, could I?"

"Of course not," I say with a chuckle that is more of a groan. I wrap my hand around my shaft and give it a couple of long strokes. "And I can assure you that he is more than happy you came to say hi."

She angles her body, so she is watching me pull on my cock, stretching it to its full length. She looks like a queen, propped up against a bunch of pillows, completely naked with one leg bent up and the other straight out toward me. She's not told me what I can and can't do this morning, so I lean forward and kiss her foot. I swirl my tongue around her big toe and then suck it into my mouth, all the while staring into her eyes. She bites her lip, and her hand slides across her breasts. Her nipples are puckered, and my mouth waters with the desire to suck on them. I stroke my cock a little faster, and she trails that hand down to her pussy, opening herself up for me to see. Last night, I couldn't see anything, and I didn't need to. I could feel and taste my way to her swollen bud. The vision before me, though, is absolute perfection. Her plump lips spread wide by fingers tipped with wine-colored nails. The nub she rubs tight circles around sings to me while the smell of her arousal makes me wild with need.

I kiss her foot again and then shift my body, so my shoulders are lined up between her legs. I kiss one perfect leg and then the other, moving my way closer to her pussy with alternating kisses. She pulls her lip back between her teeth, and when I nip at the tender skin of her inner thighs, she lets out a small yip that makes me smile. Neither of us has spoken, and the only thing I want breaking the silence is her moans. Ironically, the moment I taste her on the tip of my tongue, it's me who lets out a moan. Then I dive in, devouring her until she is panting my name. Before she can come, I trail kisses up her stomach. She is soft in all the best ways, and I worship her softness before I get to her breasts and give them their due. She grips my arms and digs her nails into my flesh, but I don't mind. I plan to make her do much more before this night is through.

Continuing my way up her body, I stop directly in front of her face. I lean close enough to kiss her but don't. Her head tilts to the side in question, and I smirk. "Tell me what you want, Pixie Girl." I expect something along the lines of "Kiss me" or "Go back and finish what you started," but she doesn't say anything. Her pupils are fully dilated, just blown, and I have no doubt she'll gladly follow any direction I give. No matter how much I want to bury myself in her, though, I want it to be her call. She surprises me.

Without warning, she pushes me backwards and straddles my lap. She leans over me and locks her lips with mine, pushing her tongue between my lips. I moan in satisfaction. Hell yes! This is exactly what I want from her. I silently encourage her with a lift of my brow. She leans over further and dangles one of her heavy breasts in front of my mouth. I gladly wrap my lips around the nipple and tug at it with my teeth. Her hips glide back and forth against my cock, and the feeling is even more glorious than it was before because there is no barrier between our skin. Her slickness coats my cock, and all it will take is a slight shift in angle for her to slide onto me. When she grabs my hands and places them on her hips, I know she's thinking the same thing. Gripping tightly, I lift her up and she grabs my shaft to line it up with her entrance. I want to slam her down onto me completely, but I don't. I give her time to adjust to my size, holding her up until she lowers herself onto me. I was wrong earlier. This is the sweetest torture.

"You're so damn perfect," I say. "You fit like you were made for me. So tight and wet."

She smiles down at me and then starts moving, muscles tightening in succession. Her walls move up and down my cock like a snake, and I'm lost to the feel of her. Fuck, I don't remember ever being this perfectly molded to someone. I'd been with Rosie for so long that we were basically going through the motions near the end before she got sick, but we were never so in sync like this feels. I lift my hips, and she slides down. I rock my hips down into the bed, and she lifts off until just the tip remains inside of her. It's pure ecstasy. When she moans, my balls tighten. Her pleasure is an aphrodisiac driving me on. The small whimpers she makes have me gripping her hips and holding her still so I can pump up into her fast and hard until she's calling my name.

"Oh my god." Her screams are the sweetest music. "Garrett, don't stop! Shit."

"Come for me, Pixie. Come all over my cock." My words come out hoarse and guttural. I want to feel her pulsating around me. I want to know that I'm the one who's made sex pleasurable for her no matter how negative her early experiences were.

"Garrett. Fuck! That's...Shit! That feels...Oh my god!"

Her body goes rigid, and her walls clench around me. "That's it, beautiful. You feel so good when you come. You squeeze me just right, like you want to take me with you." Her moans quiet and her breaths even out some as her torso falls forward. I don't stop rocking my hips up into her, but I slow the rhythm to let her catch her breath. Eventually, she opens her eyes and looks into mine. "You take me so well. You have all the control here, and you're doing so well with it."

"That was," she pauses, her eyes drifting closed, and a moan comes up from her throat. I let her breath, but I'm not letting her off the hook.

"That was what?" I slide my hands up her sides until I can reach my thumbs to her nipples, and I rub the tips until they're puckered hard. She lifts herself up some, still not speaking, and I let my tongue glide over one of her breasts before I latch on, sucking the nipple between my teeth. She hisses, and then leans her head back, her hands buried in my hair.

"That was the best thing I've ever felt!"

"Really?" I ask with a raised brow. She nods and then lowers her face away from my gaze. "Give me permission, Pix."

"Permission for what," she asks, her breaths getting ragged again from our slow fucking.

"To make the next orgasm even better."

"Better?" Her voice pitches higher with her moans coming more frequently.

I nod and keep my eyes locked on hers. I have no doubt she'll gladly let me do whatever I want right now, but I want this to be her choice.

When she gives me a slight nod, I shake my head. "Use your words, and tell me." She scrunches up her nose and glares at me, but I never stop fucking in and out of her. "Tell me, Taylor. What do you want? Do you want me to make you come even harder?"

Her breath hitches, and she nods her head, eyes wide. "Yes."

"Then tell me to make you come. I need to hear you say you want it."

"Dammit!" Hearing her cuss, like she does when she's mad at me, makes me chuckle, and her glare is even harder.

I reach between us and find her clit with my thumb, rubbing the nub in time to my thrusts. It is so swollen that she is nearly writhing within seconds. She makes the cutest mewling sounds. "Tell me," I whisper in her ear when she's lost the power to hold herself up again.

"Don't stop," she says against my chest.

"Those are not the words I asked for." I take my hand away, and she groans. I shake my head. "My stubborn little pixie. Always so defiant." She lifts her head and grabs my hand, pulling my thumb into her mouth. She licks the tip and then sucks on my thumb while staring into my eyes with a sly grin. My stomach tightens, but I will not be swayed. I slow my thrusts to an almost stop. Her bottom lip sticks out in a pout. "Just say the words."

"If you shatter me, who will put me back together?" Her question comes out so quietly, I nearly miss it.

I stop moving completely and lift her face to look at me. "Hey. I don't want you broken, Taylor. I have no intention of breaking you."

She sits up but leaves us connected. "I thought I was broken before. I imagined you putting me back together." She shakes her head and gives me a shy smile. "I was wrong. I wasn't broken, but I want you so bad, more than I've ever wanted anything, and this," she says, gesturing back and forth between us, "this is more than I could've believed possible."

"Hey," I say, cupping her cheek. "This is a lot for me too. You're the first woman I've wanted since my wife passed. You make me feel whole. You don't treat me like a pariah, or worse, like I'm going to fall apart at every turn." I grab both of her hands and kiss them, keenly aware that she's still squeezing my cock tightly inside her. "I want to make you happy and not just for a few moments."

Smiling, she rocks her hips, causing my cock to stand fully erect again where it had begun to wane with the seriousness of our conversation. "You are smooth-tongued, Cowpoke."

"If I remember right, you liked my smooth tongue," I say with a wink. I know she's trying to distract from the uncertain emotions happening, and I won't force it. I'm a patient man.

She narrows her eyes, and then they crinkle with laughter. She leans down and nips at my lip. I wrap my arms around her and hold her mouth to mine, snaking my tongue inside to meet hers. We both moan, and the rhythm of our bodies synch again.

"Garrett." She looks into my eyes, and I don't dare look away. "Make me come so hard I forget everything but you."

"Fuck," I growl out and flip her around until she's under my weight, her leg hitched up over my hip. My strokes lengthen until her nails dig into my back. "Not yet, baby." I pull out of her, and she looks up at me with a questioning pout.

"I want you on your knees in front of me." As soon as she flips over, I grab her legs and pull her to the edge. Dropping to my knees, I run my tongue up her slit licking every drop of her arousal until I bury my tongue in her tight hole. "You taste so fucking good," I ground out, and she moans. Standing, I grasp her hips, pulling them high. "Put your chest on the bed, Pix. You're gonna like this." I line up with her and push forward until I'm fully sheathed inside of her. "Mmmm" My strokes lengthen and speed up until I'm pounding into her. Her gasps become moans and then turn to screams. She tightens on my cock, but I don't let up.

"Oh fuck, oh shit. Yes. Yes. Yes." Every word from her lips is single syllable and then she goes silent, body limp. I don't stop. She's going to come back to me still coming. This old man's got a couple tricks up his sleeve, and I plan to spend the rest of the weekend showing her many of them.

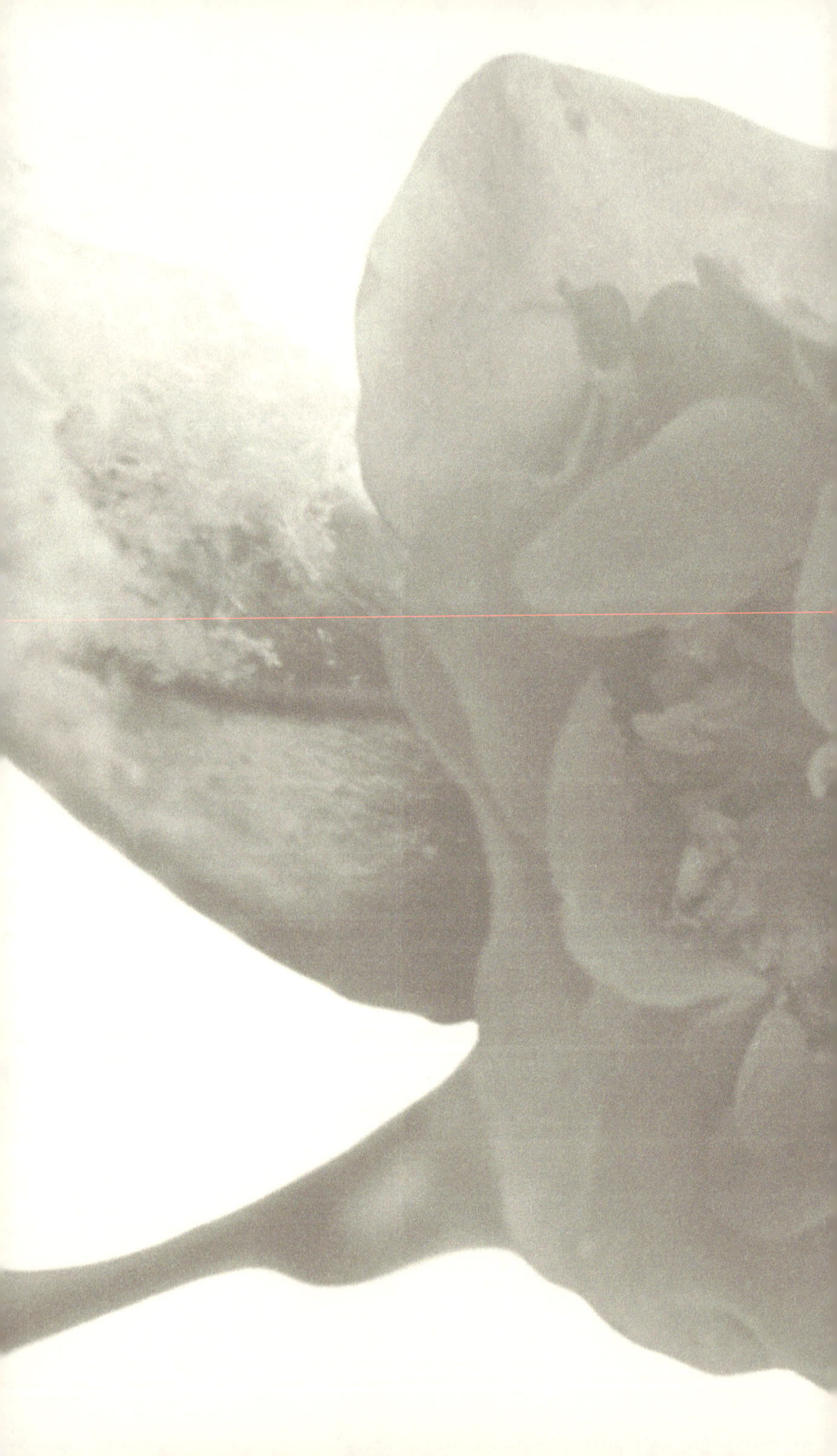

SHARING SECRETS

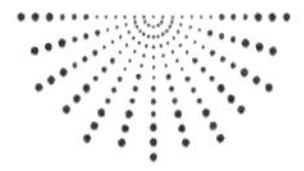

Garrett

"We're good," I say through the satellite phone.

Jacob's voice on the other end is frantic. *Pa, we've been losing our shit.* I'm sure they have, Morgan especially. A pit settles in my stomach. I should have called as soon as I got here. That should have been my first thought, but it wasn't. From the moment I found her car out in that ditch, all I could think about was getting my hands on Taylor to make sure she was safe. Nothing else mattered. This morning, though, with Jacob's reprimanding tone and Morgan's worry, guilt gnaws at my insides.

"Yeah, sorry. I found her car in a ditch and freaked. Once I got here to the cabin to find her safe, exhaustion set in. We had dinner and slept." Shit, why did I mention sleeping. My eyes flit around the cabin. Jacob knows there's only one damn bed in here. As the silence gets heavier, Taylor comes out of the bathroom.

"Is everything ok?" she asks. I give her a smile that I know isn't as convincing as I'd like. When I'd told her about the satellite phone this morning, she'd responded with a groan, like she'd have loved to have known it existed yesterday. While I initially wished she had known, I can't regret any parts of last night, not past her initial fear of being stranded and worry for Jordan. I also can't say I wouldn't have still driven out here to see for myself that she was all right. One look at her beautiful face, and I know I would have.

Is that Taylor? Morgan's voice comes through the phone. Jacob must have her on speaker. I hand Taylor the phone and step into the kitchen to let her handle the questions however she'd like. If she doesn't want to tell them about us, I'll respect that because I'm not even sure there is an us. Fuck if I don't want there to be an us. Thankfully, the fridge is full, and I can focus on something else. There's eggs, bacon, bread for toast, and Orange Juice. I rummage through the cabinets, opening and closing each one. "Shit!" I say much louder than intended.

From behind me, Taylor says, "I think the old cowpoke just realized there no coffee." I take in a deep breath and let it out before turning my most menacing scowl on her. Anyone else would've cowered at the look, my children included, but not Taylor. When I look over my shoulder at her, she just gives me a smug smile and shrugs.

I start to move in her direction, but her next question stops me. "Any idea when the snow's supposed to stop and the roads clear?" Her tone is much more hopeful than mine would have been, and my heart sinks. Is she in a rush to get away from me? Turning my face away before she can see how much it stings, I put my hands on the counter. "Damn, really?" My hands grip around the sink. "Ok, we'll let you know when we're coming down from the mountain. I still had a signal back at Slate Ridge, so I'll text when I get there." Taylor's hand touches the middle of my back, and I hang my head. "Sounds good," she says before disconnecting the phone.

Her arms wrap around my waist, and she lays her head against my back. "Snow should end tomorrow, but it's likely the road won't be cleaned until Monday."

I take a deep breath and let it out before asking the question likely to break my own heart. "Are you in that much of a rush to get away from me?"

"What?" Surprise laces her tone before she turns serious. "Garrett, look at me, please."

I know it's serious when she uses my name. Even after all this time, she still doesn't like to call me Garrett. Reluctantly, I turn to face her and try to school my expression. Her lips are pursed and her brows have drawn together like she's going to tell me off, but then her features soften. Cool fingertips press along my jaw, pulling my face down to look at her directly when I've turned my attention to a spot over her head.

"If I had wanted to get away from you, Garrett Daniels, I'd have taken the truck and left you here to dig out my car once the snow stopped. If I had wanted to get away from you, Cowpoke, I'd have made you take us back down the mountain last night." She pulls my face down until I'm eye level with her. "What I wanted was to get away from that conversation where someone mentioned sleeping arrangements. I'm not ready for everyone to talk about us when we've not really talked about us. You know?" She's still holding my jaw, so I keep my mouth shut and nod. "Now, let me put you out of your misery."

With those words, she turns toward the stove and pulls out the pans to make breakfast. Then she reaches into the cabinet and pulls something else out. I try to look over her shoulder, but she grabs it close to her chest, hiding whatever it is from my sight. I grab her waist on both sides, tickling her, and she screeches. Holding her against me, I lean down until my lips are at her ear.

"What're you hiding, Pixie?"

She looks back at me and flutters her lashes before holding up the most beautiful thing I've ever seen.

Taylor

With fully bellies, we sit on the more comfortable seats, and my mind wanders to last night when I'd climbed the man like a tree. *Jesus Christ, that was hot!* I can't get the image out of my head, and heat makes its way to my core. It doesn't help that Garrett is sitting in front of me and has taken my foot in his hands, massaging it like there's nothing in the world he'd rather do.

"What're you thinking about?" he asks, his voice soft.

I shake my head, trying to clear my thoughts before he somehow reads them and begins to think me a whole harlot. My nose crinkles at the word. *Where the fuck did that come from?* I'd never say anything like that to anyone else, so why do I do this to myself? I'm definitely going to have to call my therapist when I get back to Gretna House. That's the only answer.

Garrett's palms find my cheeks, drawing my attention back to him. "Earth to Taylor. Come in Pixie."

I swat at his chest playfully, but as soon as I make contact with the thin material of his t-shirt, my fingers burn with the need to feel his skin again. Heat climbs up my neck as we stare into each other's eyes.

"Nobody here but us chickens," I say softly. I try to shake my head but he holds me still. I give him a stiff smile, and he kisses my forehead. The gesture is so sweet that I lean into him and let him wrap his arms around me. While I may have been thinking terribly naughty things about him moments ago, there's nothing sexual in this embrace. It's completely meant for comfort, and it hits the spot.

After several moments, he speaks again. "Now, before I say something stupid and corny like chicken is my favorite thing to eat, tell me a dream you have for yourself? What does the future hold for Taylor Wright, the pixie?"

I snort out a laugh before choking on the very idea of articulating my dream. It's not that I think Garrett will laugh at me. He may be brusque, but he's not a complete asshole. It's just that it doesn't fit the mold of what most people mean when they talk about their dreams for the future.

"Do you not want to tell me?" He asks, reading my expression, and I look down at the floor, embarrassed to be so damn transparent.

"It's not that I don't want to tell you." I pause, and when he opens his mouth to fill the space, I put my finger over his lips to silence him. "I just...I'm not sure it's the type of future dreams most people think about is all."

He fingers cup my chin, once again turning my face up to his. "It's just us here. There is no most people. I asked about you, your dream."

I take in a deep breath and push it out through my nose before answering. "Honestly, I've only had one dream for far too long, and I'm finally on my way to seeing it happen." He watches me expectantly but doesn't speak. He barely moves, other than to grab my foot again. "All I've wanted was to see my sisters free of Phillip, and now that he's in jail, there's a real chance they'll all, mom included, be safe. That's my dream."

"That's a beautiful dream, Taylor, and one I can't wait to see come true for you and your sisters." He leans forward and wraps his free hand around the back of my neck, pulling my lips to his. I let out a contented sigh before kissing him back in earnest.

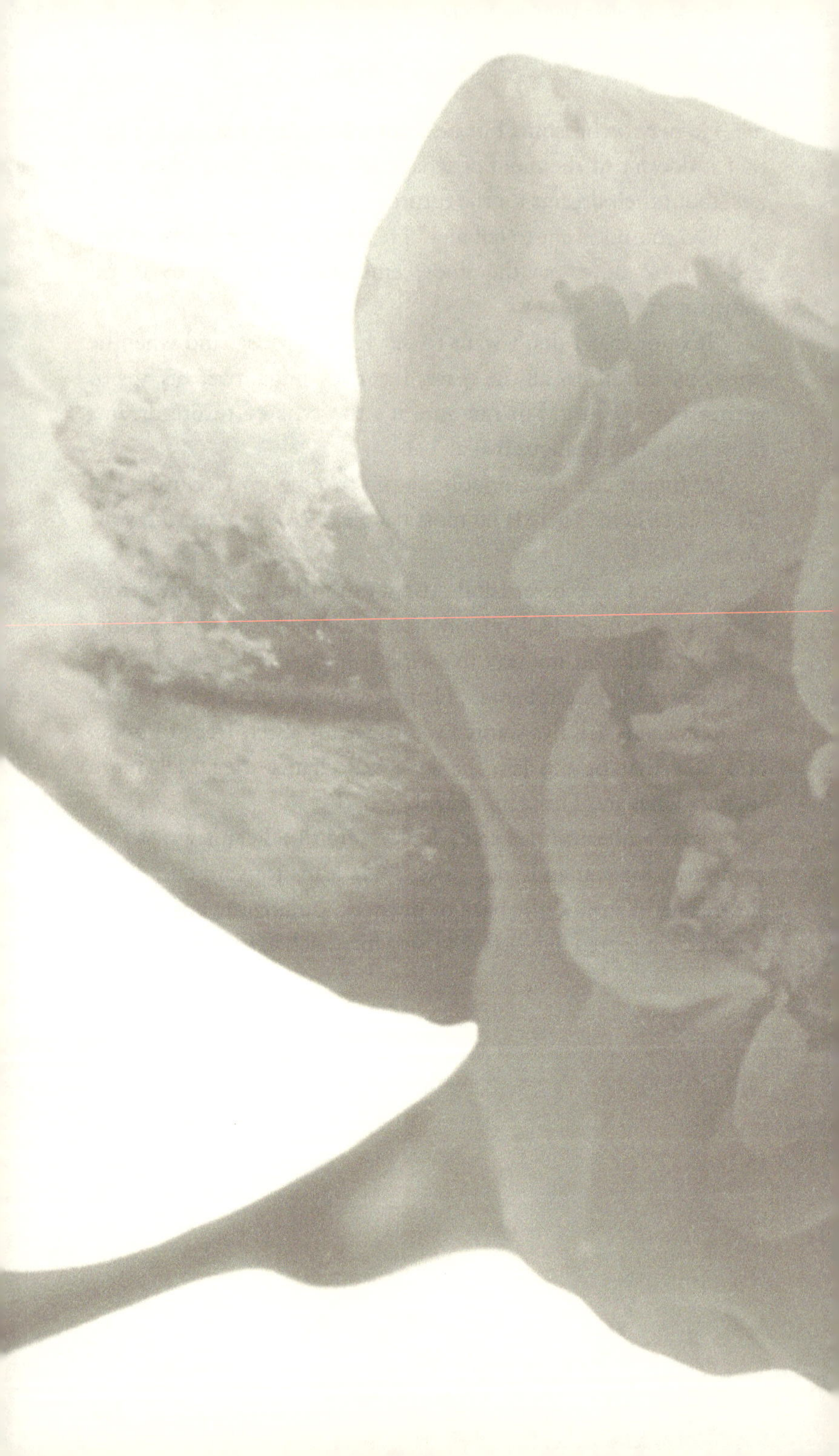

WHEN GOODBYE MEANS WELCOME

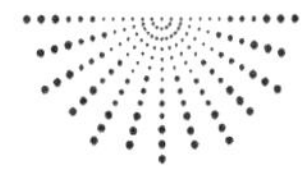

aylor

The snow stops late Saturday afternoon, and the sun comes out, warming the mountain and clearing the roads. We don't notice. We never leave the cabin and barely leave the bed until Sunday evening. I can't tell what Garrett is thinking, but I damn sure don't want to go back to reality. This weekend. This cabin. This man. It's all been a dream and everything I've ever thought intimacy with a man should be. I'm afraid that we'll go back to being antagonistic and standoffish with each other in front of everyone. I know we have to go back, but I dread the drive down to my car and then back to the house. How am I going to look Joanna and Jacob in the eye knowing I've had their dad every which way but Sunday? My only consolation is that Garrett seems just as reluctant to leave our little haven.

We eat breakfast in relative silence, my legs draped over his at the island. He runs his hands up my calves idly, like we've been wrapped up in each other for years and not just two days. It's only been two days. I've barely known this man for a little over eight months, and I've only been attracted to him for...oh who am I lying to, I've been attracted to him since our first meeting in the kitchen. But I've only realized I wouldn't turn down the opportunity to be close to him for half that time. It really was the day in the hospital when he protected me from Phillip that I knew I had to have him. Now that I have, I don't want to let him go.

"Are you ready, Pix?" His tone is apologetic.

I wrap my arms around his waist and place a kiss on his cheek. He turns his face and captures my mouth in a tender kiss, probably the softest one we've shared ever.

"In all honesty, no, but we have to go."

I give him a wan smile and turn to pick up my bag. He reaches around me and grabs it before I can. I shake my head with a sad chuckle. With both of our bags over his shoulder, he grabs my hand, and we walk out to his truck. I look back into the cabin with a sigh, my chest tight with emotion. Before I can climb into the truck, Garrett hems me in, his hands on either side of my shoulders.

"This wasn't an escape for me. It wasn't a fluke. Nothing has to change once we go home unless we want it to. I don't want it to, but I will leave it to you to decide."

His words take my breath away. They're everything I want to hear, but is that what I want? Will I feel different when I have to face his kids who are older than me? Will I feel different when I have to go back to work with Joanna? I need to talk to Jordan. I need Morgan's advice. I need to get my head together. I want to tell him that I don't want anything to change either, but I don't. Instead, I flash him a smile and let him kiss me, pouring all of my emotions into the kiss. We're both breathing heavy when we pull apart, and this time, I smile for real.

My car is fine. Thankfully, I didn't hit anything, just slid into the edge of the ditch without actually falling down into it. Garrett is able to easily pull it out with the truck, and we make our way down the mountain, him following me. As soon as we pass the Slate Ridge exit, my phone catches a signal, and message after message pops onto the screen. I wait until we're on level ground again before I dial Jordan's number. She's at work and can't talk. I send just enough via text to know she'll call me as soon as she clocks out.

When I walk into the house, Morgan wraps her arms around me. I haven't felt so much like coming home in years. This woman has become family in these past eight months. She's not old enough to be like a second mother, but she's definitely like an older sister, something I've never had the benefit of. Tears fall before I even realize my eyes are burning.

"Hey. What's going on?" Morgan asks, and I let out a sob.

"Are we alone?"

Her brows knit together as if asking why, but she admits that Jacob is staying at his house tonight to take care of the animals in the morning since no one knew if we were going to make it home tonight. That means he could turn around and come here as soon as Garrett hits the driveway, cutting down the time we have to chat.

"C'mon, I'll make you a cup of tea," she offers, and I leave my stuff at the foot of the stairs to follow her into the kitchen. As she puts the kettle on to heat, she asks the question that's been haunting me. "What's happening between you and Garrett?"

"It's that obvious, huh?"

She looks at me with a raised brow, as if to say 'duh.' I give her a half smile and lightly chuckle. "Truth be told, there wasn't really anything until that day in the hospital, well, there really wasn't much after that either." I shrug, and then go on to tell her about the possessive kiss he gave me before leaving me alone with Phillip. Though it had been soul-shaking in the best possible way, I didn't have a lot of time to dwell on it because of everything else that went down, so I had chalked it up to weaving a protection spell over a friend you know is going into danger. "Ok, maybe I read too many fantasy novels," I admit before continuing to explain how safe and cared for I felt being wrapped in Garrett's arms after Phillip was splayed out on the floor. "I just didn't know how he felt. I mean, I'm not completely sure now." She stares at me incredulously as I give her the cliffs notes version of this weekend and the look of relief and pain on his face when he found me at the cabin.

"Wait a minute. You're saying you have no idea how cantankerous, old-man Daniels feels about you?" She says the off-base description with a fond smile. There is nothing truly cantankerous about the man. I nod less than enthusiastically, and my eyes well. Thankfully, my tea has cooled enough for me to take a sip, holding the waterworks back. "The man who," she starts, holding up a finger before looking at the ceiling like she's thinking of the right words. "The man who held your hand on the way to the hospital. The man who nearly fought the orderlies to stay by your side. The man who damn near killed your stepfather for scaring you without even knowing what that asshole had truly done to you. The man who was ready to go to jail for having protected you. And the man who drove up a treacherous mountain pass in an unexpected snowstorm to make sure you were safe. That's the man you're not sure how he feels?"

She's missed adding the man who also made me feel safe, protected, cherished, and desired every moment we spent together the past forty-eight hours. "When you say it like that..." I say, drifting off.

"Garrett Daniels is crazy." She laughs when my eyes snap up, my brows creased in consternation. "Oh, he is crazy. I've known him since I was a child. But, he's crazy about you now. He looks for you every time he walks in the door. If I mention you being at the store, his face and shoulders slump like he's lost the most precious thing to him." My mouth gapes. I didn't know he looked for me.

"He barely speaks to me, and when we do speak, it is a constant battle."

"Is it really a battle? What are either of you trying to win?"

I have no answer. My brain is swimming through the muck of

possibilities. What am I trying to win by antagonizing him or responding to his snarky comments?

"Do you want my thoughts?" A smile-filled voice comes from the open kitchen door behind me.

"You didn't seem the eavesdropping kind, Jacob Daniels. I expect something like that from your father. Hell, even your sister."

He lets out a hard, mirthful 'Ha!' before walking around the island to kiss Morgan on the cheek. He then plops down on the stool next to her. "You think I lived my entire life with and around those two without picking up some useful practices."

The way he calls eavesdropping useful has me cackling a laugh. Yeah, that apple didn't fall far at all. "So, what are your thoughts?"

With a shit-eating grin, he folds his hands in front of him and says, "You're both being a couple of dumbasses."

My mouth gapes at him, and I blink multiple times unable to believe those words just came out of Jacob's mouth. He's the sweet one, the nice one, the one who tries to smooth things over for everyone.

Morgan slaps his shoulders. "Jacob Daniels!" Her voice is just as incredulous as I feel.

"What? It's the truth," he says, looking into her eyes. "They're being as dumb as I was for not doing everything in my power to find you all those years ago. Nobody should waste twenty years, or even twenty weeks fighting against their own happiness."

Morgan's eyes soften, and the love between them makes me smile, even through the confusion about my own feelings. After a few moments, though, I clear my throat. "I'm sorry, but I thought this conversation was about me. If not, I will leave you two alone to make goo-goo eyes at each other."

"If you're waiting for that shit to stop, you'll never spend any time with them in the same room together. Their googly eyes are coo coo for cocoa puffs." Joanna now stands in the open kitchen doorway.

I barely stifle a groan with a laugh. This being a bed and breakfast means the front door is unlocked all the time between certain hours. It's great when we're working, so we don't have to stop every five minutes to answer the doorbell. It's not so great when just anyone can walk in at any time unannounced.

"Is this a damn family reunion?" I ask, trying to hide my discomfort.

"Not until you join the family," Jacob says with a playful wink.

"I'm sure it won't be long now," Joanna responds. "Every snowed-in romance novel I've ever read ends that way." She pulls down two mugs and pours water from the kettle before setting a mug in front of Jacob and taking the seat next to Morgan. When she winks in Morgan's direction, my eyes roll of their own volition.

"You two are the worst!" I complain.

"Not yet," Joanna says. "The worst would be if you expected us to call you mom."

Heat courses up my neck and into my cheeks faster than I can take my next breath.

"Yeah, I'm not sure the townsfolk would know what to do with us calling our little sister turned stepmother that. What should we call you? Momster? Momma Pixie? Maybe we should ask dad." Jacob is red himself by the time he's finished the last statement, and Morgan is beside herself barely holding back her laughter.

"I'm going to disown all of you," I say.

"Who's disowning who?" Garrett's voice comes from the hallway, and I have to clench my thighs together to power through the rush of arousal his deep gravel causes.

"Now, it's a family reunion," Morgan says, an apology in her eyes.

"Am I intruding on a private conversation," Garrett asks as he sits on the stool next to me. He splays his legs a little more than necessary, so the outside of his thigh rubs against mine. He doesn't need to emphasize his presence. My entire body is aware.

"No, Pa. It was me who intruded," Jacob says with a half-smile. "Then Joanna came and interrupted my intrusion." The other side of his mouth lifts. "Then you showed up right on cue." All of his teeth show pearly white. I can't stand him in this moment.

"What are you two up to?"

"An intervention," Joanna says with a smirk, "or rather, an adoption. Either way, we were giving Taylor our blessing."

I don't even look up at Garrett. Instead, I put my head in my hands and look down at the table. I can hear the irritated crease in Garrett's voice when he finally says something.

"Do I even want to know what she needs your permission for?"

"To find happiness," Jacob says.

"To bang your brains out," Joanna says at the same time.

The three of them, Morgan included, burst out laughing. I groan, and Garrett puts his hand on my leg. I feel the tension flowing through him all while he caresses my thigh in what is meant to be a calming gesture. His hand on my leg is anything but calming. Before anyone can say anything else, my phone rings from out in the hallway, and I know it's Jordan.

"Saved by the ringtone," I say under my breath and hop off the stool, sprinting out of the room.

I have always said I do not run, but damn if I don't grab my bags and make it up to my room before the phone finishes ringing.

"Thank goodness," I say when I finally press the answer button, the door slamming behind me.

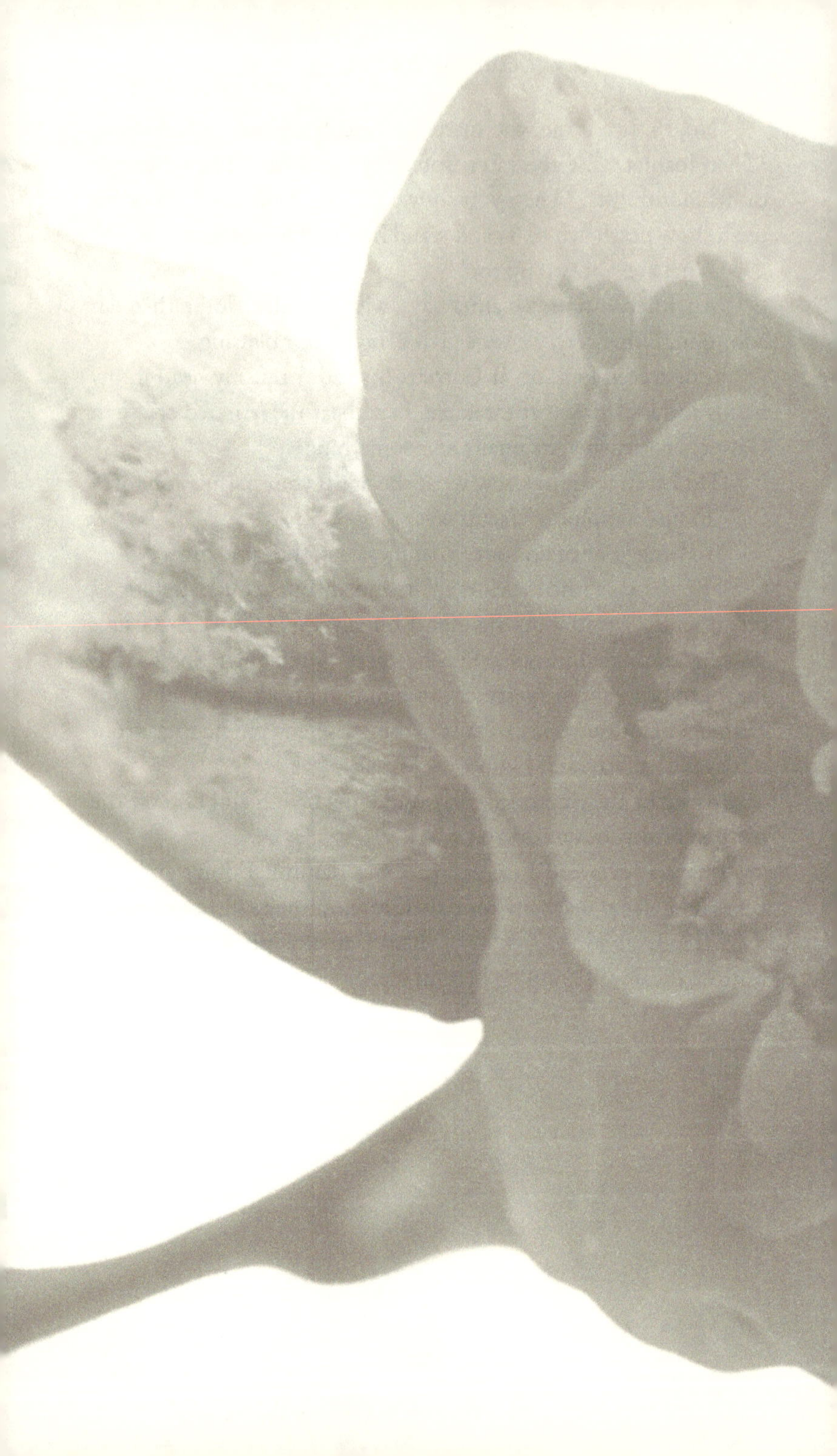

MAKE ME WHOLE

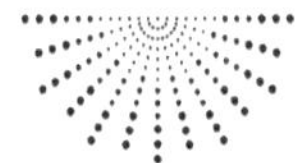

Garrett

I take a deep breath and climb the stairs. I've never wanted to choke my children as much as I do when Taylor runs off. They mean well, but it's definitely too soon. At the same time, my heart is doing flip flops knowing they approve of us. Now I just have to convince her there's nothing to be afraid of. There's a feeling in my chest I don't quite know how to define. Happiness and trepidation war with each other. Maybe we can call it some stupid ass name like nervpiness or joyidation. Still, approaching her room is like trudging through mud. She might not be ready to see me. I tell myself that my goal is simply to make sure she's okay after their ill-time and overbearing ribbing, but I really just want to see her. Her voice comes through the door before I can lift my hand to knock.

"I don't know, girl. What if he doesn't feel the same as I do? It seems so fast."

She must be on the phone still. It has to be Jordan she's talking to, as she's never mentioned any other friends. I can only imagine the off-the-wall shit Jordan is telling her after our one conversation the other day. That woman threw me for a loop asking if I was the guy with the daddy vibes. I mean, I'd let Taylor call me daddy if she really wanted to, but I certainly don't look at her like a kid. That pixie is all woman. All fire and passion and self-awareness. She's perfection in a tiny, colorful package.

"I know I'm scared, dammit! I think I have a right to be. Just because I've grabbed his balls doesn't mean I know how to grab this thing we have going by the balls. Why the fuck are we talking about balls anyway?"

I barely stop myself from barking out a laugh. I don't mean to be eavesdropping on their conversation, but I also can't bring myself to go back downstairs without seeing her first.

"Tell him how I feel is so easy for your punk ass to say. You've not found someone you're somewhere between infatuated and in love with." I realize the breaks in conversation must be Jordan talking. "Shut the hell up! I can't just walk up to him and say 'Hey, so I'm in love with you and scared as fuck that you don't feel the same.' That's not how this shit works, J!"

My sight gets blurry, and I wrinkle my nose. I shouldn't be listening to this. She wouldn't want me hearing this. I think to turn away from the door and head back downstairs finally when the door pulls open. Both of our eyes go wide, and a random tear creeps down my cheek. I look down at the ground, hoping she doesn't catch it, but I know she does.

"I have to go, J. I'll call you back later." She says, her voice quiet. I'm afraid to look into her face and see whether it's quiet happiness, quiet concern, or the quiet that happens before a storm. She has every right to rage at me for listening outside of her room, every right to be pissed that I know what's in her heart before she's decided whether to tell me or not. She does none of that. Instead, she puts her hands on each side of my face and tilts my head up to look at her. "How much of that did you hear?"

"Enough," I say. "Maybe too much." I can't bring myself to

apologize because I'm not sure she'd believe it. We're not exactly the mind-our-business family, and I'm sure she's learned that by now, especially with the twins' earlier behavior. Also, I'm not sorry for hearing that she loves me. I can't apologize for that. I want to hear her say it again, to say it directly to me. Her brows knit together, and she worries her lips with her teeth.

"I don't know what to say," she whispers, and I'm not sure whether that statement is for me or herself.

"We don't have to talk about it if you don't want to," I offer. "At least not until you're ready."

"And if I'm never ready?" I lift my eyes to see her single brow raised in a questioning challenge.

"You don't hold back for long, Pixie Girl. You're more of grab life by the balls kinda gal." I raise my brow back at her.

"You're the worst!"

"And you love me," I say before I can stop myself.

We both go silent. In fact, it is so quiet there on the landing, we might've both stopped breathing. *Fuck Fuck Fuck*. If I could punch myself in the mouth and not look ridiculous, I absolutely would.

"I'm sorry. I got carried away in our banter. You could say it back if it'd make this whole awkward moment better."

"Would it be as true as your statement? Would it sting as much?"

"Yes, and no. I'm not still trying to figure out where I stand. I've known something was developing between us for a while, or rather, that I've been feeling something for you. I just didn't think you'd be interested in this old asshole of a man who'd spent most of the past five years taking advantage of his children just to survive, to keep breathing each day. I wasn't sure I was worthy of breathing in your scent, let alone touching your skin. That kiss in the hospital was more than I was prepared to handle. I just wanted to show that guy that you had someone in your corner. When you held on and kissed me back, my heart melted, and my brain turned to mush. You've been all I've known ever since. So yes, it would absolutely be a true statement, and to hear you say it would be affirmation of what I've known since I found your car in that ditch."

I finally shut up. Her jaw is slack, and her eyes are wide, staring into mine like she's trying to read my soul through them. I give her a moment to take it all in, to accept everything I've just said, hell, to process the fact that we love each other.

"So, you love me."

Though her statement could have been a question in its wording, it is definitely a statement. The steadiness of her glare says she's waiting for affirmation. I nod.

"Use your words, Cowpoke."

I smile at her returning my words from this weekend. This is the pixie I know. This is the woman who won my heart with each challenge and soothed my soul with her vulnerability and openness.

"Yes, I do."

Before another word can be said, she jumps into my arms, literally jumps, and I barely brace myself to catch her in a way that we don't both fall over. My hands cup her ass and her mouth claims mine. There is nothing sweeter until I taste the saltiness of tears and open my eyes to look at her. She's blurry, and I realize that the tears are mine. She pulls one arm from around my neck and wipes my cheeks before planting soft kisses on them. I'm just about to tell her that we should get out of the hallway before we end up with an audience when the clapping starts. Neither of us turn to look; there's no reason. She kisses my lips once more and then releases her legs from my hips. Once her feet are on the ground, she winks before grabbing my hand and pulling me into her room. I don't even bother closing the door.

"Let them hear," I say loudly.

She giggles and pulls off her shirt, exposing her ample breasts, and I no longer hear the laughter from the stairs. My mouth waters at the anticipation of tasting her skin, her arousal. When she pushes me back to sit on the bed and drops to her knees in front of me, my cock jumps to attention, squeezing against the zipper of my jeans.

"You're so fucking perfect," I say with reverence.

At some point, before I make her scream my name repeatedly, we close and lock the bedroom door. It's dark out when I hold her in my arms, both of our bodies sated. there's no doubt in my mind that I love this woman. I don't even want to go home if she won't come with me. Apprehension twists in my chest at the thought of her refusing to be there with me. I hold her a little tighter.

"Are you alright, Cowpoke?"

I both love and hate that she is so attuned to me. I smile in the dark and try to relax my body.

"You can pretend with the deep breathing, but I know better. What's wrong?"

"You're not going to let it go?" I ask with a chuckle. I already know the answer, but I have to ask anyway.

"I'm not letting you go, so no."

I kiss her forehead. "I just had a thought that..."

"What was the thought? Maybe I can help it not do whatever it's doing."

"If anyone can make it better, I'm sure you can. I just don't know how to really explain it."

"Let's try something my therapist does when I can't find the words."

I hate the fact that she has to see a therapist because of that piece of shit stepfather and her neglectful mother. I may have neglected my children for a few years, but they were already grown. Ok, maybe I wasn't the most attentive before then, but I did everything in my power to protect them.

"You're tightening up again, Mr. Daniels."

I growl against her ear.

"That growl will get you nowhere right now. Save it for later, and tell me the emotion that made you tense up earlier."

I don't say anything right away. I don't really want to talk about this right now. Her patience, however, is much better than mine, and she waits me out. "Fine. Apprehension, fear, whatever name you want to give it."

"Good. If you can name the emotion, then you can say what caused it. Where did you feel the fear in your body?"

"Huh?" Though I hear the words fine, I'm not sure I understand what she's asking.

"What part of your body responded first to the emotion? Where were you affected? Your arms? Your legs? Your neck?"

"Oh, my chest. Right behind my sternum."

"What was the last thought you had before you felt the first prickles of that emotion in your chest?"

I froze again not wanting to say the words. She turns in my arms to face me and rubs her hand up from my stomach to my chest.

"So, it has something to do with me then?" I nod in the dark knowing she can't see me. "I feel your head moving, so I'm taking that as a yes. I can sit here all night and say you have nothing to fear from me, but I know better. I still have fears around you, around this, around us. I don't always know when they're going to pop up or how to respond to them, but they're there. You're not in this alone, Garrett. I'm here with you."

Before I can stop it, a single tear streams down the side of my face and into my hairline. This woman has me feeling all the emotions I thought myself no longer capable of, and I want them all, even the fear. I tighten my arms around her and kiss her forehead.

"I love you, my Pixie Girl," I say against her hair. "Will you come home with me?" That last part comes out barely above a whisper, and though part of me hopes she didn't hear me, I feel better having asked it.

"I love you too, Cowpoke, and I'd like nothing more than for you to take me home with you."

Five and a half years ago, my whole world fell apart. A year ago, I started putting the pieces back together. Three days ago, I found the glue. Tonight, her words make me whole.

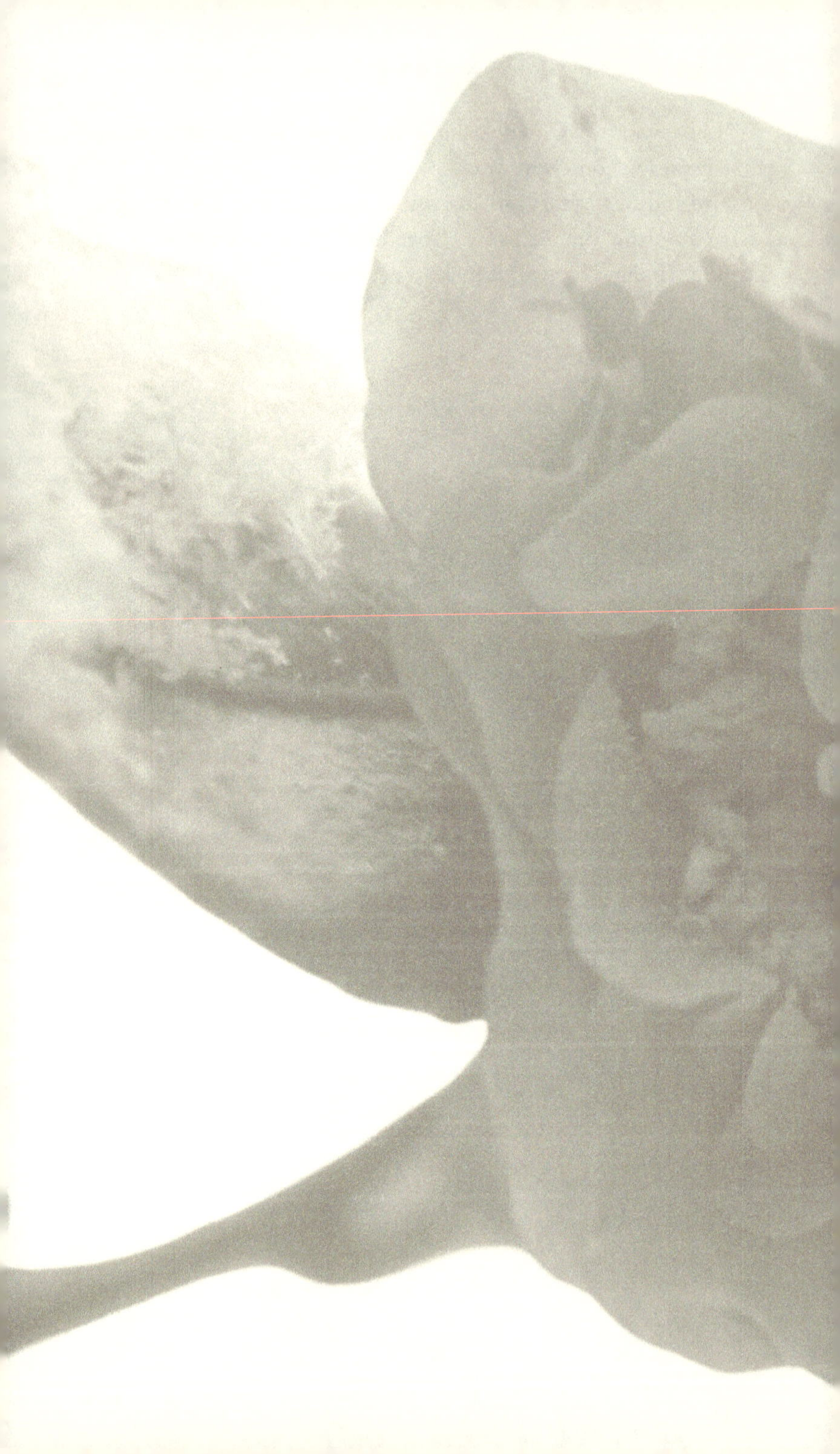

LUMBERSNACKS

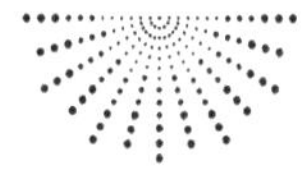

*T*aylor

"C'mon, cowpoke, it's going to be a blast."

"You ladies will be ogling all the shirtless men and their axes. Why would I want to be there?"

"You're welcome to take your shirt off and let me ogle you." He glares at me and I laugh, tossing him his flannel jacket with a wink. "C'mon, I don't want Jordan to be sitting around waiting for too long."

"Woman, you have me wrapped around your little finger and surely know how to take advantage of that fact."

I giggle. "But I make it worth your while," I coo against his lips, reaching around to grab his ass. He has on those jeans that hug him just right, and with his silver fox beard growing in, I'm going to have to beat the women off of him, but it'll be worth it.

"And you will tonight," he growls before dancing his tongue with mine.

I pull away from him with a laugh and head toward the door. "No ruining my panties before we even get there."

Jordan is standing outside the gate when we arrive. She looks beautiful in her pink snow bunny ski jacket with the white tassel pulls. She has her goddess locs braided to each side to hang down the front of her shoulders. With her jeans hugging her thick thighs and ass poking out underneath her jacket, she looks ready to take on the cold ass day.

"I love those boots. Where'd you get them?" I yell from behind her. She turns to glare at me before smiling at Garrett.

"Hiya, Daddy Cowpoke. How've you been?"

"I was great until your bestie here decided to drag me along to the meat market."

I roll my eyes at him, and Jordan laughs. "It's only a market if the meat is on sale. I do need some, though. My fridge has been empty a while."

Garrett rolls his eyes this time, and Jordan and I both burst out laughing.

"You two have only been a thing for a month, and you already have twin eye rolls. Soon, you'll be finishing each other's sentences and dressing in matching outfits." She laughs at her own joke and then stops suddenly with a scheming gleam in her eye. "I know," she says, and I cringe. "I'll make you two matching t-shirts that say Pixie and the Cowpoke. I'll even put a silhouette of a couple on it. People will think you have a band and want your autograph." Her laughter catches the attention of everyone around who turns to see what the crazy woman in pink is laughing at.

Garrett shakes his head at her, the corners of his lips turn up slightly, belying the exasperation he's trying to portray. I wrap my hand around his elbow and pull him forward toward the gate.

"C'mon, Madame Comedienne," I say with a faux French accent. "Let's see if we can't find you a lumbersnack, so you can leave us to our non-matching t-shirt happiness."

I've never been to the Lumberjack Festival, or Lumbersnack Fest as Joanna fondly called it when she first told me about the event. Supposedly, there are many mini-events taking place around different parts of the lake. There are vendors posted up in the neighboring town, and Christmas Tree vendors have come in to provide trees for the log rolling and splitting competitions. They will also have trees for sale. I promised Morgan we would get one for Gretna House, and I want to get one for our house. Garrett doesn't know it yet, but I plan to decorate the entire house and host a Christmas party, even if the only people who come are our little family and close friends.

I'm pulled from my holiday happiness daydream by Jordan's "Oh my gawd, that is a fine ass right there!" I look up to follow her line of sight and see a man with long, dark brown hair squatting down to retrieve a wrapped pine tree that slid off of the truck they're unpacking. The sign on the side of the truck reads Branch Family Trees.

"You're a mess," I say to her, snuggling up against Garrett whose eyes are probably rolled so far back in his head, he can't see where he's walking.

"I may be that, but his ass is fine," she says even more exuberantly.

The man turns and looks straight at us. Jordan quickly turns away, and I crack a huge smile, pointing my finger at her. He looks her up and down and smiles with a tilt to his head. Jordan hasn't looked back, but if she had, she'd have found the front was just as fine as the back. He has a nicely cropped beard, beautiful teeth, and perfect fucking eyebrows. I'll admit I'm a little jealous of this man's brows.

"You're staring, Pixie," the grumbly voice next to me announces. "If you start drooling, I'm going home."

I know he's lying. He'd be even less likely to leave me alone here if he thought I was interested in anyone out here. My cowpoke isn't insecure, except maybe a little about our age difference, but he does have a slightly jealous streak at times. He calls it protectiveness, and maybe there's a bit of that, but really, it's his desire running away with him. He loves every inch of my plump frame, so he assumes everyone else will too. I can't blame him, though. I am a delicious.

"I'm checking out the merchandise for my bestie who's too shy to do more than stare at backsides."

"I remember you having a thing for backsides too."

"Oh, don't get me wrong, I do, but I have the best one in town in my bed every night. Not to mention the rest of the man it's attached to." I walk my fingers up his chest and pull down on his beard until his mouth is right in front of mine. "Trust me when I say I'm not shopping for anything here except a couple Christmas trees." Then I kiss him, pulling his bottom lip between mine and nipping on it before I walk off to follow Jordan. When I turn around, Garrett has walked toward the guy with the trees. I don't know whether to cringe or cheer. He strikes up a conversation with the man and then turns a wink in my direction. I catch up with Jordan, and we watch the men from a distance. Lucky for her, the blush that has crept into her cheeks is nearly imperceptible to the random people walking past us because her cheeks are glowing as she glares at Garrett. He's going to get an earful when he finally joins us, and I inwardly chuckle. Today is going to be a fun day!

Garrett

"That was so much fun!" Taylor's excitement fills me with warmth, and I smile. I will gladly spend the rest of forever giving her all these first-time experiences if they keep her this happy.

Taylor and Jordan giggle back and forth as they talk about everything they saw at the festival. Each of them had tried their hands at axe throwing after watching a slew of other women miss.

These two are super competitive and insisted they could do it. Jordan's made it into the wood. Taylor's, on the other hand... Well, hers dropped onto the floor with a thud. My pixie is beautiful and creative, and strong in so many ways, but coordinated is not it. I chuckle to myself at the way she stomped her foot just like Tinker Bell does in the movie. Not surprisingly, the lumberjacks were Jordan's favorite, especially that guy we'd met early this morning. She'd basically melted each time he looked her way at breakfast.

I can't help but look over at Taylor, though I should be watching these windy county roads. She's glowing, and it takes my breath away. She must feel my gaze because she looks up with the brightest smile and grabs my hand, interlocking her fingers with mine.

"What would you like for your next adventure?" I ask.

Her eyes rake over me, down to where my cock has begun to harden under her scrutiny. She bites her lip before reaching over to run her hand up my thigh.

"Oh, hell no," Jordan screeches from the backseat. "You two save all those sexy looks and touches until after you drop me off!"

Taylor gives me a wink, and I bark out a laugh. For a moment, I forgot Jordan was in the car, but it's obvious Taylor hadn't.

"Don't worry, Jordan, I'll punish her for that later."

"Ugh," she groans, covering her ears. Taylor snickers from the passenger seat, and I pull my lips up, trying to hold in my laughter. "It's one thing to live vicariously through my best friend. It's another to hear you talk about it, Daddy Cowpoke."

The look of disgust I catch in the rearview mirror opens the floodgates, and laughter boils out of me. These two are truly a breath of fresh air. I grab Taylor's hand and kiss the back of it at the same time my phone rings.

I give a sidelong glance at Taylor's beautiful face. It's the county DA's office, and I'm not sure I want to answer it. This day has been too perfect for bad news. Her smile falters, and Jordan must sense the growing tension because she also falls silent.

Squeezing Taylor's hand once more, I grab the phone and pull it to my ear. It's hard to say how long I hold my breath, but I have to pull over to the side of the road when it finally releases. Taylor's hand touches my arm as soon as I end the call, and there are tears in my eyes when I look at her.

"They found him guilty. Twenty-five to life."

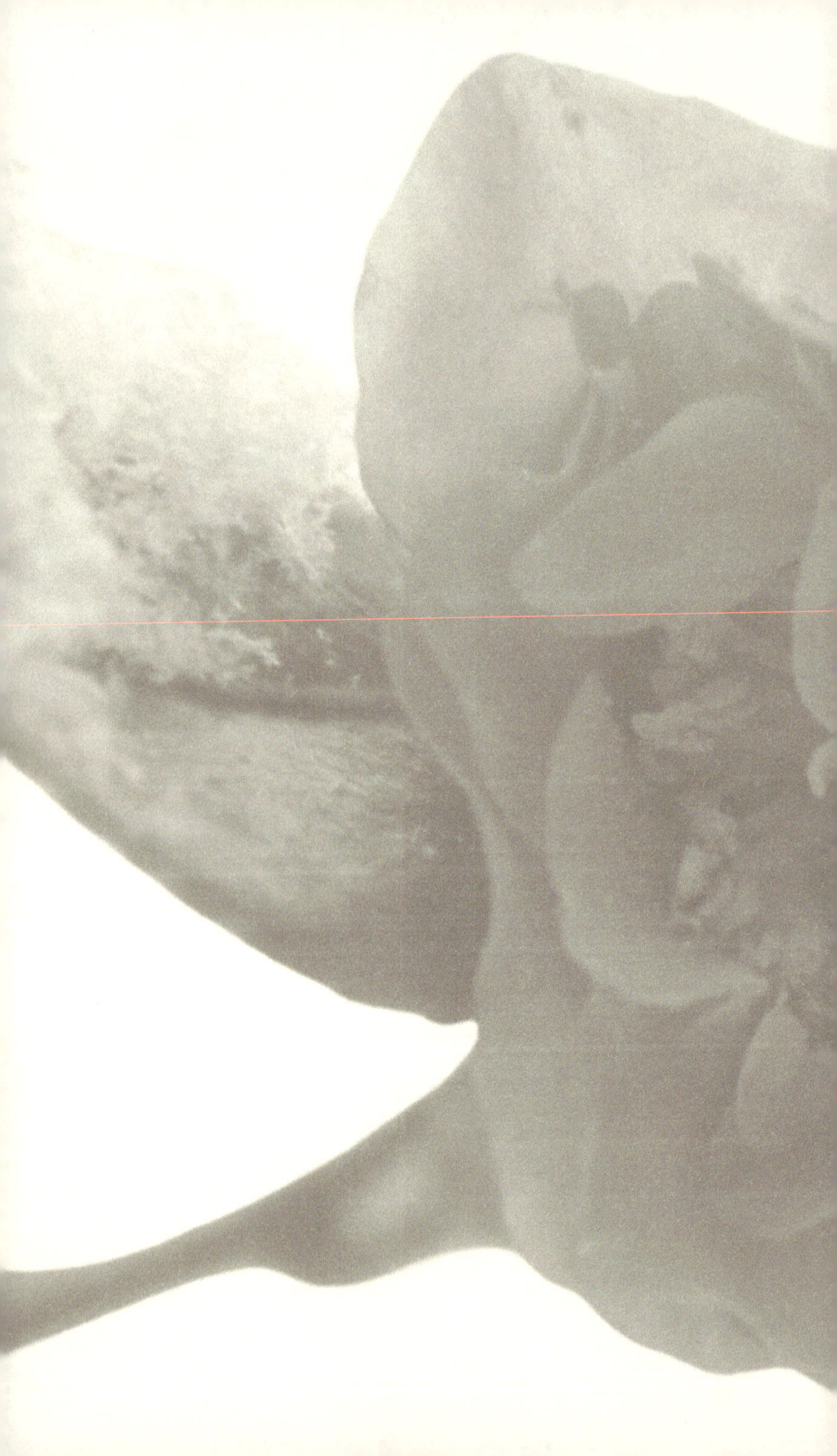

CAN YOU KEEP QUIET?

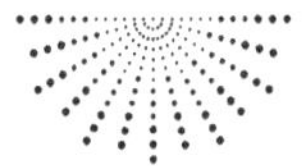

*G*arrett

I'm supposed to be working through the books and preparing for inventory, but listening to Taylor move things around in the stockroom has me smiling, and one thing I never smile about is using this damn computer. That woman, though. That spitfire of a pixie. Yeah, she makes me smile every damn day.

We've settled into a smooth routine since Joanna left for the rodeo, fell in love, and decided she wasn't coming back home. I won't say I don't miss my baby girl, but I'm as thrilled for her happiness as I am for Jacob's. I simply wish she wasn't so far away. My eyes shift to the couch along the wall where she'd broken my heart while trying to mend her own. Maybe it was selfish of me, but I just never thought she'd leave Cole County, so I acted like an asshole. I shudder at the memory of how that day went when something crashes out in the storeroom.

"I'm alright. I just dropped a box," Taylor calls from the back aisle moments before I turn the corner, blood pumping and jaw tight. For a moment, I see her laid out on the floor, boxes and buckets strewn around her. I have to blink several times to clear the vision. By then, her hands are pressed to my cheeks, bringing me back to the present. "Just breathe," she says softly, letting her hands slide up into my hair. "I'm alright."

I pull her into my arms. "I thought...I saw...Oh God, Taylor, I saw you on the ground."

"I'm right here, whole and happy." Her smile is warm. "I'm not afraid of that memory. Do you know why?"

My head tilts to the side. I can't imagine. That was a crazy day, argument with Joanna aside. The ambulance ride, her injuries, fucking Phillip showing up to torment her. My hands ball into fists at her waist.

"The reason I don't fear all the horrors of that day is because it also holds one of my favorite memories ever." She stands up on tiptoe and reaches around my neck. I have to lean down a bit, so she can link her fingers together. Rubbing her cheek against mine, she whispers near my ear. "That was the first time you kissed me and made the whole world disappear."

I kiss her then with all the love, all the passion, all the fear that had flooded me at the sound of the crash. She holds me tight, not letting the kiss end, and I walk her backwards toward the small worktable at the end of the aisle. I need her, need to feel her alive and well and mine. Thankfully, she's wearing one of those long, flowy shirt dresses since she came straight from Gretna House without changing. I squat down, sliding my hands up her thighs and lift her ass up onto the table.

"Garrett," she screeches quietly. "Someone could come into the store. The door's still open."

"Then you're going to have to keep quiet, Pixie Girl." I don't give her a chance to respond before sliding her panties to the side and pushing two fingers inside. "So wet already?" I ask with a raised brow, though my eyes have drifted closed at the delicious feel of her squeezing my fingers.

"You kissed me, Cowpoke. What was I supposed to do?"

The admonishment in her words doesn't have the same power

when they're breathy as I work my fingers in and out of her. A soft whimper leaves her lips, and I whisper a 'shhh' into her ear. She turns her face to bite my neck, and I pull out my cock, ready to slide it into her. No sooner do I hit home and we both sigh at the connection than the bell for the door chimes. I give her a wink and rock my hips, which earns a swat at my chest. I chuckle and repeat the movement.

"Garrett," she whisper-yells.

"Yes, love," I purr, sliding in and out of her pussy in languid strokes.

"They're going to hear us."

"Not if you're quiet." She swats at my chest but quickly slides her hands around my waist, digging her nails into my ass as I pick up the pace. I can hear the customer out in the store, and Taylor's wide eyes tell me she's heard them too, but she doesn't tell me to stop. "Be out in a minute. Just holler if you need anything," I yell from our hidden spot down the back aisle.

"Garrett!"

"You don't want them coming back here looking for us, do you?" I wink and pull her hips off the edge of the table, so I can piston into her. She glares at me, but a smile flits across her face before she bites her lip. A tiny moan escapes, and I shake my head. "Do you want me to stop?" I whisper. She shakes her head vigorously. "That's my pixie," I praise and keep pushing us toward the edge.

"Garrett, shit." Her voice is a hushed whisper, and I will never get over her saying my name like that.

'Hey, where are the buffing pads for floor sanders?' A disembodied voice asks from the other room.

I barely hold in my groan at the distraction. I don't want to think of anything else besides the way Taylor feels around my cock. She's so close based on the way she's squeezing me and the sounds of her arousal. I grunt out some directions, hoping that's the right aisle.

"Goddamn, you feel so fucking good," I say, my mouth pressed against my arm to stifle the sound.

"So close," she whines.

'I think I got everything.'

"Be right out," I somehow manage to say without sounding as breathless as I feel. While I liked the idea of us potentially being heard, I hate that there's someone right outside the stockroom door. "Fuck!" I say, swiping the empty boxes off the table top onto the floor.

'Dude, you alright in there?'

"All good," I ground out. "Give me one minute."

"Fuck, I don't want you to stop," Taylor says, and I groan because I don't want to stop either. "Go and hurry back," she says, pushing herself upward, like she might push me away. "I'll stay right here." I pull myself from her and slide my rock-hard cock into my jeans before fastening the button and walking toward the door.

Opening and closing my hands a few times to release the tension from not finishing, I walk out into the store. "Sorry. We're getting ready for inventory and then I knocked something over that I had to clean up." I frown at myself. This person doesn't need details or an explanation. I ring them up without another word and watch as they exit the store, my only thought is getting back to finish what I'd started.

All my salacious thoughts grind to a halt when I find Taylor sitting in the middle of the office floor instead of where I left her. Her phone is in her hand where she's staring at it like a lost puppy as tears stream down her face.

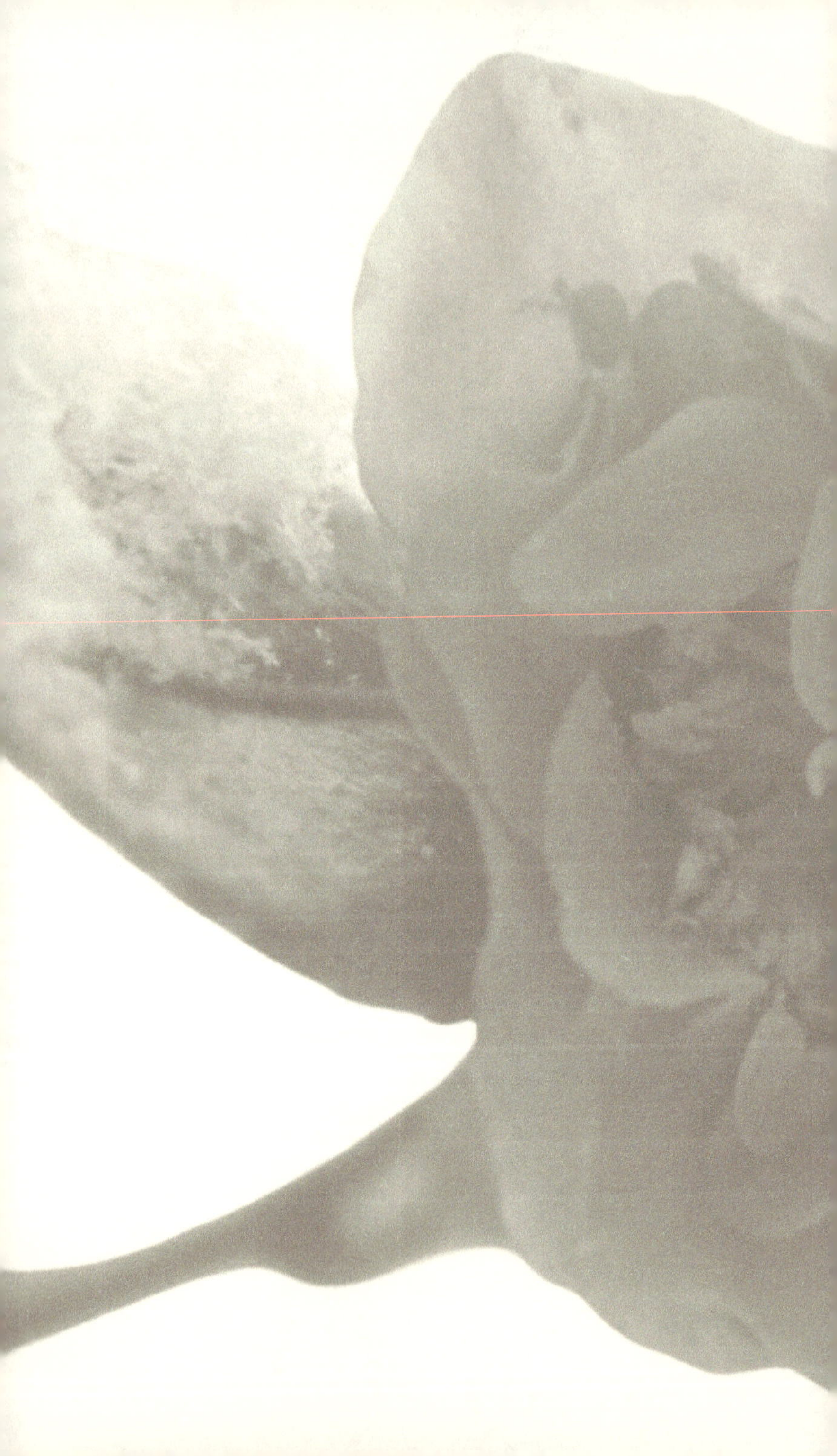

PLEASE FORGIVE ME

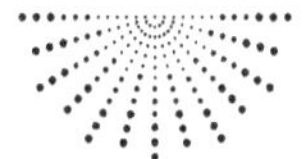

Taylor

My hands are clammy as we sit in the car outside of the courthouse again. I honestly never thought I'd be back here again once we'd testified against Phillip. I wipe my palms on my jeans for the fifth time when Garrett grabs my hand and kisses it. Giving him a nervous smile, I open the door and climb out. He's at my side before I can take two steps toward the building, and his reassuring palm is on my back when we walk through the sliding door and into the foyer. Other than the trip through security, he never leaves my side. I want to tell him how grateful I am, but I can barely put one foot in front of the other.

We enter Suite 203 moments later, and yet it feels like we've walked through water to get here. Time is dragging and speeding by simultaneously. At the front desk, the receptionist looks up at us with a smile that I can't return. I have no control over my emotions right now, no idea how my face is supposed to function or what I'm supposed to do with my hands.

"We're here to see Ms. Sullivan," Garrett says when I don't answer right away.

We're immediately taken to a conference room down the hall

where we sit waiting, Garrett holding my hand in his lap, his thumb making slow passes across my skin. I know it's his way of trying to comfort me, but my brain won't calm down. Our conversation from last night plays through my mind as we talked through the possibilities and all we'll need to do to make this work. Still, there aren't any guarantees. It could all go to shit. They could reject me. I deserve for them to reject me.

My stomach roils as we go through the process of standing, greeting, shaking hands. I hardly take in any of it. I don't remember any words that are exchanged, except for Garrett's final promise. It's the same one he made last night.

"Whatever we have to do to make sure everyone is alright, we will. I'll even go to therapy if it's needed. Whatever it takes."

When Ms. Sullivan mentions the scrutiny we might fall under, I stop in my tracks. We've been walking down a long corridor, but I can't take one more step. "With all due respect, Ms. Sullivan, if even one person would have scrutinized us, if they had even taken a close look at our family, we wouldn't be in this situation today. I welcome the watchfulness and hope you don't fail to do your job because I won't fail at mine." While her eyes remain locked on me, her expression softens. Finally, she nods in acknowledgment and leads us to the door at the end of the hall. Hushed conversation comes through the wood, and my breath hitches. Garrett squeezes my hand one last time before letting go and stepping to the side, so I'm the only person they see when the door opens.

Silence fills the space as I stare into eyes like mine, eyes full of apprehension and anger. I know those emotions well, and I hate to see them reflected back at me. My own eyes sting while they take me in, scrutinizing every inch of me. I could have dressed as the woman I am, the hospitality guru who helps run the hottest BnB in Colliers Town. I could've presented myself as a woman who is loved in all the best ways by friends who've become family and a man who's taught me to fully live again. Instead, I chose to dress as me, the defiant eldest daughter, who used color and bold print to mask the dark. Several moments pass before recognition kicks in, and hurt immediately follows.

"Taylor?" Marybeth's small voice squeaks from Brenna's side. The three of them have been holding hands since the door opened. I can only imagine Brenna suggested the stance as a show of solidarity. No one told us what the girls had been told about who was picking them up today, but their response says it wasn't me. So, when my baby sister looks up at me warily with her big brown eyes, Phillips eyes, the tears I've barely been holding back flow down my cheeks as I nod. She immediately drops Brenna and Justine's hands and runs to me. I drop to my knees and wrap my arms around her.

After several moments, I pull her away and let my hands roam over her face, taking in every inch. It's only been two years since I'd last seen her, but she already looks so different. Unable to handle the emotions, I stand, pull her back into my arms and look at my other sisters. They've remained rooted in the same spot, neither of them taking their eyes off of me or Marybeth. Uncertainty is written all over Justine's face, like she's still not sure what is about to happen, or maybe she's worried about me. That's the vibe Brenna's exuding. Her anger and distrust is palpable, and it guts me.

"I'm so sorry," I say, my voice thick with guilt and sadness.

"You left us without saying goodbye," Justine says, hurt evident in her tone. I nod. There's no denying it.

"You left us with him, with them. You promised to always protect us, and you left." Brenna's accusations are meant to cut, and they hit their mark, nearly making me double over.

Before I can respond, Marybeth pulls away, looking up into my face. "Where have you been, Taylor?" I swallow. Is there a good answer? Is there anything I can say that will wash the anguish from my sisters' faces and make everything right?

"I've been in Cole County, dreaming of ways to take you all away from that house."

"Did you know?" Brenna spits at me. "Did you know that he was arrested? Did you know what he did to me, to Justine, to mom?"

Something shuffles behind me, and I turn my face to see Ms. Sullivan watching us, her expression unreadable. Then I catch sight of Garrett, and the compassion in his eyes is almost my undoing. Without a word, he reminds me that I'm no longer alone. I'm no longer a victim. I am loved, cared for, and supported. My fortitude, which had been waning, returns, and I face my sisters again.

"Yes, I knew he had been arrested. He was arrested in the hospital where he'd gone to torment me after an accident. I had to testify against him, to tell everyone in the courtroom what he'd done to me for years, what he'd threatened to do to you if I didn't do what he wanted. If I didn't let him..." My voice cracks. "If I didn't let him abuse me." I take a deep breath when Marybeth wraps her arms around my waist. "I couldn't take it anymore. I was dying inside, and that wouldn't have helped any of us. I'm so sorry."

"They locked Mom away," Justine says. "She went crazy when dad..." She pauses, and I have to force myself not to cringe at the word. "When Phillip was convicted. She locked herself in the bedroom and wouldn't come out. Finally, Brenna," Justine says, turning to look at our sister whose face is so much like our mother's, like mine.

"I couldn't take it anymore. We had no food, and the water and electricity had been shut off because mom never paid the bills while Phillip was locked away. I went to the neighbor's house and asked for help. They called the cops. I didn't want them to call the cops. I just wanted something to eat. I just wanted to piss in a clean toilet. I just wanted a shower." By the time she finishes the last sentence, tears are streaking down her face, and a sob erupts from my lips.

"I had no idea," I say. "We got word of Phillip's conviction and then his sentencing. That was all we knew until Ms. Sullivan called yesterday."

"Who is we?" Brenna asks, distrust settling into her features again.

Shit! These past months, I've gotten so used to thinking about Garrett and I as a team, as one, that I hadn't even considered the use of 'we' as a problem. My sister's pursed lips and crossed arms, however, tell me I was wrong.

"Who is we, Taylor?" She asks again.

I let out a sigh. If I expect them to trust me enough to come home with us, I have to find a way to get them to understand. "I met someone at my job, and he's the one..."

Brenna interrupts, "He?"

With a nod, I finish my sentence. "He is the one who protected me from Phillip in the hospital, which is how he got arrested."

"Protected you how?" Justine asks, curiosity evident in her tone.

My lips tilt up. "He beat the shit out of him and left him in a pile on the ground." Marybeth looks up at me, her lip pushed out, and my chest tightens. "Sorry, baby," I say, pushing the loose hair from her face.

"What're we supposed to do with no mommy or daddy, Taylor? I don't want to go back and sleep in that place with all those other kids."

I shake my head. "I don't want you to go back anywhere." Though I say the words to the little one, my eyes lock on Brenna. She's become the default leader of the family, and she will be the one to decide. "I'm hoping you'll come home with us."

"There goes that us thing again."

"Do you want to meet him? No, let me rephrase that. I want you to meet him."

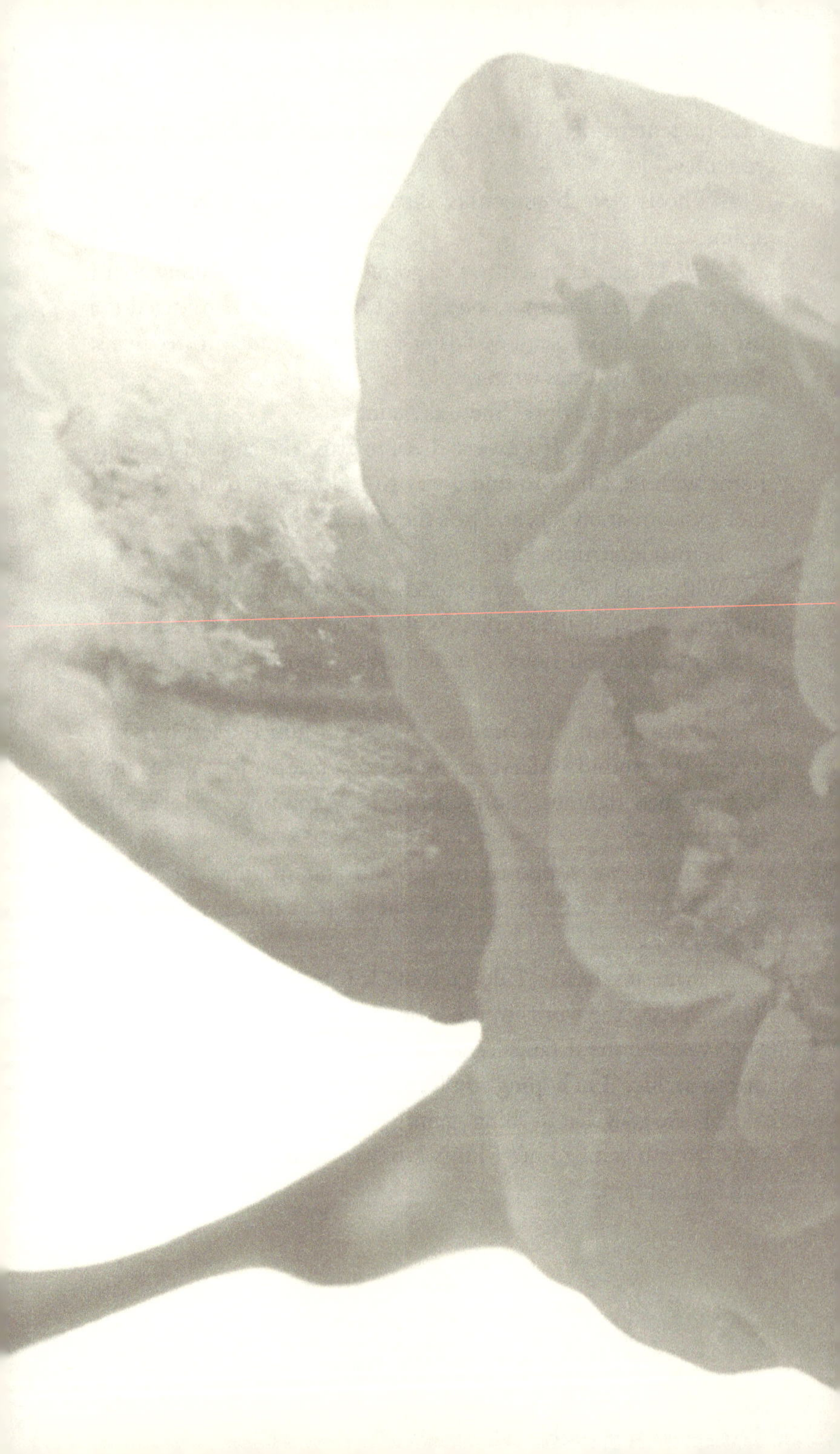

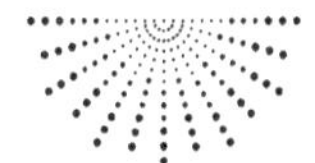

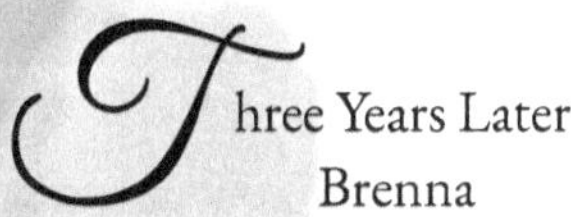

hree Years Later
Brenna

As we make our way down the long and windy, country roads, I can't help but smile out at the landscape. I never thought I'd feel so content coming back home. Hell, I never thought I'd think of this place as home. It's not that I didn't try my hardest not to grow attached, not to allow myself to grow comfortable. Vigilance was the goal when my sisters and I were finally free of the nightmare that was our home life. Now, I can't wait to get back to the house.

My first year of college has been an experience, one I never imagined having. I've learned so much about the world and myself. It's been liberating to not have responsibility for my sisters and not having to live in constant fear. As the trees pass by in a blur, I smile at how quickly my life changed once Taylor and Garrett brought us home with them.

"What are you thinking about over there, B?"

Jordan's voice startles me. Somehow, I forgot she was driving. A chuckle bubbles out of me, and it feels so good to laugh. There were so many years I barely smiled, and now I find myself laughing just for the sheer joy of it. My therapist calls it euphoria, but I really feel like I'm just making up for lost time.

You deserve to be happy, Brenna. Garrett's words play through my mind. I had been angry with Taylor. If I'm being honest, I was always angry with everyone. He found me out near the pen where they let the boarded horses run. Something about watching them frolic would bring me peace like nothing else. I wished to be like those horses with no worries. I wanted to be able to trust I'd be safe. Happiness was never even something I imagined. I guess I was most angry with Taylor because she'd found happiness. She'd attained it by leaving us, and I hated seeing it when I couldn't feel any of it.

Jordan makes a noise next to me, something that might be called static, before she says, "Come in Brenna. Over." Another bit of laughter escapes.

With a sigh, I admit, "I was just thinking about how one little sentence can completely change your life."

She turns her head toward me, one brow lifted in question. "That was no little sentence he got," she says, "and in my opinion, he deserved so much more."

My mouth drops open as I register that she thought I meant Phillip's jail sentence. I hardly ever think about that man now. "No," I say with a shake of my head. "Though that sentence made a huge difference in how things have worked out, I meant an actual spoken sentence." Her mouth makes a small 'oh,' and she falls silent. "It's ok, J. I don't expect you to read my mind. You and Taylor have that level of relationship."

It's her turn to laugh. "You and she are a lot alike, you know."

I smile. I used to think so. In fact, I used to emulate my big sister, wanting to be just like her. Then I got old enough to realize what Phillip was doing, and I'd grown to hate her, changing everything about myself to not draw his attention like she had. Guilt starts to gnaw at my stomach, and my hand presses to my sternum.

"Sorry. You can tell me to keep my opinions to myself," Jordan says.

"It's not you. It's just...I was so unfair to her. I blamed her for everything for a long time."

"Honestly, I probably would have too if I were in your shoes. An abuser does whatever they can to make the victim look like a willing participant. She probably looked guilty as hell to you."

"Yeah, but I was wrong, and I can't kick the guilt. It's something I still need to work through with my therapist."

"I'm glad it's helping, but it doesn't answer my initial question about your smile earlier. I don't think guilt is what had you smiling. I know your horrors. Tell me what brings you joy."

I take one last look out at the passing trees, basking in the knowledge that we're almost home and say, "Truthfully, I'm just happy to be home. That realization surprised me for a second, but that's the truth of it. I can't wait to see all my sisters, and I'm so glad I was able to come surprise Garrett for his birthday. It was his words that helped change my entire perspective a year ago, and I'm so grateful."

Jordan sniffs, and I turn to face her in my seat. "I'm also grateful to you for being there for Taylor when she escaped. You and Morgan and Joanna. You all helped her get to the place where she could be there for us." Her breath hitches, and I lay my palm on her arm. "Though I hate not having a mother who could look out for us, I'll gladly take all the big sisters I can get."

"You got us, B, and we're not going anywhere," she says as we pull up the dirt road that leads to the farm.

My sisters are all on the porch before Jordan puts the car in park, and a booming voice fills the space as I climb out of her car. "Why's everyone outside? What's going on out there?" I smile, knowing the words are more curious than anything else. Holding up a finger to silence Justine and Marybeth who are poised to run down the steps, I stand at the bottom of the porch. "Is the party out..."

Garrett's voice trails off when he sees me, and I hold my smile. He turns to look at Taylor who simply lifts up and kisses his cheek. The look of love on her face nearly breaks me, but I stay cool. "I thought you were at school," he says, taking one step down the porch, eyes squinting.

"About that," I respond, "a little birdie told me that someone here was celebrating a big birthday, and I couldn't help but think how selfish it would be for me to not send a gift." I put my hand on my hips and then bend at the waist with a flourish of my hand, repeating the words from one of his and Taylor's favorite television shows. "I am the gift." He barks out a laugh and opens his arms. Without hesitation, I run into them, nearly jumping up the porch steps.

"The best gift," he says, settling his chin on my head. Seconds later, he releases me. "Now, go greet your sisters. They've missed you." I step around him and walk the rest of the way up the stairs straight into Taylor's arms. Seconds later, Justine and Marybeth are wrapped around both of us in a group hug of limbs and tears. "Oh, and Brenna," Garrett's voice calls from the dirt lot where he's standing next to Jordan. I turn his way as best I can with my sisters hanging onto me like koalas. "Welcome home, kid."

Tears fill my eyes as I nod my thanks, unable to speak. He'd said those words to me three years ago, and I'd told him to go fuck himself. I'd said I'd never call this farm home and that I couldn't wait until I could leave and never come back. Garrett never faltered, even when Taylor tried to reprimand me, to protect him from my anger. He remained steadfast and patient, and then he and Taylor sent me off to college like the parents I'd always dreamed of, with tears, new linens, and well-wishes.

"Nowhere else I'd rather be, Poppa Cowpoke," I say before hurrying into the house.

LEYA LAYNE

Leya Layne's love of a Happily Ever After started with Disney. Then she found romance novels in her early teens thanks to a bag of Harlequin novels hidden under her grandmother's dresser. She got her HEA fix for the rest of her teen years thanks to a well-worn library card. Though she is currently publishing contemporary romances that have been described as Hot Hallmark, don't be surprised to see her delve into historical or paranormal in the future. The possibilities are endless, but the one thing she'll promise is that they'll all be spicy!

Follow Leya all over social media:
https://linktr.ee/LeyaLayneAuthor

See her website for forthcoming releases and trigger/content warnings:
https://bisabelwrites.com/leyas-content-is-for-18-only/

You've Got Bookmail

Shar's Story

Love with a Vengeance

Carol's Christmas Awakening

Clarissa and the Wallflower

Breadcrumbs

Josefina

Cole County Anthology Series (Unpublished Dec 31, 2025)

Something Old (Magnolia Cove Anthology Book 1)

Waiting for You

Coming in 2026

Yearning for You

Trying for You

Reaching for You

Elinora

Raquel

Whiskey Falls (The Distilleries Anthology Book 1)

Fireproof

#JustRight (If I'm really feeling froggy…if not, 2027)